THE RELUCTANT REAPER

DENARII PETERS

First Published in Great Britain by Crystal Clear Books 2025

Copyright © Denarii Peters, 2025

Denarii Peters has asserted her moral right under the Copyright Design and Patents Act 1988 to be identified as the author of this work.

This book is a work of fiction and, except in the case of historical fact, any resemblance to actual persons, living or dead, is purely coincidental.

No paragraph of this publication may be reproduced, copied, stored or transmitted in any format save with written permission or in accordance with the provisions of the Copyright, Designs and Patents Act 1988, or under the terms of any license, permitting limited copying issued by the Copyright Licensing Agency, 33 Alfred Place, London, WC1E 7DP.

No part of this book may be used in any manner in the learning, training or development of generative artificial intelligence technologies (including but not limited to machine learning models and large language models whether by data scraping, data mining or use in any way to create or form a part of data sets or in any other way.

Published by: Crystal Clear Books: www.crystalclearbooks.co.uk

ISBN: 978-1-7394272-9-0

Cover Image: ID 115480366 © Passigatti | Dreamstime.com

Author Photograph: Elizabeth Whitehead

Here's a dedication to thank Jenni for all her dedication. My very best alpha beta reader.

Acknowledgements

First, I'd like to thank everyone who bought (and hopefully enjoyed) my short story collection Will You Walk into My Parlour and has come back for more.

Thanks again to Sue ("Can we have a comma here?"), my super editor, to Linda, who has unerringly guided me through the publication of both books (and more to come, I hope!), and to lovely Liz Whitehead for her brilliant cover photo ("Stand still, Denarii!").

Finally, thanks go to my long-suffering PA (alias my other half), who works just as hard as me, doing all the admin behind the scenes, spotting the odd plot fault as well as putting right my somewhat wayward spelling and grammar. He also takes care of that most vital of tasks: keeping me in coffee!

Denarii Peters
https://denariipeters.substack.com/
June 2025.

CHAPTER 1

That last shot came far too close, spattering my face with cold, slimy mud. As I crawled through the gorse, the thorns a thousand prickling points of pain, my clutching fingers tore at the scrubby grass on the edge of the abyss. I cried out as a nail ripped free.

With nothing but unresisting air beneath my other hand, I fell over the precipice; one more sad ghost to wail in the wind whistling around Greystone Crag.

Tumbling, falling; clothes snagging on sharp shards of granite, I wrapped my arms around my head and bounced like a cannon ball down a mountain, crashing into boulders; drowning in an ocean of pain.

My eyes opened to a pale sky arching above me: dawn. Cold, damp but still alive, I lay on my back at the foot of the crag.

How could I have survived such an impossible fall? I held my hands up in front of my face, turning them over and over. Nothing more than a dozen deep scratches, a missing nail, bruises and a few drops of dried blood: almost no damage at all. Laughing out loud, I hugged the rocks as I hauled myself to my feet; breathed a sigh of relief as my legs held me. Every muscle ached, but no worse than I had endured in the past falling from a horse. What a shame there was no one around to tell about my remarkable escape.

Ah yes, it was indeed an escape. But was I safe? What had become of my pursuers? Had my tumble down the cliff convinced Elias Robertshaw and his men I was dead? Even if it had, I couldn't stay where I was. Once the light was strong enough, they would search the base of the cliff for my body. If they were to discover I was still alive, my miraculous escape would have all been for nothing. They would arrest me, try me and hang me. I was a wanted man: an important fugitive. The bounty on my head would keep the thirstiest man in ale for months.

Last night I had come within a whisker of being caught. This part of the country was getting far too hot for me. I needed to find somewhere out of the way to hide up.

Should I consider moving on?

Well, it wouldn't be easy. It's difficult to be a successful highwayman if you're not acquainted with the highways! Perhaps the best option would be to make my way to the Farrier's Arms, where I hoped for a friendly reception. It was a fair way off so I would have to get a move on.

CHAPTER 2

Keeping an eye out for any pursuit, I clambered over rocky terrain until I reached the edge of the dusty road which led away from the cliffs. As I tramped along, I cursed myself for being such a fool as to trust Luke. We'd worked together often but I should have sensed this time something was wrong.

"It'll be easy, Ross. The merchant's a fool. He's got a pile of gold he shouldn't have, and he's got to shift it quick."

Why didn't it occur to me to ask where Luke got this information? I hadn't heard any whispers myself. Was I so blinded by greed? "Are you sure he won't have an armed escort?"

"No, he won't. He has to do this in secret. It's the proceeds from a cargo of smuggled brandy and lace. He can't risk anyone squealing to the Customs men. So, the only people he can rely on are the two men already involved and his coachman."

"And you're certain he's taking the route over Greystone Crag?"

"Yeah, along the Bishop's Road. Come on, Ross. You and me, we can ambush him as he crosses between the cliff edge and the trees. We'll make more than enough money from this to lay low for a while. You could even use some of it to get yourself well in with that lass you fancy." He raised his eyebrows.

It was all so tempting. And by midnight we were in place, awaiting our prey.

Only, as the coach drew level with me, I realised I had fallen into a trap.

Luke rode up from behind the vehicle but instead of levelling his pistol at the coachman, pointed it at me. At that same moment another man appeared, galloping back along the trail towards us, the door of the coach flew open, and I was under fire from three sides.

The first shot missed me. Another ploughed a furrow across the right shoulder of my jerkin. Fearing the sting of a third, I threw myself to the ground using my horse as a shield. She rolled over. I scrambled away. Seconds later, over the cliff I went.

CHAPTER 3

By mid-morning I was standing outside the inn I had known for years, from long before taking up the career of highway robber. The landlord, Pete Noyles, was a tall, stout man as honest as a bent farthing. Half his spirits came from the wreckers and smugglers on the nearby coast. Most of the rest were stolen from other hostelries, but his beer was the genuine article. He brewed it himself in the long, low building to one side of his inn. It was dark, tasty and, when he had not watered it, as strong as they come.

His daughter, bonny, blue-eyed Tessa with her long, wild tangle of blonde hair, had for a good while been a particular friend of mine. It was her I hoped to see.

Entering the tavern by the side door through the warm, busy kitchen, I was careful to ensure Martha, the landlord's shrewish wife, did not notice my arrival; she was none too happy about her daughter's friendship with a man like me. I slipped through into the bar and walked straight into trouble.

Luke saw me the same instant I saw him. I'm not sure who drew his pistol faster, but both were cocked in seconds and the shots rang out together.

He fell and so did I, but he stayed down.

Having always been a crack marksman, I wasn't surprised my shot had pierced him through the heart. His had only taken me high up in the left shoulder but I was in pain nonetheless, forced to clasp my hand tight to the wound as I collapsed into the nearest chair.

Noyles stepped out from behind the bar. He towered over me. "You shouldn't have come here. I told you before: you're not welcome."

Still a little groggy, I mumbled something about having nowhere else to go.

He looked around him. "I can't risk the High Sheriff's men finding you in the bar, so I'll hide you for a few hours. But no longer."

He wasn't fooling me. I knew his daughter would not let him make me leave.

Draping my arm over his shoulder and grumbling all the while, he helped me up the stairs. As he laid me down on a narrow bed, tears were falling from Tessa's wide, blue eyes.

I reached up and caressed her cheek. "Hey, I'm all right. It's only a flesh wound. Just get me a surgeon. He'll soon sort me out."

She glanced towards the door. "You'll have to hang on, Ross. My father's afraid the tavern is being watched." Her words sent a shiver down my spine. I had to get out of there. I couldn't stay if...

How long had I been out cold? I struggled to concentrate. Voices in the corridor: Noyles was talking to someone. "Tonight. It has to be tonight, before Robertshaw and his men find him here. Tessa mustn't know, though. She's sweet on the lad."

Sweet on who? Oh, on me! Yes. I began to smile.

Then it dawned on me what her father had said. "Do it tonight." Tonight? Do what? The conversation continued but I only caught snatches of isolated words. Until there was one sentence in a low, deep, rumbling voice, as if spoken by a man with a huge barrel of a chest. "I guarantee no one will ever find the body. The currents are too strong in that spot. It'll be washed way out to sea, food for the fishes, and we'll be back here with your brandy by morning." I heard the jingle of coins changing hands.

It struck like a physical pain. Noyles was arranging to get rid of me; to have me killed, my body dumped in the sea. I had to get away. Right now. It didn't matter where.

I sat up, expecting my shoulder to be on fire. But it didn't hurt a bit. Maybe my comment to Tessa was right: it had been nothing but a flesh wound. Luke had only winged me.

I placed a foot on the threadbare, green carpet. Had those red stains always been there? Maybe I'd lost a little blood when they'd carried me to the bed.

"Good evening." A slender woman with brown eyes and long, dark hair stood in the doorway. Strange. I hadn't noticed her enter.

"Who are you, madam?"

"My name is Caroline."

"Pleased to meet you, Caroline, but I'm sorry: I can't spend time chatting. I have to get out of here right now."

"Indeed you do. And I agree: we don't have much time. This is not a safe place for either of us." She took a step to the side, as though inviting me to walk past her. Being the suspicious type, I'd have preferred her to go first.

Never had I seen anyone so out of place at the Farrier's. Her pale blue gown, fashioned from the type of gauzy material only the wealthy wear, was somehow old fashioned. Her cloak was too thick for the time of year, while those fancy, high-heeled shoes would not have lasted five minutes on our rough roads.

I thought I knew all the local gentry, but this lady was not familiar. What did she imagine she was doing, alone in a tavern bedroom with a notorious highwayman?

It was a mystery sure enough but one I hoped I could use to my advantage. She would make the perfect hostage.

I walked round her and approached the door. I couldn't hear anyone in the passage but that didn't mean no one was out there. I raised my hand to the latch.

"I'm leaving now. And you're coming with me. We're going to walk out of the inn together."

I waited for her to protest. Instead, she gave me a broad smile. "What a splendid idea. Why stay any longer? Let's be on our way."

This made no sense. Was she volunteering to be my hostage? I knew a lot of women found me attractive, but this was ridiculous. She had to be part of some elaborate trap.

Checking the escape route was clear, I strode over to the window but there was nothing to be seen, other than a pair of mangy nags and an untidy stack of beer barrels.

"Do you want to go out through there?"

Was the woman insane? No one could have squeezed through an opening as narrow as that.

Turning to face her, I repeated my first question. "Just who are you, lady?"

"I've already told you. My name is Caroline, Caroline Trenby."

Trenby? I knew of no family in the district by that name. "Where are you from?"

"I was born and brought up at Middleham House, near Witholme."

The temperature in the room plummeted. This woman definitely had to be insane.

"The only Caroline Trenby I've ever heard of perished with all her family when the manor house burned down. That must have been over a hundred years ago."

"Has it really been that long? My, how time does fly!"

"Are you trying to tell me you're a ghost?"

"It takes one to know one, don't you think, Mr. Ferris?" With her open hand she indicated the bed.

A body lay across it. And a lot of blood. It was my body. It was my blood. And I was not moving, not breathing.

I stood over myself, staring down into my own wide-open, unblinking eyes. I extended my arm, trying to touch the cooling flesh, but my fingers refused to make contact, instead hovering a hair's breadth above. I was outside and I realised in that moment there was no way I could ever be inside again.

And I discovered a ghost cannot cry; you can shed no tears for your own lost life. My hand fell back to my side and, as it did so, the waves of sadness ebbed away.

So, this was death, was it? How very surprising: not at all what I had expected. And who would have thought the grim reaper was not a hooded man with a scythe but an uncommonly pretty lady!

In silence she waited for me by the door. As I followed her through it, I realised there was nothing more to hold me in that place.

Although the passage was deserted, I sensed drifting shadows and whispers in the air.

Frowning, she drew her cloak tight around her and hurried towards the landing. "Come on. We can't stay here." I was confused. What was this all about? Why was she suddenly in such a hurry? Even so, I followed her.

We descended the stairs and crossed the tavern's bar. As we neared the low, stone exit, without any warning everything changed. The room was now filled with strangers: crowds of men and women wearing bright coloured clothes and speaking words in an odd accent. One man was sitting on a stool at the far end, playing a stringed instrument for which I had no name. He was singing a sad lay, a tale of mischance.

I wanted to listen to him, but Caroline urged me on.

"Close your ears, Ross. You mustn't pay any heed to it. It's only a future echo, nothing to do with us. We've been here too long as it is. You should have chosen somewhere safer to die. We have to leave this place. Right now!"

She was already too late. Unable to take a further step forward, I tarried. The ballad was the story of a woman who had died at the hands of a sheriff's man. He had come in search of a highway robber. Finding only a corpse he could not hang, he had taken his pleasure with the woman then murdered her and, with mocking words, laid the body beside that of her dead lover. When the singer reached his chorus, his audience joined in. They sang out the name of the woman.

"I can't come with you, lady." Reeling, I backed away from my guide. "Didn't you hear him? This is all my fault. I have to stay here and save my Tessa."

"I'm sorry but there's nothing you can do for her. Those events have not yet happened. And you couldn't alter them anyway. It's sad but that's the way things are. Now, please hurry along."

"I don't believe you. I'm staying right here." Why didn't she see I couldn't leave now? I wasn't about to go anywhere while Tessa needed me.

Caroline bit her lip. "I can't risk hanging around. If you really want to become a wraith haunting this inn forever, I ought to let you. This is not a good place and if you do stay, you will soon enough find plenty of bad company. I was warned you were going to be a difficult case: wilful and stubborn. And they were right."

"Calling me names changes nothing, lady. You can do what you like but I'm staying here. And I am going to save Tessa."

But around me everything was different again; the scene had returned to normality. Noyles was serving smuggled rum to two men at the bar and Tessa, very much alive and laughing, passed beside me, her arms full of tankards.

I reached out to her. "Tessa, listen. You must get away from here!"

But she looked straight through me.

Caroline had reached the door. She beckoned to me. "I've got an idea, Ross. Why don't we take a look outside? Maybe we can head off the sheriff's man before he reaches the tavern."

I had completely forgotten about dying and becoming a ghost. I didn't know what to think but Caroline's words sounded like the right thing to do.

The door did not open but somehow we found ourselves outside and the night was far too hot, even for the time of year.

As we crossed the yard, five horsemen galloped towards us. Leading them was Elias Robertshaw.

Crying out, I tried to grab the bridle of his horse but an invisible force propelled me away from the tavern. Unbalanced, I fell forwards. Enormous hands with too many fingers and long, curved claws closed around my arms, tight as shackles. I could see nothing beyond the wrists of my assailant, and what I did see was not flesh but deep red scales.

The air around me began to taste of sulphur. Grey-white ashes clung to my clothes.

CHAPTER 4

Time does not exist in Hell. It is taken from you along with everything precious. I could not bring to mind a single friendly face. Around me the only music was the rise and fall of screams, an unending siren of pain.

The air was hot, too hot, and stank of sulphur; the horizon a bleak, parched desert of stone and dust. I was alone.

My ears continued to be assaulted by a barrage of wails and whimpers. Ashes drifted in the air. Was someone being burned? Would it be my turn next?

I looked down at myself and saw straight through to the ground above which I hovered. Where there had been flesh and bone, there was nothing now but a thick mist. I had less substance to me than a dust mote in the wind.

A flickering, the isolated brilliance of a single tongue of lightning, and with it a voice echoing all around me.

"Let's see what sort of punishment you deserve, shall we?"

The horizon faded away and, in its place, a disembodied face appeared. And it was watching me. I wanted to flee, to get away from it, but I had no command over my being. The face was not human. It was comprised of overlapping red scales with a suggestion of two blunt horns breaking through the forehead. And the eyes were swirling whirlpools of gold.

"Are you the Devil?" My voice was little more than the whisper of autumn leaves; his laughter the crackling of a bonfire built to receive them.

"You flatter yourself. What is so important about you?"

I wanted to curl up into a ball and bury myself beneath the dust, but I was fixed in place, an unmoving exhibit splayed out for the amusement of my tormentor. But fear has always made me want to talk. More than one enemy has described me as flippant.

"Are you going to burn me now?"

He wrinkled his nose. "Oh, really. I had hoped for better than that from you. They said you were more interesting than most. But they were wrong; you're just one more boring, unimaginative soul."

The next instant I was screaming, one more voice in Hell's cacophonous choir. Flames leapt up all around me. The pain was beyond description; so unbearable had I not been dead already I swear I would have welcomed death. I have no notion of how long it went on but suddenly it was over, though the memory of it would become a scar I knew I would carry with me for all of eternity.

I forced myself to look at the creature and was lost in the whirling gold of his eyes.

"See what I mean? Boring, boring, boring. The problem with pain such as you have just experienced is that it can be nothing more than a transitory illusion when you no longer own the body being burnt."

I wasn't so sure about that. It had felt real enough to me. I could never have imagined greater agony.

The face was peering harder at me. "You're going to have to come up with something better than a mere eternal blaze to warm your lost bones. It simply won't do, you know. Use that shrewd brain you're supposed to have; I've administered nothing but burnings for far too long!" He sighed. "Ah, if only I didn't have to rely on your imagination, but alas it's against the rules for me to suggest anything myself."

"Are you saying you want me to tell you how to punish me?"

"What else have I been saying to you for the last year or so?"

A year? Had I been surrounded by those flames for such a long time? It couldn't have been possible, but why would he lie?

"We can't stay here forever, you know."

A flicker of hope flared inside me. "You mean Hell is not for all time? I'll be going somewhere else soon, will I?"

"Oh, you will go somewhere else but it will still be Hell. Don't you know anything about this place?"

"No, why don't you explain?" Had I gone too far? Was he about to return me to the fire?

But no. Instead, he gave me an ugly smile, showing off a double row of razor-sharp teeth and canines bigger than those belonging to the most vicious and rabid of dogs. "There are seven levels to Hell. At the moment we are situated on level three. Your permanent place will be on level five or perhaps even level four; your actions in life don't rate you at anything lower. I am the unfortunate daemon charged with categorising you. And you are supposed to co-operate with me. By now almost all of the intake from your time period have been classified. We're lagging some distance behind." As he sighed, a cloud of faint yellow gas swamped me. Had I a working pair of lungs, I would have choked to death. "Right. I think we will have to try something a little more drastic to wake you up a bit."

We were no longer in Hell. And the daemon was no longer only a face. He had taken on a near-human form as he came to stand beside me. But the eyes remained the same strange, too large orbs, glowing like pale golden suns.

I stared round me. "Why have you brought me here? This is North Farm, my sister's place."

"Indeed it is and two days have elapsed since you died. As you can see, no one here is mourning your passing."

"They'd be too busy. They have the cows, the chickens and the corn field to look after. And it goes well with them. I know Jayne is happy." Across the hedges a small group of people were digging the land. Among them were Francis and the children. "My nephew and niece. I haven't seen them for, oh, it must be three years now."

"Why is that?"

"I had a quarrel with Francis; he said I was a bad influence and my presence would only bring trouble down on his family. I was so angry with Jayne because she stood by him and said nothing when he barred me from the house."

"He was right, though, wasn't he? You did bring trouble."

"Did I?" I was puzzled. Everything around us was so peaceful; a dozen hens scratched for bugs and worms in the shadow of the barn, a marmalade cat was curled up on the windowsill and an old dog lay in a patch of sunlight beside the farmhouse's doorstep. "I see nothing wrong."

"Wait. Here it comes right now." He pointed at the road leading into the farm.

Two horsemen rode through the gate and dismounted. "Elias Robertshaw? What on earth is he doing here?" I would have run across the farmyard and challenged him if I wasn't fixed to the spot. "He's the High Sheriff's man. He shot at me the night before I..." The word would not come.

"Yes, I know. Let's follow him and see what he does, shall we?"

While his comrade stayed outside holding the bridles of the horses, Robertshaw pushed open the farmhouse door.

I cried out and took a step forwards. I felt the daemon's claws close around my wrist and we were beyond the door, standing on the flagstones of the kitchen.

My sister was leaning across the table, her arms dusty with flour as she kneaded a pile of creamy dough. As Robertshaw strode towards her, the song she was singing caught on her lips. "What do you want?" She sounded surprised but not alarmed. Not yet anyway.

Robertshaw's hand was on the butt of his pistol. "I want the spoils your brother left with you."

"What are you talking about? I haven't seen Ross in ages. He left nothing with me. I'm sorry but you've had a wasted journey." She released the lump of dough and took a step back from the table, wiping her hands on her apron. "Let me fetch you a tankard of ale. You must be thirsty."

That was typical of Jayne, to be concerned for others. We had always been so different.

Robertshaw drew his pistol and aimed it at her. "I don't believe you. Ferris must have hidden his ill-gotten gains somewhere. They're not in his lair nor at the Farrier's either. I've checked both places. So, where else would he have stashed them if not with his beloved sister?"

"I've already told you they're not here. We have nothing belonging to Ross at the farm. He doesn't come here. My husband will not permit it."

I watched Robertshaw's eyes narrow and his stance shift a little.

Fear for my sister flooded through me. "Jayne! Jayne, get out of there!" But my cries were as silence in the room.

Time slowed to a near standstill.

Jayne was so alone. Her eyes wide, she fixed them on Robertshaw as her hand reached for a carving knife.

I saw the bullet fly from the barrel of the pistol. If I could, I would have run in front of it and taken it into me but all I could do was watch.

A growing, red stain spread outwards. For a long moment she stared down at herself. She fell; her body striking the edge of the table; the knife falling through dying fingers. With her last breath she called to the children and Francis.

Robertshaw glanced around and cursed. It was clear he could see nothing of value. Putting away his pistol, he strode out of the kitchen. "Nothing! The bitch had nothing. Ferris must have had another place." He mounted his horse and, without a backward glance, he and his companion galloped out of the farmyard.

"Jayne, oh Jayne!" I was weeping dust-dry tears.

The daemon coughed. "Well? Was that more painful than the flames or not? I could do with knowing."

"What are you talking about? My sister is dead." There was something I had to know. "Where is she now? Has she gone to Heaven? Oh, please tell me she's not suffering as I am."

"Why would I tell you that? Uncertainty is a knife edge. The last thing I'm here to do is give you solace. No, think of your sister's children instead. Think of the tears, the loneliness of her husband. They had such a good marriage, didn't they?"

"Take me back to the flames. I deserve them." I would have said anything to get away from that place of such sorrow.

I expected to be returned to Hell. Where else could he take me? Nothing on the temporal plane could hurt me as much as the scene I had just witnessed. And yet... I found myself in the Farrier's Arms.

It was busy, as usual. The talk and the laughter were loud and raucous. At the bar a ruddy faced Pete Noyles poured smuggled French brandy into small glasses, while Tessa weaved her way between the tables, her arms filled with overflowing tankards. The rich bouquet of roasting meat vied with the hoppy aroma of beer. As always, the only concession to caution was two men sitting at a table by the grimy window, compensated with free drinks for their task of keeping an eye out for any customs man who might decide to check on what was being served. It never happened, of course. Pete Noyles knew who to bribe.

I became aware of a strange sensation: an aching, a pulling from the floor above. "I'm up there, aren't I? This is the night I..." Again, I could not say the word.

The daemon nodded. "Yes, two hours ago, almost to the minute. Now watch. Things are about to get interesting."

Above the buzz of conversation, I heard the sound of hooves, many hooves. The two men by the window had no time to shout out a warning before the door burst open. It was Robertshaw and he was not alone. A posse, four strong, erupted into the room after him.

In the sudden silence the sheriff's man ordered the drinkers to leave. "We've no quarrel with any of you. It's Noyles we want. He's harbouring a fugitive."

Tessa dropped the tray. Ale slopped over the floor as six empty tankards rolled this way and that.

Customers fled into the night. The sheriffs' men fanned out, overturning the tables, smashing the furniture, breaking everything in sight. The man I had seen with Robertshaw at North Farm forced his way behind the bar and, while Noyles watched, smashed up the stock. Beer poured onto the floor, and a brandy bottle crashed against the wall close to where I stood beside the daemon.

Robertshaw grabbed Tessa round the waist.

She struggled, wriggled, but he held on.

He laughed. "Come along, missy. Let's us two go upstairs and find Ferris."

"No, no! He mustn't take her up there. He's about to..." At first the words stuck inside me then exploded out as a shout so loud it must have carried not just to Hell but to Heaven as well. "Stop him! Don't let him rape and kill her. I can't bear the thought of what he's about to do." I prayed he wouldn't make me see Tessa's body and mine entwined together, our cold, dead arms around each other as Robertshaw looked on and laughed. "Please don't force me to see any more."

The world stopped: frozen as though a picture on a wall.

The daemon's countenance was creased with confusion. "You shouldn't know about this. You died before it happened. You had already been gathered in; how can you know about something that occurred after you left?"

"It was when I was leaving. A woman, no, a ghost was with me."

"You're talking about the one who came to collect you?"

"I think so. She was called Caroline. We came in here and there was a man..." I told him every detail I could remember. I recounted how Caroline and I had almost been trapped in the Farrier's; how the words of the singer's ballad were now coming true as I witnessed Robertshaw dragging my poor Tessa from the bar.

I swear I saw the daemon shiver. "That sounds like a future echo. Oh, my. This changes everything. We must return to Hell without delay."

I don't believe anyone could ever be as grateful as I was to find myself back in Hell.

"What happens now?" I trembled as the flames began to reappear.

The daemon waved his hands at them and they vanished again. "I need some advice. The woman who collected you said nothing of any future echo. It's possible she didn't understand what it was or at least misunderstood its significance. You know, it's quite deplorable how low the training standards have slipped." It was as though he were no longer talking to me but musing aloud. "Hmm, you had better stay here for now, Ross. I'll be back when I've found out a bit more."

He left me. I was alone on the stone plateau, surrounded by a timeless, featureless, silent wasteland with nothing for me to look at, nothing at all to do and no one to talk to. And even if there had been, I had no voice to speak with. The boredom, heavier than any physical weight, was crushing me. I might not have been in pain, but this frustration was agonising. With no body I couldn't pace or exercise nor even fidget.

I dreamed of a wind to blow me away over the horizon; better to be a silent, drifting wraith than a tethered, empty husk of nothingness. But the wind never came; no insect crawled, no cloud hid the relentless sun, no variation occurred in the unending view.

After what felt like an eternity the daemon was back.

I cried out in delight. If I could, I would have embraced him. Being so lonely, any company would have had the same effect. However, my short-lived elation was displaced by the torture of absolute dread. What might he be about to do to me now?

"It has been decided. First, I am to take you on a brief tour of some of the fates of those condemned to spend eternity in this place, but I am not permitted to say which of them might resemble your own. This visit will last only a few seconds, mind, but it will be enough. After that, the powers that be in Hell intend to employ you for a while, either until we have caught up with the future echo or unless you prove yourself so useful, we decide to retain your services."

"I don't understand."

"Why should you? These echoes are something of a mystery to us too. They are so rare. But when they do occur, souls caught up in them always have some part to play in what is to come. For good or ill, Ross Ferris, you have gained yourself a reprieve."

CHAPTER 5

Days or perhaps weeks later, my mind scoured and my will broken, I was once again floating above the silent plane. The daemon had indeed escorted me into the deepest part of Hell. What I had seen there was so terrible it was almost beyond my powers of description. The tour had begun with a glimpse of a writhing, seething mass of disembodied hands and impossible long arms. I could still see them rippling across a liquid surface of molten iron, beckoning in unfortunate souls towards their final reckoning. This, the daemon said, was the Final Door. It was there I lost the last of my courage.

The daemon laughed at my distress. He would take me no further as each soul's torment is different, designed for them and them alone. The form my own would take was still locked inside me. It would be released and set upon me only when the time was right. Until then, it would nestle deep within: a curled viper; a vicious beast with many heads, claws and teeth, awaiting its moment. Awaiting my arrival.

Then the daemon whispered to me of how patient my fate would be. And I knew I would do anything to keep it waiting; anything not to have to return; anything to remain this side of that dreaded door.

"I will leave you now, Ross, but we will meet again; you have been assigned to me and I will complete my task. Eventually. Who knows? You might even have come up with a fitting, imaginative end for yourself by then: perhaps something I might find worth discussing with my colleagues. In the meantime, you have an appointment. The management have made a decision on what you might be capable of doing. Let us hope they are right for your sake."

I thanked him, though I didn't know what for.

He gave me another of his hideous smiles. "Farewell. Oh, I nearly forgot. Enjoy!"

He was gone and I was alone again. But something had changed. Oh! I had been given a body.

I stood up on legs that ended in feet. I was no longer drifting. My skin was cold since no blood flowed beneath it, nor was there a pulse in my wrist. But it was a body nonetheless. For the first time since I had died, I had gained something. And, though I was never a vain man, I did so crave a mirror!

CHAPTER 6

I stumbled along an endless, grey corridor, the air too hot, coughing at the acrid, overpowering stench of overcooked flesh. It felt as though I was melting.

Where was this strange place? What was I doing here? My last memory was of lying on a narrow bed at the Farrier's Arms. But I was not there now. And what had become of the wounds I suffered? Why did I have this awful feeling of dread?

Somehow I knew there was an interview I must pass though I hadn't the faintest idea what the job might be. But something terrible was going to happen if I didn't get it.

I glanced down at the clothes I did not remember putting on. They were smart: a swirling, dark cloak over an expensive, tailored suit. However they did not belong together. The calf length boots gleamed and the silver buckles glistened as though someone had spent hours burnishing them. And I was wearing spurs. The only thing lacking to complete the outfit was a pair of pistols.

Around me rose blank, grey walls. No windows. No signs gave clue to the type of business carried on here.

The corridor had no corners. I could see no end to it. Several doors made of plain, unvarnished wood led off. Still no windows. It took a moment to dawn on me there were no handles either.

My feet carried me to the nearest one. It felt like the right place. Was I supposed to knock? Should I leave? And if I did try to leave, which way should I go?

The door began to open. It was so slow, silent, gradual I drew back for an instant. All my instincts screamed. This door might lead into some dark place where only a fool would go.

Even so, the invitation was extended so in I went.

The walls inside were the same shade as those outside. Beneath my feet lay a grey tiled floor and across the space from me sat three people, a mismatched trio: two men and a woman sitting on upright chairs behind a long, mahogany desk. On my side nothing. No chair. No carpet.

I approached the table, spurs clicking like rasping talons against the tiles. "Good afternoon." My voice echoed in the near empty space.

"Oh, is it afternoon?" The woman with the pale, heart shaped face was about my age. She wore a black and red hooped jersey and a raspberry-coloured beret perched on her short, bobbed, dark hair. Her piercing, green eyes stared hard at me. She nudged the man on her right. "You didn't tell me it was afternoon." She spoke with a slight accent, similar to that of the French smugglers I remembered from the Farrier's Arms. They would arrive with barrels of brandy and items made of fine, gossamer-thin lace. Tessa was always wanting me to buy her a shawl or a scarf. I always told her it wasn't worth the price.

"I don't think it is afternoon." Glaring at me was an older man with a bald head so shiny it reflected the light. He was dressed in a tatty, threadbare, tweed jacket with leather patches on the elbows and had a pair of horn-rimmed pince-nez balanced on the end of his nose. "What evidence can you present for your contention that it is indeed afternoon?"

"Er, I don't have any evidence." I cast my eyes over the unbroken walls. There were no windows, no shutters, nothing. It could have been midday or even midnight for all I knew. The only illumination in the room came from a large, plain lantern held to the ceiling by thick, dull metal chains.

"Do you often give opinions without evidence to back them up, Mr. Ferris?"

"No, sir. I was attempting to break the ice." I tried without success to give a light laugh.

"Ice? I haven't seen any of that for such a long time."

"Be quiet, Nadine. Mr. Ferris doesn't want to hear about your problems, do you?"

"I don't mind. Erm, I'm afraid I don't..."

"No, you must never be afraid. It's such a futile emotion," the other man, swarthy with olive skin and a single golden earring, cut across me. He was wearing a tunic heavy with gold and silver brocade and a tricorn hat with a long, curling white feather. Folding his arms, he allowed his chin to fall onto his chest, where it remained.

"Look, I know this might sound strange, but who are you? And what am I doing here?"

"You are here so we can evaluate you; see if you will be any good at the job. We can't give it to just anyone, you know."

"Yes, well, perhaps, madam, if you could remind me what the actual job is..."

"How can we do that before we've finished evaluating you? It wouldn't be fair to raise your hopes, now would it?"

The man with the earring began to snore. I couldn't help staring at him.

The woman shrugged. "You'll have to excuse Claude. He's always tired and this is the only chance he has to get any rest. They have him on a treadmill all day, you know. It's because he was so lazy."

"Right."

The snores were becoming louder. The woman pinched him. He snorted but still slept on.

She tapped the table. "Let's get to business. We've wasted enough time. Tell us about how good you are at lying. Let's start with a few examples, shall we?"

Stunned by the question, I took a step back and tried to come up with what I hoped would be a good reply. "I don't tell lies."

"Oh, come now. That's a really poor attempt, quite the worst I've heard in ages. You must be able to do better than that. No one would be taken in by such an obviously untrue statement. Don't be so modest, Mr. Ferris. We have a long file detailing all your petty, little deceptions."

Were these people officers of the law? Was this peculiar place part of a prison? I had no memory of being arrested.

"Never mind his lies. Is he a good enough conman to carry it off? That's the only thing we have to decide, and thus far he is not impressing me."

I stared at the bald man. "You think I'm a conman?"

"On occasions. Though, according to your file, you spent most of your time robbing coaches." She pushed a thick pile of papers across the table towards me. I was sure it had not been there a moment before.

I didn't want to touch the file. I was torn between alarm at the strange behaviour of these odd people and a desire to laugh: this interview was so absurd. I had reached the end of my patience and turned to make for the door.

"Oh dear. Are you giving up so easily?"

"Madam, I have no idea what game you're playing so, yes, I think I might be."

"If you do give up now, you'll never be given another chance."

"I'm not sure I want one."

"Very well but I guarantee you will come to regret it. You'll become just one more sad and sorry wraith."

"Nadine! Watch what you're saying!!" The bald man was on his feet.

The woman clapped her hand over her mouth.

It was too late. In that instant everything changed. I rocked on my feet for a moment, unsteady, as my memories returned. Like arrows striking a straw target, they flew into me.

I now knew where I was. I was dead. This was Hell. This panel could send me to my eternal torture. Again I stood on a cliff edge. But this time if I fell, there would be no remarkable escape.

My interrogators were back in their seats, the one with the earring no longer convincing me he was sleeping.

With a final, sharp snore, he opened his eyes. "Is it all over? Have we given this one the job?"

"Shut up, Claude. Nadine opened her big mouth and told him, didn't she?"

"Ah, how unfortunate. Well, I'm sorry, Mr. Ferris, but under these circumstances we cannot continue with the interview. I apologise for having wasted your time, not that I suppose you mind." He flapped his hand at me as though I were nothing but an irritating fly. "The door is behind you."

"No! Wait, please!!" My legs were weak. This must not be the end. "Why can't you continue? Believe me: I'm willing to do anything. Just give me another chance." I was shaking. I could feel the flames at my back.

"Anything? Anything at all?" The woman leaned towards me.

"Yes. I can't imagine what kind of work you have for a... but I... I'm... I do want to give it a go. I can tell lies, if that is what you want. Please!" My voice faded away. I had never believed I would beg for my life. But knowing the fate awaiting me beyond that Final Door made a coward of me.

"The task is far from pleasant. You may regret persuading us to take you on. A great many others have in the end preferred to pass through the Final Door than continue with this work."

"Madam, I still want to try. Really I do."

She glanced at her colleagues. "Do I go ahead and explain to him what the job entails?"

Claude shrugged. "Why not? It's that or we'll have to start all over again with the next candidate."

"Well, Mr. Ferris, you must be aware not everyone wants to come here."

"You mean there are some who do?"

She chuckled. "Not many, I admit. We are seeking a new member for one of the teams tasked with gathering in the newly dead who belong in Hell. They must persuade, cajole or deceive those souls into coming here, then send them through the Final Door."

I shivered. She was right: it did not sound a pleasant task. Or an easy one for that matter. But, despite my fear, I was now curious. "Don't you have daemons for that?"

"No. They think the task is beneath them and, besides, it's much more reassuring for the clients in the first instance. Daemons are pretty scary."

I couldn't argue with that.

"Do you still think this job is for you?" She sat back, watching me. Her fingers rifled through the papers again. "Could you trick them? Some won't even have realised they're dead. Could you explain their demise to them and then deceive them into following you? Are you certain your emotions won't get in the way when you have to gather in a child? Or a young woman? Or someone just like you? Knowing what lies in wait for them, would you still be able to look at them and smile?"

I did not know the answers. But I could not fail this test and so face the Final Door again. "Let me try. I can be persuasive. I'm good at explaining things. I can smile."

She turned to her colleague with the earring. "What do you think, Claude? Is he suitable?"

I did not give him time to reply. I felt I had the measure of these three interviewers now: two were just window dressing. I looked Claude in the eye. "I will not fail you, sir."

He sat back. "Very well. We'll give you a trial."

"So, when do I start?"

"You already have. You are now officially a Reaper, Third Class, though most people will call you a 'Hell hound'. Report to your team leader. She has recently been promoted to run the group that deals with the first quarter of the twenty-first century. I expect you will find the contrast with your own time most interesting."

Behind me the door swung open.

CHAPTER 7

I left the interview room. The door opposite opened. I was meant to enter. But for a moment I could not move. I felt dizzy, disorientated as I waited for the nightmare to continue. What had I agreed to?

I gave myself a shake. Whatever did lie ahead for me, it had to be easier to endure than what awaited me beyond the Final Door. If these people wanted me to smile, I would smile.

So, I did.

I entered a large room. Haphazard groups of mismatched armchairs, settees and even the odd chaise longue were strewn around on a grey carpet. Beside them were low tables covered with higgledy-piggledy piles of glossy bound papers. I could not have felt more out of place.

In the middle of the disorder sat a woman with long, black hair. She had her back to me. There was something familiar about her.

"Come and sit down, Ross."

"Caroline?"

"Who else did you expect? Didn't they tell you I was going to be your team leader? That's so typical of them. They never tell you anything that matters. But I'm glad you're here and I'm sure we're going to work well together."

Perhaps this was not going to be too bad after all. Despite everything, it was good to see her again. "I hope so."

"And, having had a glimpse of your records, I'm certain you'll fit in with the rest of the team without any problems. Now, welcome to our common room, although most of us call it the 'kennel'. When you're off duty this is where you'll spend the time... unless you're being trained or doing some research in the library."

As she was speaking, I looked about me. It was not the most interesting room I had ever been in. The walls and floor, like everywhere else I had seen in this place, were a uniform grey, the exact same shade as the corridor and interview room I had left behind me. The only contrast was a large, ornate mirror to the left of the door. In it was reflected a circular table surrounded by over a dozen upright chairs at the opposite end of the long, rectangular space. It would not have been out of place in the great hall of any manor house. Littered across its surface were neat stacks of paper, quill pens and inkwells. Someone must have been expecting to make a lot of notes. (I was glad I couldn't read or write, so it wouldn't be me). A large, floor to ceiling bookcase stood on the opposite side. It was filled with leather bound volumes which looked as if they hadn't been touched in centuries. Throughout the room various lanterns were suspended from the ceiling, giving off more than enough light to illuminate the space. Like everywhere I had been in this level of Hell, the atmosphere was hot and dry but not too uncomfortable, though I did wonder if it was only because I was becoming accustomed to the temperature.

As she finished, a door in the far left corner opened, sending a shaft of pale green light across the floor almost to our feet.

Caroline stood up. She bit her lip. "They're ready for you now, Ross. There's no reason to be scared. It shouldn't hurt too much and it'll soon be over. We all have to go through this."

Go through what? I didn't like the look in her eyes. I would have run if there had been anywhere to hide. Could the interview panel have changed their decision? But no. Caroline was a Reaper and she said they all had to go through this.

I must have hesitated too long. The light shot out and enveloped me in a slimy, hot, green mist. Something dragged at my unwilling feet. I slid across the floor, propelled towards whatever awaited me inside the light.

I think I may have cried out.

They had done something to me. I ran my fingers through my hair. What was that small, uneven lump at the back of my head? I was sure nothing had been there before.

I sat up. A wave of dizziness coursed through me. I groaned.

Caroline was leaning over me. "It'll be all right. Just take it easy. You'll feel better in a few minutes."

"Have I been asleep?"

"Sort of, but not the kind where you dream."

I was on a low chaise longue in a corner of the common room. A tartan blanket had been thrown over me, the bright colours incongruous against all that plain grey. I twisted my body free of the clinging fabric and perched on the edge of the seat.

She straightened her back. "We have to be on our way soon."

"Where are we going?"

"To your first assignment. Though I have to be honest, it's more of a test; to check the panel got it right and you do have an aptitude for this type of work."

"What do you mean? I didn't think there was any doubt. They gave me the impression the job was mine. They said nothing about any probation."

"No, I don't suppose they did. As I said before, they never tell anyone anything that matters. Still, I'm sure you'll be fine, especially now you've been..." More lip biting. Why was she so nervous? "Adapted. They've made it so you can recognise the souls we're sent to collect, so you won't make any mistakes. You have a piece of Hell in your head. We call it a lodestone. And it's not all bad. It lets you keep the body you're wearing, the one the daemon gave you. You are now a 'fetch': a ghost with a body who appears to the living as if you were one of them."

"Adapted?" I rubbed the bulge in my skull. So, now they'd put something inside me, had they? Yes, I had agreed to work for them. What else could I do, given the alternative of eternal torment? But I wasn't sure about this. "What happens if I fail their test? Do they mess with me again?"

"I don't know but I'm sure they won't." She was lying, trying hard to convince herself as well as me, but which was the lie? Did she know and not want to tell me?

She floated across the room and passed straight through the wall. I had seen the daemon do the same thing. Indeed, he had taken me with him. But could I do it on my own? My body appeared solid but so had hers.

I put out a hand and touched the smooth, grey surface. My fingers did not vanish into it.

"Hurry up, Ross." Caroline was now only a disembodied head, while the rest of her was on the other side. It reminded me of a trophy on the wall of a baronial mansion.

I hesitated. What was I supposed to do next? There was no handle on the door. I was trapped inside.

"Come on. Let's go. What are you waiting for? We should get this over with."

"How are you doing that?"

"Oh, this? It's simple. Just walk at the wall or door and keep on going. Trust me. You may have a body but it has no real substance, even though you can touch and hold things."

Still expecting to bounce off the wall, I gritted my teeth and closed my eyes.

I emerged into the long, grey corridor.

Some distance away another ghost awaited us. He was fairly tall, but not quite my height. He wore his shoulder-length light brown hair tied back. There was something unfriendly about the look in his heavy lidded, hazel eyes. "I'm Josh, Caro's supervisor. I'll be observing you to make sure nothing goes wrong."

From the way Caroline's eyes widened, something had already gone wrong.

He smirked at her. "You know, this is such an easy one. I see no need for you to accompany him. In fact, why don't we both stay here and give the new boy a chance to cut his teeth."

I could not miss the look of alarm on Caroline's face. I guessed this was not normal procedure. I should no doubt have had copious amounts of training before reaching this point. But I had met Josh's type before: he was the sort who would not listen to argument. And I could already tell, although we had only just met, he had taken a strong dislike to me. I wondered what I could have done to deserve it. I would have to watch my step.

With a shrug, I followed him along the corridor. "Where am I being sent?"

"You'll see. And it couldn't be more simple. There's a dead man waiting for you and he's in a room on his own, so I'm not anticipating any complications. All you need to do is talk to him. Use those skills of persuasion you're supposed to have to get him out of there. Then get yourself back here as quick as you can. When you have, I will evaluate your performance."

The grey corridor ended at the side door of an old barn. Inside, dust motes floated in rays of sunlight streaming through cracked side walls. Over in one corner heaps of hay had been piled up. Other than that, the place was empty. Except for the figure tied to the chair.

He was little older than a boy: couldn't have been more than eighteen. His dark hoodie and denim jeans were saturated with blood. Only the ropes binding him held his body upright. It was clear from the bruises, knife slashes and the unnatural positions of his limbs his death had not been an easy one. At his feet was an inside out canvas rucksack, every seam split and the contents trampled into the blood-soaked earth.

His wraith had not yet emerged.

I went over to the corpse and crouched in front of it. I had no idea what to do next. Ah well, I would just have to play it by ear.

"Leave him alone. Don't touch him!"

Startled, I rose to my full height. I had been so intent on the task in hand I had neglected to keep an eye on my surroundings.

A young woman wearing an identical, though much cleaner, hoodie and jeans and with a determined scowl on her face stood in the doorway. She was aiming a shotgun at me. "I said leave him alone!" She jerked the weapon in the direction of the far wall. "Get yourself over there."

I considered ignoring her request: I didn't think there was any way she could harm me. But I didn't want any complications. Not yet. Not ever, if I could avoid it. I didn't want to give Josh the satisfaction of watching me fail. So much for this being an uncomplicated assignment! Here I was, with no training at all, struggling to deal not only with this newly dead boy but also a living witness. I didn't know whether to placate her or ignore her. Under my breath I cursed Josh.

For now, I would do as she asked. Perhaps I might be able to persuade her to go for help. Then I could get on with my task. One thing was certain: I could not afford to fail.

The woman and I were seeing different things. As far as I was concerned, the young man's ghost was now an insubstantial shell, wrapped tighter than a lover's embrace round the cooling flesh. But for her there would only be the flesh. She had not even realised his connection with life had been severed.

She was not alone. The ghost shared her opinion. He writhed against the ropes, unaware how easy it would be to slip out of them. Somehow, I must convince him to come with me. But so far I hadn't had any opportunity even to explain to him he was dead. As with me at the Farrier's, he still believed he had survived the torture, the deep gashes in his skin and the bullet lodged in his head. He didn't realise the sticky, spreading pool of blood around his feet was all his: more than he could ever have shed and hoped to walk away. I understood. But I could not afford to sympathise.

Raising my hands I backed into the corner. As I did so, he called out, "I knew you'd come for me, Valerie."

I would have liked to explain only I could hear him, but it would just have added to the woman's confusion.

Except... I was the one confused.

She smiled at him. "I told you I would. Now we've got to get you out of here before the law arrives. Can you stand?"

Trust me to have stumbled across a true medium. And on my first mission! I didn't imagine there were too many of those around. Yet here she was, in my way. How inopportune. But Josh couldn't have known about her. Could he?

She levelled the rifle at me again. "Cut him loose. I'm taking him somewhere safe and you're coming with me."

"Maybe it would be better if we didn't try to move him. You should go and fetch help. I'm not the one who hurt him, I just found him like this. Tell you what: I'll stay and look after him."

I wasn't convincing her. She waved the weapon. "Shut up. I've no idea who you are, mister, but you're going to do as you're told. Now, untie him."

Her finger was twitching on the trigger. If she wasn't careful, any moment the gun would go off.

Crossing over to the corpse, I concentrated on trying to untie the ropes binding his hands. I took the opportunity to hiss, "You're dead!" into his ear. He took no notice (all his attention was on the woman), but it had been worth a try.

To my surprise, the ropes snaked down from his limbs. They tangled as they fell into the sticky pool around the chair. The body slumped forwards.

"Now, get him up. Lean him on your shoulder."

Was she joking? Anyone could see he was way beyond that. Anyone except her, that is.

The novelty of having a shotgun pointed at me had worn off. And I had no intention of attempting to remove the body from the chair. I wasn't even sure I could.

I was certain we were not supposed to reveal ourselves to the living, but this young woman's actions left me with no choice. I could think of no other way to get through to her boyfriend.

"You can't help him and neither can anyone else. There's no point in taking him from this room." I took a step towards her.

It had the desired effect. A shotgun makes a noise like no other. In a confined space it's uncomfortable on the ears, though I did not feel any pain as the pellets sped through my borrowed body only to bury themselves in the rear wall.

To her credit she didn't scream or faint. She just stared at me as she let the rifle fall to the floor. "What are you?"

Well, that had to be an improvement on 'who'. I was making progress.

"My name is Ross, and you would call me a ghost, which I am, sort of. I died a long time before you were born." I waved my hand toward her boyfriend, who was now leaning forward and in danger of falling off his chair. "And I'm sorry to have to tell you I'm not the only ghost here."

The young man's spirit frowned and his mouth fell open. "Are you trying to threaten us?"

"Not in the slightest. I'm just trying to do my job. I was sent here to collect you."

"Aaron isn't going anywhere. I don't care what you say. He's not going to die."

"I'm sorry. You're not listening. He's already dead."

"No, I'm not dead. I can't be. I want to stay with Valerie."

I ran a hand through my hair. I was getting a headache with the constant warmth from the lodestone. And I didn't want to do the next part: explain to both of them he had no choice.

Valerie picked up the shotgun. Did she imagine she had only missed me? Was she about to try again? It was a concern because the barn was not isolated. The sound might carry far enough through the quiet twilight for someone to hear. I had too much to do already, dealing with these two.

"Where do you want to take him?" There was something in her voice, in the way she was now gazing not at me or Aaron but at the pool of blood on the ground. It had at last dawned on her I was telling the truth.

"There's no point in lying to you. You wouldn't believe me if I told you I was taking him to Heaven. You know him and the way he has lived."

"I don't care. If you take him, I've got nothing left. So, I guess I'm coming too."

"It's not your time."

"It could be."

The rifle was upright. The muzzle dug into her chin. Her finger writhed as it put pressure on the trigger.

"No! Don't do this, Valerie. I'll be wait..."

Distracted, I turned to watch the connection between Aaron and his corpse dissolve. He was gone.

An explosion shattered the silence.

Followed by Valerie's cries of despair. The pellets bounced harmlessly off the walls. She fell to her knees. "I couldn't do it. Oh, Aaron, forgive me. I wanted to but..."

I heaved a sigh of relief. I had no idea how much trouble I would have been in if she had succeeded. We'd both had a lucky escape.

"I will see him again, won't I?"

"That depends. You must know where he's gone isn't very nice. You could do so much better. It all depends on what you do with the remainder of your life."

She grinned at me through her tears. "I'll have to make sure I'm a bad, bad girl then, won't I?" Leaving me unable to answer, she slung the shotgun over her shoulder and strode out of the barn.

I stared after her for a few long seconds, then gazed at the empty cadaver sprawled beside the chair. I didn't want to, but I couldn't help wondering if his spirit was now stranded on that empty plain, about to face the golden eyes of the daemon. Or had he been one of the "easy" ones: his passage leading straight through the Final Door? Either way, I hoped he would not curse me for persuading him to leave the temporal plane.

CHAPTER 8

I sensed a movement at the side of the barn.

Caroline was watching me. She gave me a faint smile. "It's hard, the first time. I remember mine, and at least I wasn't alone. You did well. No one can doubt you have a real aptitude for this. Josh won't have any grounds at all for claiming you haven't already done enough to pass your probation."

"Is that how it's done: throw the new one in at the deep end? You let me think I was alone when you were there, observing, all the time."

"I came as soon as I could because it's not usually done like this. As soon as Josh was called away, I slipped out. He's treated you so unfairly. He had no right to send you here on your own as early as this, without even a single training session. He knows full well every new recruit is mentored on their first few missions." She bit her lip. "Perhaps I should mention it to someone in Personnel."

"No, don't do that. It'll only make things worse. Though I don't understand why Josh has taken such a dislike to me."

"Neither do I, but you'd best watch your back. Supervisors can make dangerous enemies. But you shouldn't see too much of him from now on. As team leader, I'm the one who has to deal with the man."

Was that a shudder I saw as she turned and began leading the way down the long, grey tunnel? Her words did not reassure me. Instead, there was something in her tone which made me certain I was going to see a lot more of Josh.

On our return, Caroline introduced me to the rest of the team. There were four of us, which, she explained, was the usual number. Greg was a tall, slender man around six feet two, with hair so blond as to be almost white and eyes the same shade as chips of blue ice. He spoke in a clipped, abrupt manner. I was sure he was not English, but maybe Germanic, and I got the impression by the way he stood with his hands clasped behind his back he might once have been a soldier. Louise was a quiet mouse of a girl, with brown hair and washed-out hazel eyes. But at least she was a little more friendly than Greg, who was so aloof it was almost to the point of being impolite. It struck me I might have replaced someone who had been important to him.

I was told all of the teams (and there were a great many of them, spread out over every continent and based in every era) had the same structure: one leader with three or occasionally four more junior hounds. I realised at once that for me to have been recruited to this team, a previous member had either to have been promoted or, more likely, been sent beyond the Final Door. I wanted to find out more about my predecessor, but Caroline brushed off any attempt at gentle probing. She only wanted to talk about our missions. And asking Greg was out of the question.

Which left only Louise.

I had to bide my time and be patient, which was never one of my strong points, while I waited for Caroline and Greg to be sent out together. (I had not yet been able to work out how Josh made the decisions on who or even how many of us to allocate, but I was sure it wasn't random.)

When at last the chance arose, I interrupted Louise as she was passing the time idly turning the pages of a magazine. I suspected, if she was as bored as I was, she might welcome some conversation; an opportunity to open up.

"How long have you been in Hell?"

She shrugged. "Have you seen any clocks around here? We don't even possess a calendar. And you must have noticed every mission you're sent on it's a different season, even a different year. Time in Hell doesn't operate in the same way as it does on the temporal plane."

"No, I don't suppose it does."

"Don't worry, Ross. You'll get used to it eventually. We all do."

"Did my predecessor?"

She shifted on her chair. Her mouth formed into a sharp circle. "We don't talk about that. We still miss Anya."

"What happened to her?"

"Don't you already know? I'm sure they must have told you." She cast her eyes down onto the page of her magazine and for a moment I thought I had lost her.

But I could not let it rest. "No one told me anything. When I was first assigned, Josh sent me straight out into the field. And Caroline did little more than introduce you to me. You must agree it's only natural I would be curious about the team."

"Nothing is natural here. Haven't you realised that yet? All I will say is that we were very different then. Anya was our team leader, Josh and Caro her deputies, while Greg and I did as we were told. We worked together well."

"What went wrong?"

"Anya broke the rules. She got involved with someone. You have been told that's not allowed, haven't you?"

I nodded.

"They were betrayed. We all knew it was Josh who squealed on her. And he got his reward: promoted straight to supervisor. Caro was made team leader, even though she didn't want the position. I became a Reaper, Second Class which, I suppose, makes me her deputy. We never saw Anya again."

Her mouth was now set in a firm, thin line. I understood. Who would want to say out loud that their friend had been sent behind the Final Door?

"And Greg?"

"What about Greg? He hadn't been with us long. So, he's the same as you, a Third Class, not that there's much of a difference between one class and another. Caro gets to give the orders, which she hates, and has the use of a private study room, which she never goes near."

"No one told me there were any private rooms in this place." How interesting: somewhere to get away from everyone was sure to come in useful. It was certainly something I had been lacking.

"Yes, it's one of the doors at the back of the library behind the section on twentieth century technology, but like I said, she never goes there. And before you get any ideas, it's out of bounds to anyone of a lower grade."

So that was where those doors led. There were dozens. I had noticed them on my earlier tour of the facilities with Caroline. She had said, "Nowhere important" when I asked about them. I was now even more determined to explore. There had to be many other places I had not been shown. But it would be unwise to press Louise further. In any case, from the way she rustled the pages before holding them up, I guessed she'd had enough of talking to me.

Before going on my next mission, I was at last sent for some training. Well, better late than never. Though I soon discovered it was all a complete waste of time, not to mention rather boring. Someone should have pointed out to the tutors you can't teach people how to lie. They've either got the skill or they haven't; tricking others is innate, not learned. And the hounds are selected from people who possess those abilities. Everyone is a con artist in this part of Hell.

Yes, a con artist and a joker. I was quick to discover the limitations of the body I was wearing. It was tempting to think there was little difference between it and the one I had in life; I was about the same height, had the same dark hair and blue eyes. I still had my moustache and even my beard, though neither grew any more. There were even a couple of improvements: all the scars I had collected during my career were gone and, of course, this body could pass through walls and doors as if they were thin, gossamer curtains. I did miss having a heartbeat though, and sometimes it would have been pleasant to have been able to take a deep breath but, on the whole, I guess I had gained more than I had lost.

It was strange never feeling hungry or tired. I'm sure I would have missed enjoying a drink or a good meal much more had they been put in front of me, but ever since the first moment I had been in Hell, I had seen neither.

We had arrived at what our tutor said would be "our last formal session". There were five of us in the group: three men and two women. We had been kept busy when we were together so had little opportunity to get to know each other. Anyway, it wasn't considered necessary. We were unlikely to ever see each other again. After the training was over, we were to return to teams operating in different parts of the world and covering different centuries.

We entered the room to discover chairs placed around a central table. In front of each of us had been set a glass and a bottle. Mine contained brandy, fine French cognac. I had always had a weakness for the stuff.

Our tutor had in front of him a tall, cut crystal carafe filled with red wine. He poured himself a glass before nodding to us. "You've done well so I believe a little celebration is in order. Enjoy!" He raised the glass to his lips. Why did I not notice he took only the tiniest of sips? Was I so absorbed by the thought of the pleasure to come?

The man opposite me was the first to drain his glass, which had been filled with a green liquid. I had never tasted absinthe. I thought perhaps I might ask for a sip, but first...

The heady aroma of the brandy swamped my senses and the taste... Oh, was I even still in Hell? I couldn't help myself; I drained two glasses in quick succession. I was just about to pour a third when the woman to my left gave a little squeal and jumped to her feet.

Then it happened: a spreading stain and I was sitting in a puddle. My clothes were dripping. I had never been so mortified. I would never have disgraced myself so in public.

And it was the same for all of us. The drinks were no longer inside the glasses, the bottles or our bodies. They were pouring out of us from every orifice.

"Sit still!" commanded our tutor. He waved his full glass at us. "I hope you now understand why you can never give in to temptation while out on assignment. There may be rare occasions when you will be permitted to drink, even to eat. It might be a necessary part of your cover, a step taken to prevent suspicion while you are surrounded by the living, but in general this will be the result. I will leave you now. There are clean, dry clothes next door: gentlemen to the left, ladies to the right. Class dismissed."

I swear I heard him chuckle as he passed through the wall.

We three men dressed in silence, all of us too embarrassed to meet each other's eyes. Unsure what to do next, we returned to wait for the ladies and say our farewells. The table was now empty, no longer any sign of glasses or drinks. The chairs and the floor were dry.

"How dare they do that to us?" Miriam, one of the women, scowled as she rearranged her skirts. Then, after giving it a thorough inspection, she perched on the edge of her chair.

"Just one more indignity in this place! Did you hear him laugh?"

We all nodded at Michael's question.

But he hadn't finished. "I'm sick of all this. The job stinks and, as for the rest of it, I'm not sure how long I'll be able to carry on doing it. My first mission was a kiddie, a twelve-year-old boy, who'd killed his ma. Not a nice child, I agree, but still, it makes me shudder when I think what's lying ahead for him."

Miriam lowered her voice. "We all feel the same. There must be a way out. There's got to be."

Michael cleared his throat. "Well, I've heard there is. Someone did get away and not so long ago. It was a woman; her name was Anya." He stared hard at me. "Wasn't she from your team?"

Ah, so Miriam and he were a double act, were they? Well, it wasn't going to work with me. You can't extract information from someone who knows nothing.

"I arrived after Anya had gone. I think I'm the one who has taken her place. But I'm sorry: I was told she didn't escape. She was sent through the Final Door for breaking the rules."

Michael pulled a face. "I heard she was sent there but she never arrived. The rumour..."

I cut across him. "Rumours! What are rumours? They're not facts. They're more like wishful thinking." But I remembered the look on Louise's face, the way she had hidden behind that magazine. Had she been keeping something from me? Did she suspect Anya had indeed gone missing?

I gave myself a shake. This wouldn't do. False hope had to be worse than no hope at all. Hadn't it?

I had disappointed my interrogators; they had hoped for more. From the way Michael was observing me, it was clear he thought I knew more than I was telling. And that was not all. Where had Miriam and he heard Anya's name? We had not discussed our teams at or around our sessions. Could it be Anya was the subject of a much more widespread rumour? If that were the case, could there be the tiniest of chances she really had found a way out?

I was in the right place to find some answers. And I was determined, if there were any to be found, I would do my utmost to uncover them. Perhaps this incident with the liquids had taught me more than our instructor had intended.

For a while after that, my missions were pretty straightforward, executed with Caroline and sometimes Greg or, less often, Louise. But the day finally came when I was assigned to my second lone mission. I hoped it would be easier than dealing with Valerie had proved to be.

CHAPTER 9

Everyone was avoiding the fifth seat from the left in the front row. A young couple occupied seats three and four; the man in seat six was reading a thick, dog-eared paperback with a lurid cover. On the row behind, a restless child brushed the back of five then jumped away, startled by something he could never have explained. As a uniformed guard with a sniffer dog paused by the seat, the Labrador growled deep in its throat.

The dog and I were the only ones who could see the occupant of the fifth seat. She was in her late twenties and had blonde, curly hair and the widest of blue eyes. She had put out a hand to pat him, which was why he growled. Sensitive living creatures are often uneasy when they are touched by the dead.

The flight for Dubai was announced on the public address system. The couple giggled as they gathered their baggage and headed for the departure gate arm in arm. The word "honeymoon" floated in the air behind them.

I took the newly vacated seat four. "Good afternoon."

Ignoring me or not realising I was addressing her, she continued to stare straight ahead. Death can be somewhat disorientating at the best of times.

Despite not yet being able to read it, though I was learning, I unfurled a newspaper. I needed the camouflage. Unlike her, I was visible to the people around us. Having a conversation with thin air never looks good. "My name is Ross. What's yours?"

I half expected her to ignore me again but instead she replied, "Jennifer."

Good. That was easier than expected. First step over: contact established. Tick. Now all that was left was to explain to her she was no longer alive and persuade her to come back with me.

She swivelled in her seat to face me. At that moment, had I been breathing, the air would have caught in my throat; I would have gasped. She was, as many would say, a "complete dead ringer" for someone I had once known. Watching her from the side it wasn't so obvious, but now, so close, so visible, I wanted to call her Tessa.

But Tessa was no more: a life cut short over two hundred years ago. She should have inherited her father's tavern, taken a good husband, had children, instead of dying at the hand of Elias Robertshaw. Waves of anger and sorrow rose in me at the thought of how he had raped and murdered her.

It was all such a long time ago now. Robertshaw would be beyond the Final Door; his suffering far greater than any I could have inflicted. I smiled at the thought of how much pain he must be in. My situation was better. But if it was to stay that way, I had better get on with what I had been sent to do.

When Caroline allocated me this routine assignment, I saw nothing special about it. All I had to do was gather in a soul. This one died around six hours earlier in a baggage tunnel beneath the airport terminal building. There had been a shoot-out over the drugs Jennifer and her friends were attempting to smuggle into the country. Of the four in the gang, one was now in hospital and would in all probability join Jennifer soon. The other two survived and had been taken into custody.

Time to get on with my task. Again, I reminded myself this woman was not Tessa. I should not waste my sympathy. She was a bad woman who deserved the fate which awaited her.

"Where are you trying to get to, Jennifer?"

She replied with a frown, the tiny lines around her eyes so like Tessa's used to be when she was confused over something, which she often was. I had liked Tessa a lot. Perhaps, given the way I was reacting now, I had liked her more than I realised at the time. After all, it had been her to whom I fled on that final day when I was injured and afraid; an action which had cost her so much.

"I think I might stay here a while." Jennifer glanced at the destination board then back to me. "There's nowhere on there that appeals."

I knew there wouldn't be. She was not capable of leaving. If I did not take her with me, she would haunt this place forever. But if I could get her to leave the terminal building, my task might well be over. The cold night air blowing through her would waft her away from the temporal plane. All the way to Hell.

"Would you care to take a walk with me? You've been sitting here such a long time."

"I don't think so. I'm quite comfortable where I am."

I had to get on with my task. If I failed, Josh would make sure I had an eternity to regret it. So, why was I hesitating?

"Come on. A little stroll will do you good."

She rose to her feet and we headed for the tunnels. She showed no surprise as I guided her through the wall. I hoped no one saw us. But if they did, the chances were they would only rub their eyes and blame jet lag, alcohol or tell themselves their imaginations were running away with them. Once Jennifer caught sight of her bullet riddled body, I was confident she would come to terms with her condition and it would all be over.

But when we got there, the tunnels were not swarming with police and airport officials. The only people around were baggage handlers.

We reached the place where she had died. I watched her, expecting her to need a little comfort, a little reassurance. We stopped.

"There. You understand what has happened now, don't you, Jennifer?"

"Understand what?"

For once the authorities had acted with indecent haste. Perhaps her corpse had been in the way. Whatever the reason, all traces of the gunfight were gone except for a few holes in the walls and a slight reddish stain on the concrete floor. There was nothing to alarm Jennifer; nothing for her to see at all.

My only evidence was gone. What other proof could I offer her that she was dead and it was time for her to move on? There was no point in remaining in that draughty tunnel. I was already attracting curious glances from a couple of cleaners. I did not want to be challenged. What excuse could I offer for being in an area off limits to passengers? "I'm trying to stop you being haunted" was more likely to result in me being escorted off the premises than Jennifer.

But our seats had been taken; now occupied by two members of a group of young women dressed in strange clothes. They were all wearing flimsy, pink costumes, and acting in a far more rowdy way than anyone from my own time would have considered respectable.

Jennifer laughed at the sight of them. "I'm having my own hen party soon. I'm getting married in July."

I did not want to know that. By July she would have been in Hell for over three months. I ought to return to my original plan. I ought to persuade her to leave the terminal. I ought to suppress my emotions: this woman was not Tessa!

But still I wavered.

We sat together in silence on the back row.

After a while she stood. "I want to visit the tunnels again."

"Why not? I could do with a walk. Let's go." She thought she was just doing it for something to do, a break from the departure lounge. I knew it for what it was: the need a ghost has to haunt the place of its death each day at the same hour it died. It's a vulnerable time. The spectre can become quite visible for a short period. And Jennifer did. For several minutes she became a pale presence. And standing straight, still as a statue, with her hands in tight fists by her sides, she threw back her head. And howled.

There wasn't a thing I could do about it. She was now unaware of anything around her. I could shout as loud as I liked but she wouldn't hear me until this was over. I backed away round a corner and hid behind a baggage cart someone had left there.

That first night we were lucky. No one saw her. But it wouldn't last. If I didn't deal with this soon, before long the terminal would indeed earn a reputation for being haunted. She would become established. And I would have failed.

Her howling over, she could not remember what had just happened. There was little point in trying to tell her; she would not have believed me. And I could still not get myself to persuade her to come with me. Could not think of the right words to explain. Perhaps if I gave her a little space...

I wandered through the huge building. I had never been inside an airport before. There had been lots of pictures, even a film or two, shown during the orientation sessions after basic training; the boring ones which were supposed to prepare me for working in my assigned time period. Close up, the aeroplanes fascinated and appalled me in equal measure. There had been nothing remotely like them in my own century. I must have spent several hours watching those leviathans manoeuvring on the tarmac through the terminal's huge, thick plate-glass windows.

Caroline had told me this was going to be an easy job: one I could do on my own. I had been pleased I would be spending a few hours away from both Hell and the rest of my team. Now I wished they were here with me.

Another howling session. This time two men watched with their mouths wide open, before racing away. Things were getting out of hand.

The door out of the terminal might as well have been a hundred miles away given the progress we made towards it. Jennifer sat close to me and began to tell me about her life. I watched another flight to Dubai take off. The sniffer dog growled at both of us this time.

I tried to hint, to suggest she was not alive, but my attempts were clumsy. Jennifer was so like Tessa. Was this my first real test? The one Nadine had hinted at during my interview? The one which would make me loathe my job? Whatever she had done, I did not want this young woman to go to Hell. But we could not stay in the departure lounge forever. Caroline knew where I was, my whole team knew, Josh knew; everyone knew. It was not a choice: they would push us both through the Final Door.

By the third day we were still sitting there. I imagined the excuses Caroline must be inventing. But when they did come, I had decided it would be for two unwilling souls, not one.

Jennifer was going to cost me my future. Yes, this woman and I were set to go through the Final Door hand in hand. And would it be such a bad solution? I was already sick of being a Hell hound; sick of it all. How could I go on sending the souls of people who had lived lives no worse than my own into eternal torture?

The third howling. She was getting good at this. She had discovered it was possible for her to float off the ground and raise her arms as though she wanted to embrace anyone watching. Her clothes became bloodstained, and a hole ran through her forehead. She was exaggerating. I never knew a ghost could do that.

Nor had I known it was possible for a spirit to attract and court an audience. She extended her area of activity every time she made an appearance. Would Tessa have done such a thing?

Well, she had possessed a wicked sense of humour. It was one of the things which had attracted me to her. She might well have found frightening people in a tunnel under an airport an amusing escapade. On the other hand, she might have found it rather silly and boring. As I did.

Dubai called again, the second of the two flights that day. How many had there been since I arrived?

Jennifer and I sat there together. There was no sense of time passing, being punctuated only by the compulsion she felt to go and haunt the tunnels. I had long given up trying to find a way to tell her why they had sent me. I had failed in my duty. Surrendered my right to remain on this side of the Final Door.

A feeling of exhaustion overwhelmed me. Soon another hound would be sent to find me. Perhaps it would be Caroline. I wouldn't make it difficult for her. I'd just remain here in the airport beside Jennifer. For the moment it was enough for me to be able to sit and look at her face: the face of Tessa. The woman I had always denied to myself I had been in love with.

"Who's Tessa?"

"Tessa?"

"You keep calling me Tessa. Is she your wife?"

"No, I died a long time before I could take a wife."

She laughed but it emerged as a nervous, high-pitched squeak. "Why, what an odd thing to say. This Tessa's your girlfriend, is she?"

"She used to be. Over two hundred years ago."

Silence. Her eyes ranged over my face as though in search of some hidden secret. "You believe in reincarnation, do you?"

"No, two hundred and some years ago she was the wayward daughter of an innkeeper, and I was the highwayman who used to serenade her beneath her window."

At that moment Jennifer did something she had not done before. Her hand hovered over my wrist. "You don't have a pulse."

"Neither do you."

She sat back. Her face turned to the departure board and, from her expression, it was as though the destination "Hell" was up there, written in letters of crimson fire.

"I'm..." Her seat was empty.

I stood, uncertain what to do next.

"She's gone, Ross." Caroline walked out of the shadows. "I came to find you before Josh decided to send me. You've been here for six days. It's been far too long."

I closed my eyes. How could I let her lead me home to Hell? It was the last place I wanted to be. How much longer would I be able to withstand the thorns that pricked at my conscience, driven ever deeper into my borrowed flesh?

"I'm not coming with you, Caroline."

She raised an eyebrow. "You think you have a choice?"

"What's there to stop me? I could wander off and lose myself in the tunnels under this place. It wouldn't be boring. There's always something going on and the aeroplanes are fascinating. I'd become a nice, quiet spirit, haunting without causing a fuss." I smiled at her. "All you have to do is say you couldn't find me."

She glanced around. "What a pretty, little daydream you've been having. But Ross, do you really think it's as easy as that?" She leant towards me and reached out. She touched the bump in the back of my head, just above my spine.

A shock wave travelled right through me.

"This is from them. And it does so much: it lets you keep that rather handsome body, it tells you when you've found your target but, most of all, it informs them where you are and what you are doing."

I suppose I had known the truth all along, but it hurt to hear it spoken. "I am my own betrayer, am I? Do they also know what I'm thinking and what I'm feeling?"

"No, no. Only where you are and if you are getting on with the mission. Your thoughts are still your own." She hesitated. "They must be."

So, she didn't know. She just hoped.

CHAPTER 10

"'Is this a flame I see before me?' No! No, that's not right. It's a dagger. 'Is this a dagger!' What's the matter with me? Why can't I remember any of the script? I should know that bit by heart. I've lost count of how many times I've played Rom... No, not Romeo. I'm not here to play Romeo. What's wrong with me today?"

As he slunk off into the wings, the veteran actor's shoulders slumped. I already felt quite sorry for him, and I knew his confusion was only going to get worse. He'd played a lot of different roles on this stage and right now they were clamouring for a bit of him. They all wanted to be his last performance, the one before he faded away.

It said a lot for how good an actor he had been and also much about how little there was to his own personality: so shallow it could be submerged into any character he happened to be playing. I imagined he was not the easiest friend. Or lover; his marriages only lasting the length of his current role. When his public gathered to mourn him, they would all have someone different in mind.

I knocked on his dressing room door; no need to alarm him by walking through it. We had plenty of time: it was the middle of the night, and he was the only person left in the theatre. The audience long departed, the other players and stage crew already in their beds, no one was going to disturb us while I got on with my task.

"Come in."

He was sitting in front of a mirror, half of his face covered in greasepaint, a cotton wool ball clasped in his fist.

"Who are you?" He didn't bother to turn to look at me. He just glanced at my reflection in the glass. No doubt he thought I was one more dedicated fan desperate for an autograph.

I wasn't. I'd never even attended any of his performances. And it was too late now.

"My name is Ross, Mr. Barnes, and I'm here to ask you how you're feeling tonight."

"I'm fine. Why shouldn't I be?"

"You have noticed those deep wounds in your chest, haven't you?"

"Scratches, mere scratches. I've put some big plasters on them and they don't sting at all." He frowned. "How do you know about them? Can you tell me how I got them? I can't seem to remember."

"You were in a fight with your leading lady's husband after last night's performance. He followed you both into this room. He brought a sharp knife with him."

"Oh, I don't remember that. Was he badly hurt?"

"No, you never even landed a blow. He stabbed you through the heart within the first couple of seconds."

"What?" It was starting to dawn on him. Once he fully understood he was dead, my unpleasant duty would be fulfilled. I could take him and get back to...

He froze, his hand midway to his mouth. The cotton wool ball he had released floated in mid-air like a smeared multicoloured cloud. The door did not open but I knew we were no longer alone.

"Good evening. It's Ross, isn't it?"

The newcomer smiled, revealing a set of perfect white teeth to go with her unnaturally beautiful face. There was more than a suspicion of curving, white feathers rising from behind each shoulder.

"Yes, my name is indeed Ross. I'm here..." I'm not often lost for words but wasn't at all sure what I was supposed to say to an angel.

She chuckled. To make a similar sound would have delighted any musician. I didn't see her walk but she was now over by the mirror. Unlike myself, she did not have a reflection. Perhaps her perfection would have been too much for the glass to take.

She tilted her head. "You're no doubt wondering what I'm doing here interrupting your work. Well, have you any conception of how many souls in Heaven think Paradise is being in the Globe Theatre with the curtain about to rise on a performance of Hamlet? Not to mention, having the author available for curtain calls afterwards? Even more of them want to be there when Shakespeare presents his latest offering and, when he found out our friend here had just become available but was to be denied him, he threw the most dramatic of tantrums. He said he wouldn't stop sulking until he could cast Mr. Barnes in the role of his latest anti-hero."

"That's a shame, isn't it? You must be aware there is no question about it. Mr. Barnes is definitely one of ours."

"Yes, you could make that argument. And we did. We offered Mr. Shakespeare a choice from all our available stock but it's amazing how few great actors make it to Heaven. It's all that temptation surrounding them, you know: people telling them how wonderful they are. It's no surprise they become arrogant and lacking in self-restraint. And then they all have so many vices and such bad memories when it comes to marriage vows. And you would never believe how temperamental they are. So, as usual, we are going to have to bend the rules and stretch a point on this one."

"You can't do that."

"Why not?"

I wanted to give her a clever answer but the only words that came to mind were, "Because it's not fair. There are so many millions of souls in Hell, all condemned by their actions in life. You haven't let any of those unfortunates off, have you?"

"You mean people like you, Ross?" She raised her right hand and from her fingers dangled a pair of golden scales. "The Ancient Egyptians have a good way of explaining things. Let me demonstrate." Her left hand touched the actor's chest. A human heart is not the prettiest of sights even when it's not bleeding. She placed it into one pan of the scales. Then she rolled her shoulders, reached up and drew a long, white plume from the tip of her right wing.

It was no contest. The feather might as well have stayed in the place from which she had plucked it.

"There. As you can see, you are quite correct. If how he behaved in life were the only consideration, I would hand him over to you right now. Indeed, if that were the case, I wouldn't even be here." She sighed. "But there are other, more important factors to take into account." She breathed on the feather and the pan containing it sank a little. "There is the weight of all the pleasure he gave to his audiences during his long lifetime." Another breath. "The esteem in which he was held." A third breath. "And the dedication he gave to his roles."

"I was dedicated to my role too."

"I have no doubt you were, Ross, but, be honest, who would ever miss a common highwayman? Who would have expressed a desire to see him in action? Did you leave anyone behind who would have been prepared to plead your case?"

I swallowed. Perhaps there might have been one, but she wouldn't have carried any weight. And my poor, murdered Tessa had to have been beyond the Final Door for a long time by now. It was painful to me to think of her and the eternal torment she had to be enduring.

The angel opened her hand. Instead of falling, the scales, the heart and the feather all vanished. "This conversation is very pleasant but, like it or not, Ross, you've had a wasted journey. This man's soul is coming with me. If it's any consolation, he won't be as happy as you might expect. Because he doesn't deserve Heaven, he won't receive a Heavenly afterlife. He will spend eternity unable to resist performing. He will be a wonderful spectacle for his many audiences, but he will be forever discontented. Sometimes Hell is not a place: it is a frame of mind. In fact, he might well have been better off going with you." She yawned. "Time we were all gone from here. This one has still got to learn his lines from Mr. Shakespeare's latest script. I do hope all this trouble was worth it."

"Before you go, will you answer a question for me?"

"That depends on what it is, whether I'm permitted to or not, but I don't suppose there can be any harm in you asking."

"Is there any possible way a condemned soul might be able to escape from Hell?"

"Ah, now that would come under the category of privileged information, which is way above my rank." She folded her arms. "Hmm, all I can tell you is I've heard rumours. If I were seeking a way out, I would look for a place where there are many souls close together. Follow the crowd, Ross."

"I asked you for an answer, not a riddle."

She shrugged then rearranged her wings. There was a faint whispering in the air as though a giant swan had fluttered its feathers. "Tell you what. To make up for your disappointment and any inconvenience at the failure of your mission..." She waved her hand over the actor, still frozen in front of the mirror. "I'm going to give you a little gift."

I didn't know what to expect, perhaps a single feather with the perfect point for calligraphy. I doubted an angel would own physical objects any more than I did.

"There is a certain woman."

My mind was flooded with an image of my Tessa, standing on a rocky shore, her long, blonde hair blown over her shoulder by a gust of cold, Cornish wind, one slender hand resting on a grey boulder, the other holding down the skirt of her long, blue dress. "She's dead."

"Well, yes, she would be nearly three hundred by now if she wasn't. But the point I'm making, my friend, is you are wrong about her."

"How do you mean?"

"She is not, as you fear, somewhere in the wasteland beyond the Final Door of Hell. Oh yes, I know all about that. You see, in life Tessa did just enough good, by the smallest of margins, to avoid that most unpleasant of fates."

After so long in Hell I had forgotten how it felt to be happy. "Does she ever think of me? Does she miss me at all?"

"No. If she had any memory of you, it would make her sad and no one is allowed to be sad where I come from. But you can remember her now and know where she is and that she is content." The angel turned and placed a hand on the shoulder of Kenneth Barnes, once and soon to be again Shakespeare's favourite thespian. "Time to go, sir. There's a stage with an audience and a brand new production waiting for you."

Barnes' wraith rose up out of his body and the empty carcase slumped forward over the dressing table. The angel nodded to me and a moment later I was alone.

I took her gift and placed it in a corner of my heart. I might have to go back to Hell, but I was returning with a tiny fragment of Heaven.

And there could be more. Barnes had just come off stage when he died and not had time to tidy away the clutter of items on his dressing table. Among them was a Patek Philippe gold rimmed watch.

I smiled as I tried it on my wrist. Perhaps the talk of Tessa had reminded me I was, underneath it all, a man who had once been a thief. It looked good against my skin. And in Hell we all so missed being able to tell the time. Why shouldn't I take this with me?

I unfastened it and slid it into my pocket.

The grey tunnel back to Hell seemed longer than usual this time. But whether that was due to the guilt at what I knew to be a forbidden act, or only nerves because it had been so long since I had done anything dishonest, I wasn't sure. Besides, it was such a tiny piece of defiance. The watch would doubtless not even be missed by Barnes' heirs or, if it was, it would be assumed someone at the theatre had filched it. Theft by ghost sounded ridiculous even to me.

But something was wrong. The tunnel was too long. I should already have been entering the common room. And with each step the watch became heavier in my pocket and hotter too, as though it were on fire.

Ahead of me was a blank wall. I stepped through it... and found myself back in Barnes' dressing room.

I shook my head. "All right, I get the message. There's no need to insist."

I laid the object down in the same spot from which I had removed it.

On my next attempt the tunnel took me to Hell in seconds.

CHAPTER 11

Caroline was waiting for me. "I don't know what you did, and I don't want to know. A petty fiend has been here with a message. I'm to inform you there will be no punishment this time because the instruction not to do it was missed out during training. But do it again and you will definitely be punished." She gave me a sharp nod. "Is that clear?"

"Yes, but all I did…"

She shook her head so hard I was afraid it might come off. "Don't tell me. I wasn't to ask. It's clear it was something so terrible you mustn't repeat it. Now, come on. We've got an urgent mission and we're to go right away."

I couldn't help it. I just had to say, "No peace for the wicked, then."

We arrived just as a bright red Ferrari smashed through a set of wrought iron gates as though they were made of paper. It screeched past us before wrapping itself round the base of an oak tree with an ear-splitting crash. This was going to be a pretty short mission: the driver had stood no chance of survival.

Except… the door flew open and the driver clambered out. He was huge, growing taller by the second. The air around him filled with the stench of camphor, asafoetida and sulphur. He glowed with a brightness so dazzling we were forced to avert our eyes; he shimmered like a mirage viewed through a mist. Horns protruded from his head. His feet were cloven hoofs. The heat radiating out of his body felt like a blast from an industrial kiln.

All of the grass in a wide circle around him was singed, the branches of the oak tree charred. He extended an arm, and with one long, claw-like finger, pointed at the car. The vehicle melted at once, creating a pool of molten metal which flowed away from him. He made a sound like the loudest of growls combined with the deepest rumble of thunder.

He began to rotate faster and faster until he became a vertical line between Earth and sky. And he was gone.

For a second or two a blinding trail of light plunged down, deep into the ground, which trembled and thrashed as though it were in the throes of an earthquake. Too shaken to move or speak, we remained skulking in the shadows for several more minutes, four ghosts from Hell scared beyond words by a denizen of its darkest regions.

I was the first to recover and helped Louise to her feet. Her legs had given way when she saw the car melt. "What is a daemon doing here? They never come onto the temporal plane. I didn't even think they could. It's too cold for them up here, isn't it?"

Caroline coughed, which was not surprising. The air was still full of the foul stink the creature had left behind. "I don't understand. If a daemon was to be involved in this, I should have been informed."

"Perhaps it was clearing the way for us. Perhaps there was a ghost here which had been so evil in life we couldn't be expected to deal with it on our own." I was burbling nonsense but couldn't help myself. "Yes, that must be it. Maybe the daemon transported the soul straight through the Final Door."

Greg snorted. "Not a chance. That lot don't help our kind. They just wait for us to slip up then get ready to welcome us to..." He shuddered.

None of us wanted to investigate the cooling puddle of metal, glass and leather.

Louise began walking away from it. "How do you suppose the living will explain this mess when they come across it?"

"My guess is they'll blame a lightning strike at the same time as an unpredicted earthquake. I don't see what else they could say about it. I just hope that thing doesn't come back." Caroline closed her eyes for a long moment. "Right. That creature can't be anything to do with our mission. Hell wouldn't expect a group of just four hounds to deal with something as far beyond them as an out-of-control daemon. They'd know we wouldn't stand a chance: we're nothing like powerful enough. So there have to be other ghosts here we can deal with who have overstayed their welcome."

This was not what I wanted to hear but she had to be right. We were here to complete a mission, not for the benefit of our education. We did not need to observe this daemon to be reminded of what awaited us if we failed. No, we were here to locate and claim at least one ghost who had so far avoided Hell.

I glanced along the road beyond the pattern of skid marks and burnt rubber which now marred its surface. The gates the car had burst through, now a tangle of twisted metal bars, were strewn across the entrance to a long, tree lined drive with a large building at the far end. "Over there looks promising."

"You could be right, Ross. I can't see anywhere else we can go." Caroline set off at a brisk pace and, as usual, we trailed behind her.

An elaborate wooden sign was set back among the trees announcing our location as "Oaklands Country Hotel and Golf Course". Passing it, Greg clambered over the ruins of the gate and walked a little way along the drive. "It looks to be a rather nice place. Come and see for yourselves."

We joined him. The building, constructed of honey coloured stone and shaped like a letter E, comprised three storeys. A large expanse of windows sparkled in the late afternoon sunshine. Long, well-tended lawns and beds filled with flowers of many colours extended either side of the drive. In front of the hotel was a crescent shaped, gravelled area which had an ornamental fountain in the form of a dolphin at its centre. It all looked well cared for, comfortable and luxurious. I had no doubt the tariff would be outrageous.

We walked up to the building together. There was a slight depression filled with charred material just before we began crossing the gravel. I guessed the daemon and his car might have had something to do with it. Perhaps it was the remains of a previous collision. Once beyond that, we arrived at a set of white marble steps which led up through a wide portico to a pair of gilt handled oak doors.

I now understood why, when we had arrived, we had found our bodies were so well dressed. Greg and I both sported lightweight lounge suits, his blue and mine grey, and as for the women, Louise looked pretty in her floral summer dress, but Caroline outshone her in glowing amber silk. The only thing missing from the picture was any items of luggage but, since we were all good liars, we could doubtless come up with some believable explanation for that oversight. Besides, we might not be in the building all that long. Already my lodestone was giving off its customary gentle warmth and I was sure the others felt the same from theirs too. Our targets were somewhere close by.

Before we could reach the door, it was pulled open from inside by a short, plump man in a rather over-elaborate livery. His uniform bore heavy epaulettes and a multitude of gold braid and buttons. His hands were encased in the whitest gloves I had ever seen. "Welcome to Oaklands, ladies and gentlemen. Please do enter." He bowed and waved us towards the interior.

Inside the hotel, all was marble floors and dark ebony. Money, was my first thought. There wasn't a single guest in sight. We would have walked straight past the reception desk, but our path was blocked by another, younger man wearing the same livery.

"Please, do take the time to book in. We are delighted you were able to cross our threshold." An odd thing to say. And as he spoke, I felt the familiar heat in my head, the lodestone telling me this man was not what he appeared to be. Not only was he dead, he was also one of ours.

I caught Caroline's eye. She gave a tiny, quick nod. She felt it too. Perhaps this man was our target. We would have to wait and see.

The heavily made-up woman on reception, despite her bright, false, corporate smile, was also dead. She placed a wide register in front of us. This was going to be interesting. We had no money. Hell had not provided us with any.

Caroline started to say we were not staying but the woman interrupted her. "We are quite used to this, madam. We will give you your keys now and, if there are to be any charges, you can always settle them later."

This place got stranger by the minute. We all signed the book: Caroline Trenby, Louise Jenkins, Gregor Altmann, and me, Ross Ferris.

The receptionist reached behind her and pulled down two keys. "A pair of our very nicest twin rooms, one-two-four and one-two-five, on the second floor have been made ready for you. I hope they will be to your liking. If there are any problems, please do not hesitate to inform us. The reception desk is open round the clock."

Caroline mumbled our thanks, and we set off for the broad staircase. Since we had been given rooms, we might as well take a look at them. Besides, we were in no hurry. Our surroundings were far more pleasant than the place we had come from.

On our way up we passed an overdressed couple on their way down.

"Good afternoon!" All nice and polite. I did not doubt these two were living people and it was as well we were giving them no reason to suspect we were not in the same state.

The doors to the two rooms were standing open. We entered one-two-four. It was indeed a pleasant room with a view over a golf course at the rear of the hotel. It was such a warm afternoon I was a little surprised to see no one was playing.

"This is the strangest hotel I've ever been in." Louise flumped down onto one of the beds. "Some people are alive and some are dead yet they mix together as if there were no difference. And all the dead ones are still wearing bodies. Do you think it might be something to do with the daemon?"

"Yes, I was wondering that too." Caroline sat on the other bed. I couldn't help noticing she was making an impression in the covers, which struck me as strange because, however real we may appear, the truth is we are nothing but fetches. We have no weight.

I decided not to comment for the moment. We were all still on edge after witnessing the daemon's crash. "What should we do now?"

"I think we ought to take a good look round. We have to establish what's going on before we can even start to do anything about it." Caroline was right as usual.

"Shall we split up?"

"Yes, we should. It'll speed things along. You go with Louise; I'll go with Greg. Oh, and Ross..."

"Yes?"

"Do be careful. I've a funny feeling. There's something not quite right about this place." Nice to know she cared.

Stepping away from the window, I headed through the door, which had swung shut while we were talking. "Ouch! What the...!" I bounced back from the solid surface.

"Don't play the fool, Ross."

"I'm not." I stared hard at the door then extended my hand until my palm rested on it. By now the other three had clustered around me. I pushed. But the door resisted, which should have been impossible.

We all took a step back.

Caroline tried the floor, Greg the wall and Louise stood in the middle of the room, watching with a hand over her mouth. Everything around us was solid.

"This can't be happening." Caroline jumped up and down on the spot, with no more result than the thump Greg gave the wall. "We're trapped in here. We can't get out of this room."

"I'm not so sure." There was one thing left to try. I curled my fingers round the knob. It turned, I pulled the door open and stepped outside.

The corridor was empty.

"I don't like the feel of this, but we still have to make the search." Greg began walking away toward the stairs. "Though I'm not sure how we do that if we can't get into any of the other rooms."

"I can pick locks." None of us were surprised by Louise's comment. When she was alive she had been a burglar and had met her end while using too much explosive to blow a safe. "Mind you, I do need the right equipment and that's something I don't have."

Caroline rolled her eyes. "All right. We can't walk through walls and doors while we're in this place, so we'll have to try a different tack. First of all, let's establish how many of the people in this hotel are dead. That way we'll get some idea of the scale of the problem. I suggest we start in the bar." She had already given up the idea of separating into two pairs. I agreed with her. This mysterious hotel was throwing up too many surprises.

We descended the staircase the way the living do, one step at a time. It was difficult to hold back my impatience. Passing through floors and ceilings gets you there so much quicker.

It turned out there were two bars on the premises, one next to the dining room and another at the back of the building intended to serve as the nineteenth hole. The latter was empty, with not even any bar staff in evidence. The former was busy. Most of the tables were occupied and everywhere I looked my lodestone gave out its unequivocal message.

After ten minutes a clear pattern emerged. Every one of the staff was dead while all the guests were alive. Why would so many dead people be here and why were they waiting on the living?

A gong sounded. Everyone hurried to finish their drinks and make their way through into the dining room. There were about twenty tables and perhaps fifteen of them had been set for a meal. Unsure what to do, we followed the human tide into the room.

A waiter was at my elbow. "This way, ladies and gentlemen. You have been allocated a comfortable table by the window."

This was awkward, since we could not eat, but at least it was a good place from which to observe what was going on.

We sat. A bottle of ruby red wine, already opened, was in the middle of the table.

Greg poured a generous measure into each glass. "I know we can't drink it, but I can still appreciate the bouquet, can't I?" He raised the glass, gave a loud sniff and... took a huge gulp.

We waited. Caroline, biting her lip, stared at him while Louise made some inarticulate noise. All of us expected a puddle to appear at his feet, for the liquid to pass straight through his non-corporeal being as it had with mine during training. But nothing happened.

He topped up his glass. "Nice drop of plonk, this."

The waiter arrived with menus. Greg ordered a long list of dishes. It was then I remembered Caroline telling me once, he was a glutton when alive. I nibbled at a lettuce leaf, unable to believe the texture, the taste, or the way I was able to swallow it. Here was something I had missed without ever realising it. We all lost control, except Caroline who after a few minutes excused herself, saying we were making her feel sick.

I don't remember what I ate. I don't remember what I drank. I don't remember how I got back to the room.

Next morning, dizzy, groggy, I woke up with a monster of a hangover. Caroline was shouting at me, at all three of us. Had we forgotten why we were here? Did we not realise something was wrong with this place?

She was sitting on the end of my bed. I could feel her weight through the quilt. While we had been getting drunk, she had been exploring as much as she could and discovered none of the doors or windows out of the hotel would open. We were prisoners. Did we not understand what that meant?

For a moment, I just wanted her to shut up and let me rest. But then the words got through. Prisoners: all these people, some dead, some alive and now us. No one able to leave. This had to be connected to the daemon who enjoyed melting cars and creating localised earthquakes. Nothing could have sobered me up quicker.

We were in danger. All of us.

Greg went down for breakfast. He said he was hungry and saw no reason not to take advantage of his new-found ability to eat. The rest of us watched him go.

"We have to talk to some of these people: the staff in particular."

"That much is obvious, Ross, but it's not going to help if we can't prove to them they are dead."

"Are we sure they are. Dead, I mean." Louise was standing by the window, where pale morning light was picking out impossible colours in her mousy brown hair.

"Of course they're dead."

"How do you know, Caro? They aren't behaving like ghosts. They eat, they sleep, everything. And so do we!"

"Oh, so you think you've come back to life, do you? You believe the lodestones have got it wrong?"

"No, but... well, I don't know."

"Neither do I but I'll tell you something. If this is the work of that daemon, there's no way it can be good for us or anyone else. Don't you agree, Ross?" Oh, good. So, I wasn't alone. Caroline also thought the daemon must be behind this mess.

"Yes, you're right. I'm going downstairs to have another look round. Back soon."

I wanted to get away from Caroline for a while and think about what was going on. If we were to be trapped in this hotel forever, would it be such a bad thing? This place was comfortable; we were more alive than dead here.

But it felt wrong. There was something in the atmosphere. Underneath it all, you could feel a distinct edge of evil. Besides, not everyone was dead. What about all the living souls also trapped in the hotel? Did we have a responsibility to help them as well?

My feet carried me to the bar at the rear of the premises, the one with the French windows which should have opened onto the golf course. It was still early but even so a middle aged man with a chubby face and thinning hair, wearing a gaudy yellow jumper, was sitting at a table by the window. He was nursing a glass of whisky as he gazed out across the greens.

He did not look up as I approached but he didn't say anything either, so I took the seat to his left and joined him in his silent contemplation of the world outside.

"It's not fair." He replaced his empty glass on the table. "Everyone else has got what they were promised. Everyone but me is happy. I did specify what I wanted. I really did. How was I to know in advance I had to be so precise? I'd be more careful if I had my chance again."

"What part did you miss out?" I suspected the answer was obvious.

He sighed. "Why, the golf, of course. It's all I ever wanted, just the golf but what do I get? I get to look at this empty green. I say, are you the same? Did you also think when he said it was a golf hotel everything would be wonderful?"

"Yes, I suppose so."

"Then you agree with me. We were cheated."

I wanted to ask him what he was talking about but was afraid to press him. Could the "he" perhaps refer to the daemon?

"Cheated is rather a strong word."

"Well, how would you describe it? I thought he was a perfect gentleman and we had an agreement. What else could I have meant when I said I wanted to be a stone's throw from the first tee? We were on a golf course at the time."

"How did he word the agreement?"

The man stared hard at me. "What are you, a lawyer or something? I'm only a simple chap. There were other, legal people in the business who used to deal with contracts and such like."

"Didn't you think it would be a good idea to get them to look it over for you so you didn't make any mistakes?"

"Look over a contract signed in my own blood? They'd have talked me out of it." He got to his feet. "I wish they had now. I don't want to spend the rest of my life staring out at that." He jerked his chin toward the window. "My definition of Hell, this is."

As he strode away, I couldn't help thinking, if this were all that lay behind the Final Door, I'd accept it in the beat of a heart. If I had one.

I made my way back upstairs to the room. Louise was inside but not Caroline nor Greg.

"Where have the others got to?"

"Greg didn't return after breakfast, so Caro's gone to find him. I bet he's still eating. He's nothing but a pig, that man."

"Come with me. We ought to find them. I've got an idea what might be going on."

"It's to do with the daemon, isn't it?"

"Yes, I'm afraid it is."

Greg was sitting at a large table surrounded by dozens of empty plates and glasses of various shapes and sizes. He was tipsy. If any normal person had drunk all those different cocktails, they'd have been under the table.

Caroline was sitting opposite him with her arms folded and a deep scowl set on her face.

I slid into the chair next to hers. "I think all this is about an unlawful arrangement concerning the sale of souls."

She pressed her lips together in a thin line. "You're too late. I'd already found that out for myself." She tapped the table in front of Greg. "Tell him. Tell him what you've gone and done."

He shrugged and picked up a glass of sickly looking green liquid. I could have sworn it had been empty a moment before. "Like Rosh said, it'sh not lawful. I can't be held to it."

"What can't you be held to?" Louise sounded more curious than afraid. She must have been daydreaming through the briefing we were all given concerning the history of blood contracts when she was inducted onto the programme.

"He's signed away his soul in return for as much food and drink as he can consume."

"Sho what? Shtop interfering, Caro. I'm already dead. He can't harm me."

I shook my head. This was way beyond mere foolishness.

At the briefings we had been taught our side, Hell, used to draw up contracts which promised all sorts of things to the unsuspecting. But the twisted words gave them nothing at all. Even so, they would still bind them as long as they were signed in blood. When Heaven got wind of this, they insisted the practise be outlawed. Anyone idiotic enough to sign on the dotted line of such a document was by definition too stupid to understand its implications. The argument was simple: no one should be condemned to Hell for not being intelligent, only for not being good.

If our daemon was using this method to collect souls, he was not doing it with the sanction of either Heaven or Hell. He was sure to be in big trouble from both sides if he was found out. Therefore, he could not take these victims back beyond the Final Door with him. Was that why all these dead people were running the hotel? Was their purpose to serve the current set of idiots who had been tricked into signing a blood contract? It would be a rather pleasant Hell if your only punishment was to become an eternal bartender.

Besides, why would a daemon bother to do this? What use were all these ghosts to him?

There was another question too. Where had Greg got hold of a contract to sign in the first place?

I held my hand over the top of his glass before he could raise it to his lips again. "Have you seen and talked to the daemon?"

He let go of the stem and grabbed another glass, which proceeded to fill itself with a dark brown liquid. "Yesh. 'Courshe I have."

"Here? Was the daemon here?"

"Yesh but he didn't look sho ugly 'cos he'sh taken human form. Now go away. I wansh more dinner."

Caroline rose to her feet. Louise made to stay where she was, so I grabbed her arm. "Come on. We might as well leave him to it."

As we made for the door, a waitress passed us, heading for Greg's table with perhaps the largest mixed grill ever seen.

We raced up the stairs to the room. Louise struggled to get the key in the lock. After so much time in Hell we weren't used to them any more but if we were to stay in the hotel much longer, we soon would be.

Caroline ran a hand through her long, dark hair. "This is a spider's web. The daemon lures them in with his false promises but they can't get out again. They're stuck here with glue of their own making."

"I do see that. What I don't see is what he hopes to gain."

"Neither do I. We're missing something, Ross. He must have a reason."

"Perhaps someone had better find him and ask him what it is."

"Oh, no. One of us has already been ensnared. We daren't risk anyone else."

"In that case tell me what you propose. Do we sit here forever and watch Greg fall apart?"

She frowned. "You can't be suggesting we take on a daemon."

"No and I'm not even suggesting we try to, but all is not lost. We do have one or two things going for us." They were both looking at me now as though they expected me to pull a rabbit out of a hat. "Think about it. We didn't arrive here by chance. We were sent. Hell must already be aware something is wrong. The daemon hasn't been quite as clever as he thinks. This place is not going to stay a secret much longer. In the end they're bound to locate us through the lodestones."

"Yes, you're right. That does make sense. All we have to do is hang on and wait. Another team is bound to be sent in to investigate what has happened to us."

"Oh no, Louise, I don't think we can do that. It'll take too long. I'd like to try to find our friend and see if he can't be persuaded to give this up."

"You want to warn him?" Caroline shook her head. "It won't work and it could well make things worse. What would happen if he moved all this somewhere else?"

She had a point but I was certain I was right. Confronting the daemon might be our only means of escape. Another team would not be interested in our well-being.

If we didn't get out of this mess ourselves, Josh would view us as having failed. And the fate of failures was a long way from being pleasant. The one playing games in this hotel was not the only daemon in Hell.

"I'll go down to the bar, make myself available. He's bound to be capable of telling the difference between those he brought here and us."

I waited for Caroline to protest but instead she held the door open. "It's worth a try but I'm coming with you. I'll keep an eye on what happens. No, Louise, you remain here. One of us should stay out of danger."

Louise flumped back onto one of the beds. "Please try not to be too long, won't you?"

Outside in the corridor, Caroline led the way. "I'm not sure this will work. The daemon might not even be here."

"No, it's true he might be back beyond the Final Door, but I doubt it. My guess is he spends most of his time here in disguise, playing with his prisoners; enjoying the results of the bargains he's made."

"He might not want to talk to you."

"You think he would prefer to spend time with you?"

"I don't know but if we sit apart, it gives him a choice. We watch each other and be ready to jump in to help if needed."

"Nice idea but I'm not sure how that works. There won't be much either of us can do if this goes wrong."

We entered the bar together before splitting up. Caroline chose a high stool at the counter while I found an empty table not far from the door. No sooner had I sat down than a waitress was hovering over me.

"Good evening, Mr. Ferris. What can I get you to drink?"

Water. Ask for sparkling water. "A large brandy, please." Now why did I say that? I must watch myself and guard against my little weaknesses.

The brandy was smooth and rounded. There were compensations to being trapped in this place and in this corporeal body. I was half way through my second when a woman in a skimpy, black and gold cocktail dress, with her dark brown hair tied into a bun, arrived at my table. She was rather good looking.

"Anyone sitting here?"

"No. Please do join me." Acting the perfect gentleman, I got to my feet and pushed the chair in behind her. I was aware daemons were capable of taking any shape. Could this woman be the daemon?

"Thank you. I'm called Theresa."

"Pleased to make your acquaintance, Theresa. My name is Ross."

We chatted about this and that for a while. She thought she had been at the hotel for several weeks, but didn't know what day it was, as they were all the same, and so wasn't sure. There was an undercurrent of nerves beneath her air of composure. Perhaps she already realised she had made a bad bargain. I didn't ask the terms of her contract, nor did she ask me what I was doing there.

Still sitting at the bar, Caroline was laughing at something being said by a tall, fair haired man. I wondered if she was having any better luck.

With three brandies inside me I would be a fool to drink any more.

A gong sounded.

Theresa put down her sherry. "Why don't you and I go in to dinner together?"

"Er, thank you for the kind invitation but I'm not hungry tonight. Perhaps tomorrow?"

She made no protest or further attempt to persuade me. As she got to her feet I kissed her hand. We said we hoped to meet again soon, each giving a false laugh; an acknowledgement that in such a place we were certain to do so. And she walked away.

Caroline slipped into the seat Theresa had just vacated. "Any luck?"

"No. I take it your companion...?"

"Rather boring and none too bright. Let's face it. This isn't going to work."

"Do you want to eat anything?"

"No. I can't sit and watch Greg stuff his face. Besides, we should get back to Louise. I'm worried about her. All this is too much. You do know how frightened she is, don't you?"

"Aren't you frightened too, Caroline?"

"Not like she is."

We left the now deserted bar. This strange hotel was in its own way quite regimented, everyone eating together at the same time. It could never be mistaken for Paradise: there were too many unwritten rules.

As we climbed the stairs, a tight knot formed in my stomach. Louise was not as strong as Caroline or I...

Caroline began to run. Somehow it was no surprise when she flung open the door to an empty room.

CHAPTER 12

We didn't bother going in. We had to find Louise.

"The dining room. Perhaps she got hungry. She thought she'd get something to eat and, since we weren't back… She'll be fine." It was obvious Caroline didn't believe her own words. I didn't either.

We raced down the stairs, across the hall and through the bar, skidding to a halt in the dining room.

Louise was at a long table, holding court. She was wearing a ridiculous dress which looked as if it had been spun from gold and silver threads. Her fingers were heavy with rings, her arms with bangles and at least three gold necklaces and a diamond tiara completed her ensemble. She was the only female among the party. Five young men in dinner jackets looked to be hanging on her every word.

"Money and popularity," hissed Caroline.

We didn't approach her. What would have been the point? Not far away, Greg was once again surrounded by dishes heaped with food and glasses filled with wines and spirits. At another table, Theresa had been joined by the fair haired man from the bar.

"Back to the room!"

I did not need to be told twice. A waiter was heading in our direction.

Caroline was full of remorse and self-recrimination. Losing Louise was all her fault. She was in charge. She should never have left our co-worker alone.

After a while I'd had enough of it. "I'm going back to the bar to try again."

"No, I'm not losing you as well. From now on we stick together."

"Don't treat me like a child, Caroline. I can look after myself."

She stamped her foot. "I don't give a brass farthing whether you agree or not. I'm telling you we do not split up again."

I have never been good at obeying orders. "Fine. In that case, you are coming with me. I refuse to stay in here listening to you going on about all this being your fault for even a moment longer."

She bit her lip. "All right. We will go to the bar but we're not drinking. You hear me, Ross? Not a drop. We have to keep our heads clear."

Argument won, this time I led the way downstairs.

The bar was filling up again as people finished their meals and returned for after dinner drinks. This hotel had little else to offer beyond billiards, cards and alcohol. There were signs for a swimming pool and a ballroom, but no one ever headed in either direction. These people had been cooped up together for too long. Their conversation had become desultory.

A thought struck me. The man I had spoken to in the nineteenth hole that morning was not among the patrons of this bar. He had not been in the dining room either. Was he still where I first encountered him, gazing out at the greens in the darkness?

Caroline was once again in conversation, this time talking to a tall woman with red hair. My team leader had her back to me but that wouldn't last long. If I wanted to slip out, it would have to be right away.

The nineteenth hole was in darkness except for the light from a Tiffany style lamp suspended above the table in the window. The man was sitting there but this time he was facing into the room. "I've been waiting for you, Mr. Ferris." He tapped the edge of a half-filled brandy balloon. "Your tipple, I believe."

"Thank you but I don't think it would be advisable for me to drink on this occasion. Do you?"

He laughed. "You could be right. I wondered how long it would take you to see round my little deception, though I admit it was fun while it lasted. But now you do understand, there are a few serious matters for us to discuss. Please, join me."

I took the chair but pushed the glass away. "You can't keep us here forever. You also know what we are."

"Yes, I know everything about you. But as to not being able to keep you, that is another matter altogether." He looked at me over the rim of his own glass. Close to, I noticed his eyes. They glowed golden in the lamplight. "I can keep you here as long as I wish. This place was chosen because, for some reason, it's not on any of the maps. It has been forgotten for a long time. Hell knows nothing about it. Even your lodestones won't give away your location while you're here."

"We still found it, though, didn't we?"

"Indeed you did. It may be the hotel will have to be relocated sooner than I planned, but rest assured, there are plenty of other places just as far from the beaten track." He sipped at his drink. The level of the liquid in the glass did not go down.

"You should let us leave."

"Why would I want to do that? You'd only run back to Hell and tell tales on me. I don't think that's a clever idea. Why don't you join your companions instead? This place can be most accommodating. Tell me what you want. I'm sure I'll have no trouble providing it."

"No, the price is too high for me."

"Ah, but not for your friends."

"You found their weaknesses: Louise for wealth and Greg for a bottomless trough. Caroline and I are different."

"Are you? I don't understand you, Ross. Why go back at all when you know in the end they will only send you on to eternal torment? Stay here. You can have a pleasant time for ten, twenty years, longer maybe."

"What then?"

"Then you pay the piper. It won't be much different, but you will have had a little fun before the end."

"You send these people on to Hell when you tire of them?"

"Not Hell, no. I'll let you into a little secret. Hell behind the Final Door is boring: all that fire and predictable torments; nothing new in aeons. Whereas, in this place it's possible to use a little imagination, think of some new distractions." The golden pupils widened, taking in all the surrounding colour of the grey irises. "Here it is possible to be a real daemon. No restraints whatsoever."

"I see. You're telling me this is your playpen and anyone who signs one of your contracts becomes one of your toys."

"Yes, that's a good description of the situation. Now, since you can't be allowed to leave, let's see about your comfort, shall we?"

"If I don't sign, you can't touch me. And there is nothing you can offer Caroline or me which will induce either of us to be so stupid."

"Is that a fact? You have no weaknesses at all? If you're right, perhaps I will have to try a different method. It could even be said you have already accepted my terms." He swirled the liquid in his glass. "A dozen brandies, a full meal, a bottle of wine... Do I have to go on? You have taken advantage of my hospitality. How did you think I would go about recouping my outlay?"

"There is no contract between us."

"Nothing physical, I agree but perhaps an implied one. I do believe Jeanette on reception did tell you all bills would be settled later." He sat back. "There is a precedent, you know. I recall a young lady who ate some pomegranate seeds finding herself in a not dissimilar situation."

"Persephone? That's nothing but a myth."

"True and I am only playing with you, Ross. So let me make it clear: I won't accept anything less than your signature on my piece of parchment."

"You'll have a long wait."

"Time is not a problem here. Everything is slow, sedate and steady."

"Not like yesterday, then. You were in quite a hurry when you wrapped your car round that tree."

He laughed. "Oh my. No, that wasn't me." He leaned across the table. "I'm sorry. Did you have the impression I was the only one of my kind here?"

A sound from behind me. "All done, Caffiaes. You were right. In the end she was so predictable."

I half turned.

Theresa was standing behind me, fanning herself with a large sheet of paper. She laid it down on the table and it unfurled itself. The writing was blurred but I recognised the familiar signature at the bottom of the document: Caroline Trenby, in graceful, flowing, dark brown letters.

I staggered to my feet. "I don't believe you. She wouldn't do that. It's got to be a forgery."

Theresa shrugged. "I assure you it's not, but do find out for yourself. Go and ask her. You will find her in the ballroom."

I fled. From behind me came the raucous laughter of a pair of daemons.

At first following signs on the walls, after a few minutes I could also follow the music. It sounded as if a full orchestra was playing a waltz. I was walking down a long, grey corridor. It could well have been the one I was familiar with in Hell, except the doors here were more elaborate and all had handles. It was not possible to see far down the passage as there was a kind of hazy mist in the air, a hot, moist atmosphere like a steam bath. The music lured me to the third door along.

Opening it, I stepped into a huge, baroque style ballroom, its floor a chequerboard of black and white marble squares. The walls were lined with paintings and mirrors, their frames smothered with layers of gold leaf. Tiny chairs stood on spindle legs which looked as if the weight of a bird would reduce them to kindling. In the centre, young women, decked out in voluminous dresses every colour of a pastel rainbow, danced with men wearing evening suits. Servants in livery circulated with trays of champagne and tiny morsels of food.

There was indeed an orchestra, a small one playing on a raised dais at the far end of the room. I stood with my back to the wall to observe the spectacle. A waitress offered me a tall glass. Smiling at her, I shook my head. It was one thing to accept food and drink from the daemons while unaware of any debt which might be accumulating, but quite another once threatened with the legend of Persephone.

Once I spotted her, it was impossible to take my eyes off Caroline. A dazzling smile lit up her face as she was whirled round the room by the fair haired man she had been talking to in the bar. Like many of the other women, she now sparkled in a ballgown shimmering with sequins, which showed off her shapely figure. I never realised she could look so alluring. And it was clear she was an accomplished dancer too, though that's what I would have expected her to be. She had been the daughter of a wealthy nobleman, indeed due to be presented at court, when she set fire to the family home and herself in a fit of pique.

Stepping further into the room, I felt a definite tickling sensation. Catching sight of myself in one of the mirrors, I discovered my own clothes had also undergone a transformation. I too was now in full evening dress.

Crossing the room presented me with some difficulty. Couples kept swerving into my path and Caroline was getting further and further away. It was as though she were deliberately evading me.

I persisted and at last caught up with her. Her dancing partner cast me a wry smile as I cut in. She was as light as a feather in my arms, her perfume a heady aroma: a mix of flowers with a darker undertone, perhaps a soft musk.

"Hello, Ross. I suppose you're a tad annoyed with me."

"Something like that. Why did you do it, Caroline?"

"Come on. Let's dance a while. Afterwards we can sit down and I'll explain everything."

I had never learned to dance the waltz (it was only just becoming fashionable when I died) but it made no difference: here in this strange ballroom my feet knew all the steps. For a few moments my thoughts drifted. Caroline's body was warm and it felt as if we were both alive again. The rhythm of the music was hypnotic, so wonderful.

I don't know how long I was held entranced by both woman and music. It was impossible to break away. A tiny voice at the back of my head tried to caution me, when all I wanted it to do was shut up.

The music rose to a crescendo before fading away. Every dancer stood still for a moment then there was a lot of bowing from the men, fan fluttering and curtseying from the women. Polite applause broke out. The orchestra bowed too. The conductor raised his baton and... off they all went again into another dance, one with different steps.

Before Caroline could join in, I took her arm and steered her to a small table with one of the spindle legged chairs either side. Nervous it might not take the weight of my body, I pressed down on the nearer one with my hand. To my relief it held.

Champagne arrived. I handed Caroline hers and prepared to take mine. The waiter pointed out a small slip of paper on the tray. "Sign here for the drinks, please, sir."

I took the pen. I placed it on the paper. I... "Oh, no, no!"

Pushing handsome men and pretty ladies out of my way, I ran for the exit. One woman fell in front of me, her bright pink taffeta gown spreading across my path. Her hands reached up to grasp my ankles. I dodged, gained the door and threw myself into the passage beyond.

The heart I should not have been able to hear or feel pounded in my chest. I had come so close to signing. Temptation had hung in the air before me. Danced beside me. But it was nothing a contract could have given me. My desire was for a favour freely given, a willing kiss; not something tied up with a string of words signed in blood, whether knowingly or by deception.

I waited a while but Caroline did not follow me. The music was now playing a Polka. By now she would be dancing again, either with the fair haired man or some other partner.

I was thirsty but would have to stay that way. The risks in this place were too great.

What could be making the daemons so desperate they had resorted to trying to trick me into signing? I was missing something. I had to be.

Returning to the upstairs room and closing the door behind me, I sat on the edge of the bed with my head in my hands. How many more times would I have to catch myself before making an irrevocable mistake? It had been such a small slip of paper. Could all my dreams and desires have been encompassed in so little space?

I straightened up again. No, they could not and, more to the point, I had not specified what my desires were and the waiter had been holding a pen, not a knife to draw blood. Had it been an overreaction on my part? At least they had got none of the vital fluid.

Blood. I raised my hands and turned them over and over, looking at the unblemished pale skin, the blue veins in my wrists. In life I had been weather beaten, my hands a little coarse from holding the reins of horses from a young age. There had been a scar on my left wrist where a knife fight I had lost was commemorated. There should have been other scars too. If I stripped and looked at this body in the mirror over the dressing table, it would not be a familiar one. It was as borrowed as the clothes it wore.

Not my body. So not my blood.

There was more. The whole concept of this kind of contract being used in this way was flawed. It was supposed to last the lifetime of its victim: giving them whatever they wanted to enjoy in return for their soul at death. The guests here might well all still be alive, but I was not, and neither were Caroline, Louise or Greg. We did not have living souls for the daemons to lay claim to.

CHAPTER 13

Since my demise, I had learned a little of how the afterlife works. The eventual destination of a person is not determined until the very moment of their death. It can't be. A man could be evil all his life and in his last few moments run into a burning building and save a family. It might be just enough of a selfless act to tip the balance.

By contrast, a woman could do no wrong her entire life but as death approaches take a machine gun and mow down an entire congregation. The scales would tip in the opposite direction. It's all a question of degree.

The hereafter is not like a criminal court, where your judges have to prove you are good or you are evil beyond reasonable doubt. It is more like a civil court, where your fate is determined on the balance of probabilities.

The people in this hotel had been lured here long before that point. Their lives were not yet over, so Hell had no right to claim their souls. And nor had Heaven. At least not yet. These daemons were circumventing the rules, twisting the game to suit themselves. But what if their victim were already dead?

How often had they told me I was the property of Hell? My life had already been judged. It was impossible for me to make a contract to give away something which no longer belonged to me. Any such contract would be null and void. I was sure I was right, just not so sure how being right would be of any help to me. The hotel was still a trap: we were still inside it. Caroline had said there was no way out. But how could she know with such certainty? She spent only a short while exploring and might have missed something.

The front door was sure to be guarded but what about the other entrances and exits? The living guests had to be fed with something, and refuse had to be taken out of the hotel. Were deliveries made or did one of the daemons go out to fetch everything they needed?

A quiet knock at the door scattered my thoughts.

Caroline entered in a rustle of sequins. "I missed you, Ross. Why did you leave? You're such a great dancer."

"I admit I wasn't bad, but this borrowed body is so much better at it than the real me ever was."

"Borrowed body? Why look at it that way? You've got the use of it for as long as you want or, if it doesn't suit, I'm sure the daemons can find you one which is more to your taste." She pirouetted in the narrow space between the two single beds. "I like mine. It's quite similar to my original one. Do you think I'm pretty, Ross?"

Standing there before me, this woman was indeed beautiful: apart from the angel, I had never seen a lovelier vision. "Yes, Caroline, you're very pretty."

"Thank you. Now, shall I sit with you for a while? You must be feeling... lonely." She settled on the bed so close to me you couldn't have run a knife between us. "You should relax, Ross. The daemons mean you no harm."

"Is that right? They just want a little of my blood at the bottom of a sheet of parchment."

"What's a little blood? Think about it. If we went back, in the end we would be burned or worse. And we would have given our all to bring more unlucky souls to Hell so they can be tortured. Why go on doing it? You know you hate it. Why not stay here? With me."

"How long have they given you? A few years of dancing? What will become of you after that?"

"Oh, I'm sure I'll suffer the same fate but, Ross, it's a hundred years away. Imagine having an entire century of whatever you want." She raised her face to mine. Her breath was warm and sweet on my skin. "Anything, Ross, anything you want."

She was almost irresistible. It would have been so easy to lean into her; to kiss her. But who was this woman? Not Caroline. Not the Caroline I knew.

"No daemon can make such promises and, even if you could, I would want no part of it."

"I did tell Caffiaes it wouldn't work." She shrugged. "But he still thought it worth a try. You will sign in the end, Ross. Everyone does." Her face changed, hardened, lengthened. I saw myself reflected in the golden pupils of Theresa's grey eyes. "We are running out of patience. You have one more day. Not a moment longer."

She was gone, leaving behind her a piece of blank parchment and a long, curling goose feather quill with a point sharper than a needle.

I left them there on the bed. It was time to seek out the real Caroline. There was something important I had to say to her.

CHAPTER 14

The ballroom was unchanged. So were the swirling couples. But now the music grated on me. Any desire to dance had left me but how else was I to get close to Caroline?

Her partner gave way. He was a tall, dark haired man this time. I slipped my hands into the correct positions. I must not let myself be distracted by how arousing it felt holding her. The orchestra began a slow waltz, which was helpful; it would not have been easy to have this conversation while dancing the Charleston. It was odd how all of a sudden I knew the names and all the steps to dances which had only been invented years after my death. And centuries after Caroline's.

"I'm glad you came back. I was missing you."

"I missed you too. One of the daemons has just called on me. It was pretending to be you."

She laughed as though such an event was of no consequence. "Well, you're with the real me now."

"I hope so." I pecked her on the cheek.

She stopped. "What are you doing, Ross? That's not part of the dance."

"No, I suppose it isn't."

Other couples continued to spiral around us without pause.

"Come on, take a five minute break. Have a drink. After all, what is five minutes out of one hundred years?"

Her eyes widened. "The daemon told you the details of my contract?"

"Yes. Why? Shouldn't it have done?"

"The matter was private."

We made for the only unoccupied seats. A waitress was upon us before Caroline had even got her sparkling skirts arranged. Champagne again but no slip of paper this time. I took the drinks and placed them on the surface of the tiny, round table. Caroline sipped hers. I left mine untouched.

"What is it you want, Ross?"

"Isn't it obvious? We have to get out of here."

"We can't. Why don't you just accept things are better here?"

"It's all an illusion, Caroline. The contract isn't worth the parchment it's written on." I leant over the table. No one else must hear. Only her.

"The blood you used to sign it was not yours."

She shrugged but did not reply. Had she already worked it out for herself?

"I've been wondering why a daemon would do this. And I think I've come up with the answer."

Another shrug. She cast a glance at the couples once again swirling round the floor.

I tapped the table in front of her. "These are minor daemons. They don't get to do any real torturing; they only stoke the fires and rattle the chains. They're jealous of those above them and wanted some victims of their own."

She took a gulp of her champagne. "You may be right. What of it?"

"It can't last. Their victims have started dying and are therefore being judged. Both sides are now looking for their own. Think about it. That's why we're here. Hell couldn't find the exact location but got us in close and they're not going to give up. Once they do find it, this place and everything associated with it will be destroyed. Forget your hundred years of dancing. Because if you don't, you'll be waltzing on the hot coals beyond the Final Door."

She let go of the champagne glass. It bounced off the edge of the table and shattered on the marble floor. No one even glanced in our direction.

"I don't want you to be right, but I know you are." She closed her eyes for a long moment. "It was such a lovely dream, but I guessed about the signature a while ago." She rose to her feet. "How do we get out of here?"

"I don't know."

"Typical, Ross. Come on. We'd better find the other two. We need to explain the facts of life to them. Or should I say the facts of death?" She giggled.

We left the ballroom to the strains of yet another waltz.

The dining room was empty and in darkness. Greg must have found himself another bottomless trough somewhere else. We expected to find Louise in the bar, but she was not among the groups drinking their endless bottles of wine or cocktails. With no idea where else to look, I led the way back upstairs to the room.

On reaching the door, we heard voices inside. Remembering the way the daemon had acted with me, I was nervous of walking in on Greg or Louise with company. So, I knocked.

There was an immediate silence, followed by footsteps.

Greg opened the door a fraction. He gazed out then peered round us. "Are you alone?"

"Yes, it's just the two of us."

"You are you, aren't you?"

It was a stupid question but maybe one I was happy to hear. "Yes, I am Ross, she is Caroline and neither of us is a daemon in disguise."

He let us in.

Louise was sitting on one bed and opposite her on the other sat the woman from the reception desk and a chambermaid.

All the jewellery Louise had been wearing lay in a glittering cascade on the floor between the beds. It now looked cheap and garish, as though it were as fake as the contract which had given it to her.

She nodded at the two women. "This is Jeanette and this is Clara. They've been telling us about a fire."

"There's not much to tell." The receptionist pursed her lips. "It was a good while ago now."

I sat beside Louise. "What happened? Was it a bad fire? Were many people hurt?"

"Oh, it was terrible. Half the hotel was burned down. We thought it would never be rebuilt but soon afterwards the new owners arrived."

"They put things right, did they?"

"Better than right. We never had a ballroom or such a lovely pool before the fire." Clara made swimming motions with her hands. "I like the pool and, when we're off duty, we can use it."

"That's nice for you, and it's good you didn't lose your jobs. Did the new owners take on all the old staff?"

"Everyone who had... erm, yes, most of us... Well, thirteen of us."

Clara was having the usual problem, the one so often observed in people who are unaware they are no longer alive. She could not mention anything to do with death. I now understood where the daemons had found their ghostly staff. If one of these two could be made to acknowledge the reality of her situation, this whole mess might resolve itself.

I was wondering how to phrase my next question. Best to get it over with. "Where were you when the fire broke out?"

Two faces portrayed identical frowns. They looked at each other.

"Er, erm... I'm not sure I remember." Clara got to her feet. "As Jeanette said, it was a long time ago. We've been told we shouldn't dwell on it. The whole thing was so traumatic. I think we ought to get back to work now. We're not paid to chat to the guests, are we, Jen?"

The other woman did not reply. She was staring into space.

"Come on. Let's go."

"I was in my room. I shared it with Lucy. She worked the other reception shift." Jeanette's eyes met mine. "She didn't get out. The firemen didn't get to... us until it was too late. We both..."

And she was gone.

Clara blinked. "Like I said, I'm supposed to be working. I'll go now."

Greg watched her as she left the room. "Will it be enough, only one of them departing?"

"I don't know, but it's got to help."

"Shame she wasn't one of ours."

"Don't worry, Caroline. Our opposite numbers, the Pearly poodles, will now know something is going on and they'll be obliged to act. Jeanette isn't the only one of theirs on the premises."

"We should warn the daemons."

"What?" We all stared at Louise.

"If we don't, we may get caught in the middle. How would we ever prove we were not in league with the daemons?"

She had a point. The authorities in Hell wouldn't bother listening to us. A complaint from the other side would be enough to send us all through the Final Door. And we still hadn't found a way out of the hotel. Jeanette's escape route would only work for her and her colleagues.

"I don't like the idea. But I think you're right. The daemons are waiting for me to cave in and sign their precious contract. They'll talk to me."

"I'll come with you."

"Yes, two of us but no more."

Caroline's long dress dusted the steps as we descended the staircase. "How did you resist, Ross?"

"There was nothing they could give me that I wanted." It was the truth. The daemons' gifts were limited. I had not been a glutton, had never cared for trinkets, had liked the ladies but only the bright, spirited ones, the type who would never have signed one of the daemons' contracts. Even so, if they had been able to offer me a fine horse, a pair of pistols and an open road, I might have found myself unable to resist.

We arrived at the nineteenth hole. The daemon, Caffiaes, was in his usual place.

"Thought of a demand or two?" He raised an eyebrow.

Caroline and I sat opposite him. "No. We've come to give you a fair chance to get out of this place before the forces of Heaven arrive."

"Heaven? I don't think so." He smiled at Caroline. "Tired of dancing, are we? Perhaps I could stretch a point. I could be generous and give you a second choice."

"We're the ones being generous. You should check your staff. You'll find there's one missing."

He tapped the table with his long, thin fingers and stared beyond us.

Nothing happened for a few moments until there came a faint flicker of light and Theresa walked through the door.

She gave a deep sigh. "It's all true. They've got to Jeanette. I told you she was a weak link."

"Those destined for Heaven often are. They've nothing to be afraid of so their subconscious minds don't fight quite so hard to maintain the illusion of life."

Caroline's comment drew a glare from Theresa.

I leaned across the table. "You don't have long. If you leave now, you might get back to Hell before they arrive."

"Why should you care what happens to us?"

"I don't. But we can't afford to get caught in the middle. I suggest you release all your victims from their contracts and send them back to where they came from. You can leave the staff to the poodles and us. If all they find when they get here is a group of lost souls awaiting collection, there shouldn't be too many questions asked." I hoped I was right. Time was running out.

Caffiaes raised his hand and from his palm fell a stack of parchments, the edges already beginning to char. A small tongue of bright yellow flame sprang from the centre of the table.

"It's done. They will wake in the morning and think all this a dream, at least what they manage to remember of it." He stood. "We will not forget all the trouble you have caused us. When you are inevitably sent through the Final Door, we will be waiting."

He and Theresa were gone, leaving a familiar whiff of sulphur in the air.

Caroline and I hurried to find Louise and Greg. The nineteenth hole was on fire. I doubted this time it would be a conflagration anyone could extinguish.

The original events were now repeating and, without the daemons to interfere, the wraiths realised they were dead. In less than an hour they were all gone. Not one of them needed persuading either by us or the Pearly poodles, who never even made an appearance.

But something was nagging at me, and I entered the grey tunnel back to Hell with some trepidation. Dealing with this had taken more than three temporal days. If Caffiaes had told the truth, which (although it must be rare for a daemon) I believed he had, the lodestones would not have been registering our location. Our team had been missing. And if we were to avoid mentioning the daemons, it would be difficult to explain where we had been.

Ahead of me, Caroline froze in the centre of the tunnel. "They're not going to listen to us, are they? They'll think we've found some way of preventing the lodestones working and if we're given another mission, we'll do it again; only, next time we won't come back."

Greg continued walking. "No, all we have to do is get our story straight and stick to it. We'll say we didn't know the stones were malfunctioning. As far as we were concerned, everything was normal. Our only problems were a few difficult spirits and a lack of co-operation from some Pearly poodles."

I agreed with him, though since we had not met any, would have left out the poodles. I was glad, however, he did not intend telling our masters there were places "not on any of the maps". That information was too valuable to part with. Once everything had settled down, I was looking forward to spending some quality time in the geography section of the library. If Caffiaes could find missing places, what was there to stop me from doing the same?

We reached the common room. Even Greg hesitated. Standing there was only going to make things worse, so I pushed through the wall, the others in my wake.

The room was empty. There was no reception committee, not even Josh. But a large, black-rimmed envelope was propped up in the centre of the main table.

Louise gave a faint cry and drifted back into the corridor.

Greg followed her.

Caroline put out her hand towards the letter, but jerked it back as though bitten. She clenched her fist. "It's not fair!"

"No, it's not. But I suppose we'd better find out what's in store for us." I picked up the envelope. It felt warm.

CHAPTER 15

Inside the envelope was not a document but a large, ornate card with crinkled edges.

I handed it to Caroline.

"Dear fellow Hell hounds," she read. "Happy Fallen Angel Day! You are cordially invited to join in the feast. Today has been declared temporal date June the thirty-first. Do not be late! Festivities will commence at the sound of the daemon's roar. Best wishes, your colleagues from Common Room Fifty-Five."

I had to be hallucinating: the words made no sense.

Caroline waved the card in the air. "It's a Fallen Angel Day. Oh, that's lucky. Everyone will have been too preoccupied to notice our absence."

"How can it be June the thirty-first? Time isn't measured like that here."

"No, it isn't, but every so often the powers in Hell decide we have to have a June the thirty-first. It doesn't happen often or last very long. But while it is here, we can eat and drink. And there are no missions."

It all sounded far too good to be true. "What's the catch?"

As I was speaking, Greg and Louise reappeared from the corridor.

She was shaking a little. "Come on, Caro. Tell us. When are we being sent...?"

"We're not. We've got away with it." Caroline again held up the card. "This is an invitation to take part in the Fallen Angel Feast."

"Never heard of it. A feast? Here?" Greg chuckled. "Nice joke, Caro."

"It's real. There was one just after I first arrived. I even got a souvenir." She crossed the room and picked up the tartan blanket. "Nothing of any use, of course, but it does remind me of one I had in my room before..." Replacing it on the chaise longue, she patted it then turned back to us. "So, I suppose you all want to know what Hell is celebrating."

"Of course we do." I wished she'd get on with it.

"Well, as you're aware, Hell is infinite, or at least has an infinite number of rooms. It only uses a fraction of them. But every so often a point is reached when there is insufficient capacity for the ever increasing number of wraiths. So, a new area has to be opened up and prepared. That's when they declare Fallen Angel Day."

"Nice of them to include us in the celebrations."

"Not really." Caroline shook her head at Greg. "Our masters only do it because they can't spare enough daemons to supervise us. It takes almost every one they've got to sort out the new torture rooms, the fires and such like. So, they keep us all in one place and try to make out it's a thank you to us for doing our jobs so well."

"I don't think I want to join in." Louise took a seat. "Why should we want to celebrate our 'successes'? It's a horrible idea."

I was watching Caroline. "It's not a choice at all, is it?"

"Of course not. When is anything here a choice? If you don't pretend to be happy on this one occasion or, worse, if you don't take part, you will never be promoted. And I'm sure they'll be keeping a closer watch on you from then on. They're bound to regard you as being disloyal."

"I think we had better get going. The party must be well under way by now." I put out my hand to Louise. "I don't want to do this any more than you do, but it will be in our best interests to be seen." We slid through the wall and made our way towards Common Room Fifty-Five.

Before we got half way there, the air was filled with the ear-splitting sound of a daemon's roar. We had arrived back in Hell at just the right time: the party only now beginning. I had never felt less like a brandy.

The pretence dragged on for quite some time. But I was certain there were few Hell hounds in the room who were enjoying themselves. The laughter was forced, the jokes producing it old and stale. It was impossible to ignore the daemon and four petty fiends observing us.

The presents were handed out: gifts from those above us. Except the objects were not ones the recipients would have chosen. My own was a pair of miniature silver spurs. No use for anything. They only served as a reminder of life before all this began.

Even so, the food was eaten, the wine and brandy drunk. I sipped my glass slowly. Somehow it tasted bitter.

Everything about Hell tasted bitter.

CHAPTER 16

The party ended abruptly when a daemon's roar drowned out the voices and the chinking of glasses. Normality was about to be restored.

In the common room, Josh was waiting for us with a handful of files. "We've got a backlog. Suspending the missions for even a few hours has put us well behind. We're going to have to work double quick. Louise, you're with me. Greg, this one's yours. Caro, you take Ross with you. Now, hurry up, everyone. These are all straightforward missions. When you get back, I'll have more waiting for you."

Josh's speech over, Caroline and I made our way out of the common room and along the grey corridor, which brought us to another car crash. In this century they were as frequent as coaches overturning were in mine. Perhaps more frequent.

Standing by the side of the road, looking dazed, we found a pretty, fair haired young woman, perhaps twenty or so to go by her face. She had a thick coat bundled around her, so I wasn't sure what the rest of her looked like.

Right away Caroline darted over to the car to check on the man who had been driving. I expected her to be back with me before long. He was in quite a mess, the fire crew having just succeeded in separating his legs from the tangled wreckage.

Two paramedics were lifting the woman's body into their vehicle. The wraith gave a plaintive howl and hared off, chasing after her corpse. Unusual. She should have been talking to me by that stage.

I followed. She didn't seem at all surprised by her ability to pass through the wall of the ambulance. I remained outside. There are times when being a fetch who can be seen by the living is not an advantage.

But even from the road, I could still hear her. She was yelling at the ambulance crew. It would do her no good. They would only see her corpse, not the wraith she had become.

Caroline arrived at my shoulder. "He's gone. How are you doing with yours?"

A police constable was upon us before I had time to answer. "Move back, please."

We did so. We could wait for the woman.

"Did you see the accident, sir, miss?"

We did not get time to reply as the ambulance set off, dragging us with it. Our target was aboard, so our lodestones were not going to allow us to stay on that country road without her when she was headed into town.

The constable let out a startled shout. I wondered what he would tell his colleagues. He had been interviewing two potential witnesses who suddenly vanished. Perhaps he would say nothing. Faced with the inexplicable it's often the best course of action.

We glided into the ambulance. The crew of two were too busy gossiping about the affair one of them was having with a surgeon to notice us, even though our borrowed bodies were now sharing the space with them.

The wraith stood at the feet of her cadaver. She looked at us. "I can't be dead. Not yet."

Caroline floated over to her. "I'm sorry but you are. And that's the end of it. Best to come with us. What's your name?"

I was trying to work out how she could know she was dead and not react the way almost every other wraith does. She should not have still been there. She could see her body. There was no longer any impediment to her leaving, yet here she was: clinging on.

"My name is Silvia. Please, I only want a little more time." She leaned forward; ghostly fingers hovered over her corpse.

Caroline gave a gasp. I saw it too. Silvia had not been alone at the time of her death. "You were with child?"

"I'm seven months pregnant."

I closed my eyes. Could this job get any worse?

Caroline shook her head. "I'm sorry but there's nothing we can do. You must come with us."

I was struck by an odd thought. "Where are they? Why hasn't anyone from the other side come for...?"

"The baby must still be alive." Caroline drifted her fingers over the corpse's abdomen. "Has to be. It didn't have time to leave before we got here."

I knew she was right. I could sense there was something still alive within that body.

Silvia pressed her hands together. "Please let me stay."

I wanted to help her, but I had no idea how. A ghost cannot come back to life.

Caroline bit her lip. "This is beyond us. We have to go now."

As she spoke a strange sensation overcame me. The heat from the lodestone began to rise and fall, as though a small bird were fluttering around inside my skull.

My team leader had her hand to the same spot at the back of her own head. "Something isn't right here." She peered at the woman. "I'm not certain you are dead. I think you should try to reunite with your body."

"Can she do that?" I had seen ghosts saying goodbye to their cadavers: once a kiss on the brow, more often a fleeting touch of fingers. It never did anything. A corpse is a corpse: empty, cooling flesh; a spirit is a spirit and the two mix with less ease than oil and water.

Silvia floated above her body. Her fingers slid down the arm. There was a moment of twisting and turning then, in places, the two became one. It was not seamless; there were gaps. Two heads, one a shadow of the other, lay separate at the top of the gurney. But from the shoulders down, where it mattered, the layers could not be distinguished. I saw the chest rise and fall; a tiny, faltering movement.

Caroline leant over Silvia. "I don't think this will last long, a few weeks at most, then we will be back."

"I'll be waiting." The ghost of Silvia closed her eyes, shutting us out.

Caroline stepped to the side of the ambulance. "Come on, Ross. Time to leave. But first this mother and child are going to need some help from the living." She threw back her head and howled.

I saw the passenger in the front seat begin to twist round in answer to the unearthly sound.

We fell through the rear doors of the vehicle. Even though it was braking, it was still moving forwards, and I bounced along the road. Had I been capable of feeling pain, I would have been in agony: my back broken by the impact.

Caroline was already on her feet, dusting herself down. "Time to go home."

Four weeks later, to the day, we were sent back. Silvia had been delivered of a healthy baby boy only an hour earlier. Two nurses were engaged in stripping the bed, no doubt preparing it for the next occupant.

"It's such a shame she never saw her baby. I hate it when it's like this."

"Ah but you have to look on the bright side, don't you? She was brain dead but still managed to have him. At least all this equipment made that possible." She patted the silent machine which stood waiting to be removed.

How little they knew.

But where was Silvia? She should have been waiting for us but there was no sign of her wraith, either by her bed or in the nursery.

"Let's try the mortuary. She must be with her body."

"Why would she be there, Ross? After all she went through to give him birth, why wouldn't she have spent every last second she could at her baby's side? If he were mine, I would never have left him until I was dragged away." Oh, the yearning in her voice. She had died too young, too soon. Her fingers strayed towards the pale cheek of the sleeping baby.

"Don't, Caroline. I'm sorry, but you'll only make him shiver."

"You're right. But, oh Ross, isn't he beautiful? Aren't they all so beautiful?"

I patted her shoulder. "Come on. Let's find Silvia."

Outside the nursery again, Caroline turned to take a final glimpse through the window.

I tried to summon a smile. "We can't stay here. He's safe now and we have a task to perform."

But our lodestones were not giving us any clues. It was as though we were in the wrong place altogether. Where was the familiar warmth that would have led us to Silvia?

A young mother in a flowery nightgown stopped beside us. "Which baby have you come to see? Look, this one's my Rhiannon. Isn't she lovely?"

This time my smile was real. "Yes, your daughter is very lovely." I paused for a second. "We knew Silvia."

A shake of the head and a sigh. "Oh, that was so sad. I was in the next bed to her. It was a shame those two people arrived just too late to say their goodbyes."

"What two people?"

She gave a light laugh. "Actually, I'm not sure I didn't imagine them. It all seemed so unreal."

"Why was that?"

"There was something odd about them, like I was seeing them through a mist or in a dream. The man said, 'Time to go.' And the woman was even stranger. She stretched out her arm above the bed, as though she was taking Silvia's hand."

"That's so wonderful!" I thought Caroline was about to start dancing. If she had, I would have joined her.

Instead, we said farewell to the young mother, and I no doubt confused her when I added, "That was a splendid dream. I hope you have another like it one day."

On our return, I chased my own splendid dream to the library. But how do you find a place which is not known to exist? The geography section was vast: a cartographer's dream. Copies of every atlas and map which had ever existed were located among the shelves. Where was I to start?

I wasn't going to find any areas circled in red and inscribed, "land lost by Hell" or "lodestone free zone"! So, how had Caffiaes found his hotel? I couldn't imagine him having the patience to pour over ancient charts, comparing them with modern ones. I knew I hadn't. In any case, didn't maps become more accurate, not less? And wouldn't he have been noticed spending hours in this part of the library?

Daemons were not uncommon visitors, but they tended to stay in their own area, one we hounds avoided. The plaque above it read, "Torture: Methodology, Psychology and Practice." But "Pornography for Daemons," would have been more accurate. There was no doubt they enjoyed their study sessions far more than any of us did ours.

I was replacing a current map of Cornwall beside an eighteenth century one when Josh interrupted me.

"Feeling homesick, are you, Ferris? It's not healthy, dwelling on the past." He waved a thin file under my nose. "This one should have been for Caro, but she's busy. It's a hand-on from another team."

Oh? That was rare. "Is there some problem with it, then?"

"Possibly. I'm not sure."

Liar! Teams didn't give up their assignments easily: it was an admission of failure.

"Who are you sending with me?"

"No one. It looks like a one hound job to me. I'm sure you'll be able to deal with it." He placed the file on the nearest table. "I wouldn't bother reading this. It doesn't tell you anything. In fact, it's time you were going."

Not good. He was not giving me the option; he was sending me out as unprepared as possible. But there was no one to complain to. And the grey tunnel was beckoning.

CHAPTER 17

The young woman in the long, white dress tiptoed along the edge of the mock Tudor battlements, shading her eyes and gazing around, as though trying to find out whether anyone was watching. She would have been disappointed. There was no one around but me and I was standing well back, hidden among the trees in the fake forest. The time was not yet right to intervene.

Clambering onto the highest crenelation, she arched her back and jumped. Her howl as she descended was more of a whoop. It was loud enough to wake the dead. And, of course, I should know.

Down she floated, though not with any great finesse. Had the dress been a crinoline, it might have made more of an impact, but the Queen Anne style clung to her legs and the effect was, if anything, rather undignified.

I drifted over the damp grass and met her at the base of the tower. "Good evening."

"Good evening yourself. Did you see what I just did?"

"Yes, I thought it, er, quite spectacular." This might turn out to be my shortest mission so far. I could see no reasons yet for this assignment to have been handed on by another team. "You jumped from up there." I pointed.

She giggled. "Yes, I do it every evening at this precise time. At first it was a bit scary, even though I knew I couldn't hurt myself, but now it's starting to get rather boring. I've been trying to think of ways to make it that little bit more interesting."

More interesting? "You do know no one could ever survive a fall from that height."

"Yes, but that was the intention, wasn't it? Not much point in attempting suicide by jumping off a farm gate, is there?" She was not even surprised. She knew. She already knew she was dead.

I recovered as fast as I could. "You can't stay here. I've come to take you away. To be your guide."

"Oh no. I'm not being guided anywhere by you." She put her hands to the sides of her face in pretend shock. "My mummy told me never to go anywhere with strange men."

So, this must be the problem Josh had been hinting at. Well, I had better find a way around it. The lodestone in my head was giving out a clear enough signal. It was warm and getting warmer by the minute. There was no doubt this lady belonged in Hell. All I had to do was convince her of the fact.

"I'm not leaving. It's great fun here." She floated away from me, heading for the building. Having no choice if I intended to complete my mission, I followed.

She halted beside the wall and giggled again as her fingers passed through it. "I like everything about being a ghost. Do you know they set a priest on me a few weeks ago? One of those with a bell, a book and a candle, no less. That smelly sage stank the place out for days."

"I gather the exorcism didn't take." Go on, Ross, state the obvious.

"It never stood a chance of working."

"Why was that?"

She laughed as though I'd just said the funniest thing she had ever heard. "It didn't work because he called on Lady Charlotte to leave. And she might have done if she had been here but, you see, I'm not Lady Charlotte."

Oh dear. It was looking like I had got the wrong wraith. But how could there have been two young women centuries apart both committing suicide in the exact same place, by the exact same method and at the exact same time of day?

"Where is Lady Charlotte and who are you?"

She tapped her forefinger against the side of her nose. "That would be telling, wouldn't it? I know all about you." She laughed again. "I was warned. He told me, 'They will come. But so long as they don't learn anything: not who you are or where you're from, they can't do a thing.' So, I will tell you nothing. You have to take me from the place I died but in life I was never within a hundred miles of this house."

How could she know all this? We take wraiths from where they died because that is where they are condemned to wait for us. I knew of no precedent for a ghost being in a location they never visited when they were alive. Why would a spirit choose to haunt such a place?

"If you're not Lady Charlotte, why do you do her haunting for her?"

"I could say it's because I enjoy jumping off towers. It's ever so romantic, don't you think? But the fact is I agreed to do it. Charlotte didn't want to be forgotten and I understood that. So, I do it for her."

I had the feeling she was lying. If she had taken Lady Charlotte's place, perhaps that included having to do her haunting for her; not so much an agreement, more a compulsion.

I hadn't a clue how to handle this situation and doubted whether anyone else from my team would be of any help either. How could I call on this soul to follow me when I hadn't the remotest idea who she was? "Leave this place and come with me, spirit!" only works if the spectre is willing to go. This one certainly was not.

I followed her into the house and met with another shock. Ghosts travel in a bubble of their own time. I should have been seeing a house decorated in the style of the late Georgian era, not one with a television in one room and a desktop computer in another. This ghost was from a time close to the one I was currently operating in. She had to have died fewer than twenty years earlier.

"Well, mister, are you going to give up now and go back to where you came from?"

"I can't do that. Whoever you are, you don't belong on the temporal plane any longer."

"I belong wherever I want to be. And for now, I choose to be in this building. Still, a little bit of company would be nice. Why don't you stick around for a while?" She tilted her head to one side, her large, pale eyes scanning me. "You're quite cute for a servant of Hell. I wonder what you did to be sent there?"

She knew far too much. It was as though someone had given her instructions. I remembered she had said "he" told her someone would come for her. Could it have been another Hell hound? I was sure it would not have been one of the poodles. Something like this would never have been given Heavenly approval.

"Fine. I'll leave you to your haunting for now, but I will return. And you will come with me in the end."

She was so sure of herself, my departure only provoked more laughter.

I returned to base to discover I was not the only one to have such an experience. The twelve of us who had so far encountered the problem were instructed to assemble round the long, oval conference table in Common Room Twenty-Four (not that it was any different from the common room I was used to, except there was no tartan blanket!) There would be no time for any chit-chat. We were there to come up with a solution. Or else.

One of the women began the discussion. "They're being switched round. There is still a wraith in each location but they're all the wrong ones. It's as though they've been put on some kind of rota. The man I was sent to collect wasn't even from the same century. And it was obvious he'd been coached."

When it was my turn, I told my own tale. It was no different from any of the others, and I had come to the same conclusions. "Whoever is behind this has been using threats. The spirits won't talk to us because they know they're told they will end up behind the Final Door if they do"

There were nods all round the table. "So, what do we do?" someone asked.

The spokeswoman frowned. "I think if what we are doing isn't working, perhaps we'll have to consider something more drastic. I know we've never used force in the past but if there is no other solution, it might be time to try more intrusive methods to find out what is going on."

I didn't like the sound of that. Or the approving expressions on some of the faces of my colleagues.

"Isn't that a bit drastic? First, why don't we all return to our clients and try to trick them. We're all pretty well skilled at that, aren't we?"

Cranby House in the autumn sunshine. I arrived just in time for her next performance, prepared to give her a round of applause, shout "Bravo!" and tell her how clever she was. Last time she thought me "cute". I would prove I could be charming too.

There it was, right on time: the figure balancing on the fake battlements.

Oh? What was going on? Where was she? Teetering on the edge of the crenelations was not the woman in the white gown. Instead, it was a man in evening dress, complete with white tie and tails. He raised his topper and waved it in my direction then, still swinging it in the air and with a loud shout of "Yippeeeeeee", he leapt out from the tower.

I glided across the grass to meet him. It couldn't have been his first jump; he must have had some practice since he landed like a cat, on his feet.

"Good evening, sir."

"Indeed it is. Quite exhilarating, this bit of haunting, don't you know?"

"What happened to the young woman who was here a few days ago?"

"Moved on, old chap. Moved on."

I was not convinced by his act. Like the young woman he had replaced, I had an inkling he was from a time much later than the one he was pretending to be in. There was something wrong with both the cut and the fit of his coat. It had the faded look of a garment bought from a fancy-dress shop or salvaged from a long-neglected wardrobe.

"She didn't stay here long, did she? Are you also just passing through?"

"No idea. It all depends, don't you know?"

"Depends on what?"

"Ah, catching me out isn't going to be as easy as you think!" He replaced his top hat and patted it down.

"No, I don't suppose it is. You look like a rather intelligent chap."

"Indeed I am. Now, why don't you buzz off back to where you came from. We're doing no harm."

"I can't agree. You're throwing the celestial books out of balance, causing my employers more than a few headaches. It would go easier on you if you were to help me. Why don't you tell me what's going on?"

"What would you do for me if I did? Send me to Heaven instead?"

"Sorry. That's just not possible." Hell hounds are not allowed to tell that particular untruth, but in my head, I ran through all the promises I could make him: the lies I could tell.

He turned on his heel. "I ought to get back inside."

"What's the point? You'd never be able to convince anyone you're Lady Charlotte. Besides, I have all the resources of Hell at my disposal. We will soon discover who you are and, mark my words, we will take you back, first to your own haunting ground and from there to somewhere a little hotter."

He frowned and pursed his lips like he was a spoiled child deprived of a hoped-for sweetie. "I don't like your tone, young man. Go away or I will fetch some help of my own to sort you out."

Now that was interesting. Who could he know capable of "sorting out" a Hell hound? There was nothing to be gained by arguing with the man, so I returned to Hell to find Caroline. I wanted to run an idea past my team leader.

CHAPTER 18

"Going undercover? You?" I had expected quite a different response. She was on the verge of laughter. "I don't see how that could work."

"This operation is being organised by someone with a detailed knowledge of how Hell itself functions. It's got to be someone from among us. I think we should find ourselves a death; grab the ghost but pretend we haven't. All in secret. I will then haunt the spot myself and hope whoever's responsible for the swaps takes the bait."

"I don't know, Ross. It's a bit convoluted, isn't it?"

"Have you any better solution?"

"No." She bit her lip. "I don't like it though. I can't help feeling we're missing something about the nature of whoever is organising this. A Hell hound doesn't have the resources. Give me time to think about it."

When she returned a few minutes later she nodded to me. "I've discussed your idea with Josh. He said he thought you might have problems with this job, and he's prepared to give it a try."

I wondered why she felt she couldn't make the decision alone, without involving Josh. He might be her supervisor but, like me, I knew she neither trusted nor liked him. If he agreed to this plan, it would be because he wanted it to fail.

"He's arranging for you to have your lodestone deactivated for the duration so you will appear as a wraith. And he says you should go to one of the sites we've already identified as having the wrong ghost in residence."

Where else did he think I would have suggested going? Some empty location with nothing to see? The man really was a total waste of space. And it got worse. As the case was so unusual, he had decided to accompany us, at least as far as recovering the soul I was to temporarily replace. It could not have been more obvious he wanted to keep an eye on Caroline and me.

It took a while for the right set of circumstances to fall into place. At long last, a car crashed close to one of the locations on the list. Now timing was everything. The driver had been drunk and he was one of ours, destined for Hell. He had already worked that out before we even got to him.

We walked his corpse to the garden of a small, isolated house and laid it down in the bushes by the drive. Having seen the driver's wraith on its way, Caroline and Josh returned to Hell while I entered the house and waited.

The property should by rights have been haunted by a soldier who had survived the trenches of the First World War, only to come home and then die from influenza. However, the present incumbent was a woman who at the moment I arrived, was sitting on the bed upstairs pretending to expire from the fever.

Once her hour for haunting was over, she came down to discover me in the living room.

"Hello. I think I've had an accident."

She peered at me. "How did you get here?"

"My car is up on the main road. It's hit a tree. I've hurt myself. Seeing your lights were on, I hoped I might find some help here."

"Stay there." She went outside.

A few seconds later she was back. "Why don't you sit down?"

I did so. It was tempting to ask her how to avoid being collected but I had to bite my tongue (not that I currently had one). The wraith I was pretending to be would not even have known he was dead, let alone expect a Hell hound to come for him.

As she leant over me, I tried to keep my gaze level.

"I ought to let them take you."

"Is the ambulance here already?"

"I haven't called for an ambulance."

Oh no! What was I to do if she told me I was dead and was to be conducted away?

She closed her eyes and began muttering.

Around us the room grew hotter. At the same time came a flash and a bright flare. Something walked out of the shimmering air.

The figure might be in human form, but his disguise did not fool me: I had met him before.

He stared at me.

I returned the favour.

"Well, well. Hello, Mr. Ferris. What are you doing here?"

"I could ask you the same. Don't tell me all this disruption has been caused by you and your friends' games again."

"All what disruption? I don't know what you're talking about." He seated himself on a chair opposite me.

"Are you responsible for all these ghosts playing musical haunts?"

"Nice way to describe it and, yes, why would I deny it?"

"Why indeed. But do let me in on the reason you're doing it, because I don't get the point."

"First, it annoys the hell out of Hell and, as you already know, we like to do that, but it also means everyone loses track."

He was making no sense but, like all villains, it was fortunate he could not resist explaining his cunning scheme.

"It all started with a travel agent. I was shovelling a bit of brimstone in his direction while discussing my last escapade with a couple of fellow daemons. You remember it, don't you, Ross, the pleasant time we all had together at the Oaklands Hotel? Anyway, this travel agent started babbling about some clever scams he had run when alive. 'Time shares', he called them. I realised they were a diabolical idea, quite splendid. All we needed to make it work was a few stupid ghosts to keep changing places."

"And the point of that is…?"

"Well, every so often one could drop out, and my friends and I could have a heap of fun torturing them. Who was going to notice? You Hell hounds can't work out who's who, let alone who's missing." He paused for a moment and steepled his long fingers under his chin. "There is one odd thing though. We've discovered once the ghosts have changed places and left their original homes behind, they're not the same."

"How do you mean?"

"They realise they're dead."

I turned to the woman. "Do you understand what he's saying? Caffiaes and his friends will work their way through all of you, one by one. Have you ever seen a cat toying with a mouse?"

She replied with a tiny, quick nod of the head.

"I'm not saying Hell is a picnic, but in that place the punishment always fits the crime. What these daemons will do to you is a whole lot worse. Trust me." I put out my hand. "Come over here and tell me your name."

"It's Judith." Her voice was the thinnest of whispers.

"I need more, Judith."

Caffiaes lunged. His arms lengthened. His hands became clawed talons sharper than any knife. His eyes were whirling discs of gold.

I was about to be ripped apart.

With a furious, ear-splitting growl, he pulled back. Destroying a Hell hound would send ripples straight to the depths of the Inferno. And he knew it.

Snarling, he stood straighter. "If you found me, others will."

"They're not far behind."

He slumped back into the chair. "All I ever wanted was a bit of respect, a decent promotion maybe. I've worked so hard for it. But what do I get? 'Shovel those ashes, Caffiaes', 'Burnish that brimstone, Caffiaes', 'Fetch the next victim, Caffiaes, but don't you dare lay a claw on him'. What kind of existence is that for a daemon?"

"Judith Maguire. My body is under the floorboards at number six, Dunston Lane."

We both looked at her.

Again, I held out my hand. "Let's go, Judith. Are you coming too, Caffiaes?"

He grunted. However, when I arrived in the house where Judith had died (following the rest of her gang of thieves finding out she had double crossed them) he was still with us.

I entered to discover a familiar ghost. He had shed the top hat and tails in favour of a black and white hooped jumper, black trousers and a mask over his eyes. He was carrying a large sack with "swag" printed across it.

Judith's mouth fell open. She flew at him. "What do you think you're doing? This is a serious haunt, not a comedy act!"

"Don't you watch any films? All the best robbers dress like this. It's not my fault you have no sense of occasion, dear lady." He peered round her. "Hello again, Mr. Caffiaes. Time to move on again, is it? I hope you've got somewhere better for me. No offence, but this place is a bit of a comedown after Cranby House, don't you know?"

Caffiaes shrugged. "Where would you like to go?"

Silly question, considering the circumstances, but he was not the only one who was curious.

"Good. It's about time I was given a choice." Above the eye mask the brow furrowed. "Ooh, now then... What about Henry the Eighth? Someone like that: important and well dressed. Yes, I'd cut a fine figure as a Tudor."

He may well have done but, unfortunately, Hampton Court was not on offer and there wouldn't be any battlements where he was going.

I couldn't leave Judith alone in her house. She said she would sit still and await collection but I was worried; once she had time to think, she might wander off again. So, four of us went on to Top-hat's own haunt.

I had never seen such a mess. Clothes littered every surface, except the ones covered in dirty dishes and takeaway cartons. I doubted the flat had been cleaned. Ever. Judith squealed in horror and attempted to pick up the nearest piece of rubbish, then gave out a plaintive cry as she remembered she could no longer touch anything.

The wraith in residence was delighted to see us, while Top-hat began to throw a tantrum. "I'm not staying here. If you try to make me, I'll tell everyone what you're up to. How you move us around..." He stopped and stared at me.

I could almost hear the penny dropping.

His face fell. "Oh, you're not working together, are you?"

I was about to move all of us to the next haunt when Caroline drifted through the wall. "Ah, here you are. Your lodestone keeps shifting location so I thought I'd come and see what you were up to. While you were jumping around, another team came up with the same idea and solved the mystery. But it looks like you weren't far behind them."

She pursed her lips when she saw Caffiaes. "You again! I might have guessed. Well, your three friends are already being dealt with. You'd better come along with me. I'll send someone else to carry on picking up the missing wraiths."

Caffiaes made an odd sound. I thought he was on the verge of tears but instead he grinned at us. "You know, if you don't turn me in, I could be of some help to you in the future. Who knows when you might need assistance from a friendly daemon?"

"He could have a point, Caroline. Think about it. What would we gain by handing him over? Nothing at all, not even a pat on the back. And he's right. He might be some use, especially now he owes us a favour."

She began to walk away. "Do what you want, Ross. Just don't get us into any trouble."

Trouble? No, I didn't want trouble. I just wanted a way out.

CHAPTER 19

The thought I might have a daemon on my side was making me a little reckless.

Ever since Louise told me Caroline had a private room she never used, I was determined to set foot inside it. There were so few places in Hell where it was possible to be alone.

When not out on the temporal plane, we would sit in the common room among the piles of glossy magazines which were constantly being added to, pretending to ourselves we were fascinated by another tale of good or ill fortune.

No one ever slept and everyone was bored. The only subject discussed was the missions we had in common. Each person's life prior to their death was a sealed box to which only they held the key, at least while they were with other hounds. To reminisce was to remind yourself and others that it was not always like this. We had enough pain to contend with. Like many others, hope was a taboo subject.

Even the magazines were not there to make the time pass more easily. Hell wanted us to be well informed about the time period in which we operated: we should not make mistakes by being unaware of events; we should know how to react if we had to converse with those still living.

I wanted more. There had to be a clue that would lead to a way out of this nightmare. Other than the obvious one! We'd all heard the rumours about other hounds, unable to go on, taking the long walk down the corridor, heading for the torment which awaited them. But that was not for me. Having already had a glimpse of what lay beyond the Final Door, I had no desire to repeat the experience.

I mumbled something about "research" and "library." Not that I needed to. Neither Caroline nor Greg reacted, and Louise was out on a solo mission.

The long room was crammed with an uncountable number of books on every subject. But no fiction; we were not here to enjoy ourselves. There was no modern technology either. Perhaps Hell didn't trust us: the lure of a video game might just have been too much of a temptation for some.

I made my way to the section on science and mathematics; took down a huge tome which I hadn't the slightest hope of understanding. I could read and write a little by that stage, but nowhere near well enough to tackle Professor Wright's thesis on "stratospheric gravity waves" (whatever they were). Open on the table in front of me though, it looked impressive enough to head off any suggestion I was not studying.

I had to find the right moment. Caroline's office was located behind the last row of shelves. Could I get there without being seen? And if I did, which one of the seven doors was hers?

Other hounds were studying. A group of four were clustered round a nearby table. Heads close together, they were discussing an aeroplane crash.

One cast her eyes in my direction. She gave me a wry smile.

I looked away and rifled through the pages of the book. This was not working. Would I ever be unobserved?

Wry-smile got to her feet. "We have everything we need. Time to go."

There only remained a group of three hounds by the economics section. With their backs to me, they picked up journals from a triangular stand.

Was this my opportunity? I would have only moments.

Speeding through the science section: seven identical doors. Which of them was Caroline's? I would have to take a gamble.

I was about to let my hand drift inside the first door when I noticed the small plaque: "Third Millennium Group One: Supervisor: JH." JH? That must be Josh. The next door's plaque read: "2076-2100: AQ". That had to be a pair of dates and the team leader's initials, since the next one read: "2051-2075: JE". This wasn't going to be so difficult after all.

The end one was labelled "2001- 2025: CT", the time period in which I worked and Caroline's initials.

Inside, the room was much as I had expected. It was small, even a little cramped. A desk took up one side and had an office chair in front of it. Along the back wall was a two-seater settee.

I sat down and swivelled, preparing to enjoy a little solitude for a change. But… there, in front of me, was a folded piece of notepaper and on it, written in block capitals and underlined twice, the words "Ross Ferris".

I thought I had been so careful sneaking around, picking the right time so no one would notice, and all the while Caroline had known. This was obviously a little billet doux to tell me to keep my bottom off her chair.

"Damn!"

I might as well see what she had to say. No doubt it would be a telling off in the most eloquent of prose. Chuckling a little at my own foolishness in thinking I had been getting one over on her, I picked up the note. I opened it.

And froze.

"Caroline," I read, "I've worked it out. Ferris is the spy."

What?

I let go of the note. It fluttered onto the desk, but the words were still the same. I forced myself to read on.

"I can see why you feel there is not yet enough hard evidence but you must agree there is more than enough circumstantial. This daemon friend of his, Caffiaes, already has a bit of a reputation as a maverick. Maybe they are working together. I expect you to help me get rid of Ferris right now. You can't afford another fiasco like Anya."

There was no signature. But the handwriting was Josh Holdacre's.

I scrunched up the paper. Thrust it into a pocket. I had to hide it.

On my feet, half way to the door. "No, she might have seen it."

Back to the table. Trying to smooth out the creases.

But maybe she hadn't. What should I do?

Put it somewhere else: on the floor, under the settee. If she had seen it and looked for it, she would find it. If not, she would never see it. But Josh…

"Stop it, Ross!" I ran my fingers through my hair. Tried to soothe myself with my own words. Counted to ten.

I couldn't stay here. They might already be searching for me. The door was a mile away. My feet were too heavy. And there was nowhere to hide.

I had no choice: I had to return to the common room.

Through the door, I slipped between the shelves. Another hound was sitting at the table with the open book. I could not close it. Not even replace it.

"Had to deliver a message," I spluttered, grinning like a fool.

She shrugged.

I cursed my stupidity. If I had said nothing, she would not have even noticed me. Now someone knew where I had been.

Outside the common room I hesitated. Was this the right move? What if they were waiting for me?

Inside, and Caroline on her feet. "Oh, there you are, Ross. You've saved me having to come and find you."

"Why? I wasn't doing anything. I was in the library. I…"

"What is the matter with you? I know where you were, you told us. Now, come on. We have a mission, and it's got to be the strangest one yet. Josh told me to tread carefully and take only one other team member."

Oh, yes? Was this it? Had she and Josh dreamed up a trap to ensnare me?

She peered at me. "Are you feeling all right? If you weren't one yourself, I'd say you'd seen a ghost."

Everyone laughed. Except me.

"I'm fine. Now what's the job?" Not that it made any difference. They were all the same and none of them would ever make me feel "fine".

"Well, on the face of it, the usual: a simple matter of collecting a lost soul, a young girl who died in an accident. You know the drill."

Oh yes. I knew the drill only too well.

Caroline set off for the corridor.

I trailed behind, trying not to bolt, trying to tell myself she might not have seen the note, or she had seen it but didn't agree with Josh.

CHAPTER 20

We arrived in front of one of those big, old Elizabethan houses, complete with candy twist chimneys. At the end of the extensive grounds was an ornate folly; someone with too much money and too much time to waste had stuck a Normanesque tower in the middle of a grove of mismatched trees. All very picturesque but there was nothing calling to us from there. No one had leapt from those fake battlements. Not on this occasion.

I tried to tell myself this was far too elaborate to have been set up to catch me out; it had to be a genuine mission. But that didn't mean I wasn't under suspicion. I'd have to watch my step.

I followed Caroline across a lawn so well-manicured it looked as if a diligent gardener had that very day been mowing it with a pair of nail clippers.

The front door was closed. We could have drifted through, but we didn't want to risk scaring anyone on the other side. Someone was at home because an ancient Bentley and a Volkswagen Golf, with a dint in the passenger door, were parked side by side on the curve of gravel in front of the mansion.

Caroline pasted on her best smile and knocked on the imposing oak door. It was eventually opened the tiniest of cracks. If we had expected an old-style butler, we would have been disappointed. The man was in his mid-thirties and dressed ultra-casual: in a pair of black jeans with rips across the knees and a tatty sweatshirt, the image on which was so faded I couldn't tell what it was meant to be.

He didn't give us time to speak. Turning his head, he yelled, "They're here, Marion." He beckoned to us to enter. "We weren't expecting you just yet. I thought we'd agreed six o'clock."

"Yes, we are a little early, aren't we?" Caroline stepped inside.

The man stared at me. "Where's your camera? I hope you don't think you can get good enough shots with some piddly little phone-cam."

"We thought we would have a chat first," Caroline replied before I could, which is just as well as I never owned either a camera or a phone. A pistol and a rapier, oh yes, but all this twenty-first century technology left me as stone cold as my corpse.

"Like I said to your editor, 'We're not prepared to give a long interview at this stage and we're certainly not about to explain how we did it'. We don't want all the others to copy us. This is our big chance; our meal ticket. You wouldn't believe the heating bills for this place."

The house had been altered a great deal from its original plan. There were no grand rooms interconnected with each other, no great hall either. At some time in the recent past it had all been remodelled, perhaps as a corporate headquarters or maybe a hotel.

We passed through a series of doors before reaching a cosy sitting room with an old-fashioned coal fire roaring in the grate.

A short, blonde woman rose to her feet. In contrast to the man, she was dressed like a fashion plate from an expensive magazine, wearing a smart, well-tailored aubergine business suit, complete with Hermes scarf. The whole scene gave me the distinct impression I was setting foot on a film set. A lot of time had been spent composing the perfect photo shoot. It was a shame they had missed the creaky, old, iron radiator under the window. And the velvet curtains were more than a little faded, well past their best. This setup was nothing more than an illusion of wealth.

"Welcome to Vascelles House. Coffee is on the way. No doubt you want a bit of background." She frowned. "Where's your camera? I know we said no recording equipment, but we didn't mean you couldn't photograph it. How will you get us the publicity we need if you're not going to show it's real?"

"'Her', Marion. She's not an 'it'."

"All right, Simon. If you insist. Her."

Behind us the door re-opened and a pale young woman in a black trouser suit pushed a little cart into the room. Yes, the place was corporate all right. And failing corporate, if I wasn't mistaken.

She poured the coffee into small, bone china cups. "Do you need anything else tonight, Mr. Boyle?"

"No, Liz, thanks very much. You can get off home now."

As the door closed behind Liz, Marion glanced at us both. "Milk? Sugar?"

"No, thanks. We're not thirsty." We weren't about to risk disgracing ourselves by discovering this was one of those times when Hell was not going to permit us to drink.

"All right, then. I suppose journalists like you are always in a bit of a hurry to meet your deadlines."

"Something like that." I was having difficulty concentrating, feeling a little distant. And I'd taken a bit of a dislike to Marion. I was pretty sure "it" was the ghost we had been sent to collect.

"Are you sure you don't want to go and fetch your camera? We'll wait for you."

Ah. "Er... we were told to confirm the story first, establish the basics. Our best staff photographer will be coming along later. At six, like we agreed."

Caroline nodded. "Yes, that's why Ross and I are here early."

"Ross?" Simon peered hard at us. "But I thought your paper said Julie Carter and Paul Smith were being sent. When you arrived, I knew something was off. You don't look a bit like your pictures in Psychic News."

"Julie and Paul were busy. We were sent instead." I didn't think he believed me. I could now read nothing but suspicion in his eyes.

"Thought it was a hoax, did they? Well, come along and we'll prove to you it's not."

Marion led the way down a set of steps towards the cellars. The lighting was low and there was a thick layer of dust over everything. There were even a few cobwebs hanging in strategic places. It was all so atmospheric, like the lead in to a conjuring trick. There was also a distinctive smell. I couldn't place it, but it was rather unpleasant.

My nose wrinkled. I would have pinched it if I hadn't been trying to be polite.

"Is someone making stuffing?"

Caroline's question made our hosts laugh. "Sage has more uses than you know." Simon tapped his own nose.

I glanced at Caroline. We were both aware of one of its uses. I've yet to meet a ghost who finds things pleasant when there is sage around. It's the reason not many herb gardens are haunted.

Neither of us wanted to enter the room at the end of the low passage, the door of which creaked, like an over-loud sound effect from a cheap horror film, as Marion threw it open. How melodramatic!

Inside, a wall had been demolished to create a large, square space. In the centre was a huge, glass box, about nine feet on each side and six feet high. It was suspended a foot or so above the cellar floor by a large wooden block under each corner. Beneath it I could see a great many bunches of sage. The foul-smelling herb was also lying in a thick carpet around the outside of the box.

"Watch it, Ross! That looks sharp."

I jerked back. I had been too busy trying to decide if Caroline was behaving normally to notice where I was putting my feet. I had been about to step on a large, clear crystal, one of many sprinkled like broken glass among the leaves.

"That's selenite, isn't it?"

"Oh yes." Marion smiled at Caroline. "Not many people recognise it, but I suppose, given your job, you've run across it before."

We had indeed. And Louise had once spent several hours sneezing after touching the tiniest of fragments during a mission.

The only furniture inside the cube was a low, wooden stool and on it sat a girl in a stained, dove grey dress and with a mob cap covering most of her light brown hair. She couldn't have been more than thirteen. Her face was streaked with tears and her small, emaciated body shivered. In silence she stared out at us, her ankles crossed and her hands in her lap.

"Oh, how cruel!" Caroline spoke for both of us.

For a moment I forgot my own troubles. I wanted to rush over and rescue the child, if you could call taking her to Hell any kind of rescue. But, on the other hand, this was far from anyone's idea of Heaven either.

"It's only a ghost. It can't feel anything."

I was only a ghost too but I felt something. If I had possessed true corporeal form, I would have had no compunction in wrapping my hands round Marion's slender neck.

As the woman approached the edge of the layer of sage, the ghost cowered back, her eyes grew larger and it was obvious she was trembling. She was terrified yet I could do nothing to help her. I could no more cross the boundary of sage and selenite than she could.

Marion, now standing at the side of the box, pointed at her prisoner. "Well, you can see for yourselves. It's exactly as I told your editor. We have captured and contained a genuine ghost. And here's your proof."

Had we been the journalists she believed us to be, I had no doubt we would have rushed for our cameras. The girl was indeed a ghost, not a captive child. There was that familiar translucency about her: she was not quite solid and the stool on which she sat was visible as a faint outline through the middle of her body.

As Marion patted the glass, the ghost in the box threw open her mouth. Anyone could tell she was screaming but we couldn't hear a thing.

"Is that container soundproofed?" Caroline was standing as close to the sage as I guessed she could bear to be. It was a lot closer than I could manage.

"Yes, we had no choice about that. It was making so much noise, constantly crying out for us to let it go. Such an unpleasant howling and moaning. So, we put baffles both in the ceiling and between the box and the floor." She tapped the glass again. "Don't worry. It can't get to you. This stuff is bulletproof as well as soundproof. It's made several attempts, but it can't get through."

She was wrong. It was not the glass which was the issue. A ghost can drift through anything, even the steel wall of a safe, so why would a bit of thickened glass be a problem? No, it was the sage and selenite which had turned the glass cage into an escape proof prison.

"Thank you, Simon. We've seen enough." I didn't think I could take much more. It was time for Caroline and me to get out of this room and try to come up with some kind of rescue plan for the unfortunate girl.

"You are convinced, aren't you?"

"Yes, I do believe you have caught a ghost. Don't you, Ross?"

"Indeed I do. We should go back to the paper right away and send in the photographer. There's a lot here our readers are bound to be interested in."

Simon clapped his hands. "Good. Let's not waste any more time. I'll show you out."

We followed him back through the squeaking door and up into the house. It disturbed me that Marion remained in the cellar. Her mere presence was enough to cause the poor, tortured ghost further distress, but the upside was it gave us a chance to talk to Simon on his own.

I hesitated as we reached the front door. "You are aware you're being cruel to that poor girl in there, aren't you?"

"Marion says ghosts don't feel anything. How can they when they're dead?"

"You saw her face. That child doesn't know she's dead yet. She believes she's still alive and you two are monsters holding her prisoner."

"She must know she's not alive. Before we caught her, all she did was drift about in the cellar, every night appearing and doing a lot of moaning before vanishing again. I asked Marion to come and help because she's a medium and knows a lot about this sort of thing."

"Marion isn't your wife?"

"Oh no, not a chance. In fact, I don't like her at all, but I can't deny she has done what she promised. She'd been working for years on a way to trap a spectre. I wasn't sure it would come off but, well, you've seen the results. This is going to make my fortune."

It was odd. I had no proof, no reason for my stray thought, but it was there nonetheless. Simon was not the type to share a fortune with anyone. And there was plenty of room in that box for more than one ghost.

We shook hands on the steps outside the house.

Simon peered round us. "What have you done with your car?"

"Oh, we left it out on the road beyond the gates. We fancied a bit of fresh air."

"What gates? There are no gates at the end of the drive. They were taken down years ago."

Ah.

I was saved from having to reply by the sudden arrival of an old, green Audi,

Page 97

which screeched to a halt in a hail of gravel.

    The real reporters had arrived.

    Caroline gave me a quick nod.

    And we scarpered.

CHAPTER 21

We perched on the outer wall of the folly and dangled our heels over the crenelations.

I watched Caroline enjoying the cool evening air. "Now, here would make such a pleasant haunt. If only we didn't have a job to do." She giggled. "I'd like to see Marion's face when she realises she put on her best performance for us, when we're not even living people. Some medium, eh?"

"Yes, she's a nasty piece of work, that one."

"Well, no doubt one day soon, she'll get her just reward." There was something in the way Caroline said it.

I couldn't stand it any longer. "Is that what you expect will happen to me when we get back?"

"What do you mean?"

"You think I'm a spy, don't you?"

She laughed. Yes, she laughed. "A what? Have you been sniffing too much sulphur?"

"Josh thinks I am."

"Oh, Josh!" Now she was laughing so hard she almost lost her balance. "You could never be a spy. You're incapable of keeping anything secret." She stared at me. "Wait a minute. You're being serious, aren't you?"

"Yes, I am."

"But why? What's given you such a ridiculous idea? What has Josh said?"

"Not much, but enough."

She shook her head. "Josh sees spies everywhere. He's convinced someone helped Anya disappear. He hasn't even got any proof she's missing, yet he goes on with this obsession of his: this nonsense that people have escaped from Hell. In his own way he's as bad as you."

"You don't believe him, then?"

"No more than I believed him when it was Greg he was accusing. Or before that, when it had something to do with Nadine from the interview team. He's just a bit insane, that's all." She sighed. "Like we all are, I suppose, in our own individual ways."

I couldn't help it. I threw my arms around her. And kissed her.

She wriggled free. "Stop it, Ross. You mustn't do that. We mustn't... We can't. Ever. You know the rules."

I did and I would have been happy to carry on breaking them, but at that moment we were interrupted by loud shouts coming from in front of the house: Simon was yelling at someone.

Caroline slid down from the wall. "Come on. Back to work. Maybe you'll be able to concentrate properly now."

We made our way to the edge of the building. Hidden by an outcrop of ivy as well as the darkness, we had a pretty good view of the scene.

The photographer was dismantling his tripod and placing it and other equipment into boxes on the back seat of the Audi.

His companion was leaning on the open driver's side door. "I'm sorry but it's one of the most inept hoaxes I've ever seen. You can't fool professional ghost hunters like us just by projecting an image onto glass. We've seen it all before."

Simon held out his hands to her. "But it's not a hoax. Our ghost is real. Please come back inside."

"Look, Mr. Boyle, if you won't let us approach your so-called spectre without keeping all that glass between us, then we have no choice but to declare you a fraud."

"I can't let her out. She'll escape. If she leaves the box, she'll vanish. Before we caught her, we only ever saw her at a certain time each night and only in the cellar."

That made sense to me. They had captured the girl in mid-haunt and the selenite was preventing the manifestation from ending.

The reporter shrugged her shoulders and swung her long legs into the car. "Please don't call us again, Mr. Boyle. As I said inside, our colleagues have crossed swords with Miss Palmer on several previous occasions. This isn't the first stunt she's pulled."

The photographer got in beside her, both doors slammed, and they zoomed away in a hail of tiny stones.

For a moment Simon was the picture of dejection, his shoulders slumping, his hands on his head.

Then he bent, scooped up a handful of grit and hurled it after the departing car. "Marion! Marion!" He raced back into the house, slamming the door behind him.

Caroline laughed. "Call themselves ghost hunters? What a pair! They can't tell the real thing from a parlour trick."

"It's as well they can't, not that we're any closer to rescuing the girl. I don't see how this is any help at all."

There came a loud crash from the other side of the front door, followed by another and another. Was Simon pulling the house apart?

We drifted inside. There was no one in the entrance hall but...

"Is that...?" I already knew the answer. There is no other substance with quite the same colour or sheen as freshly spilled blood.

We looked at each other, then at the trail of drops and splashes. They were heading for the steps, heading for the cellar.

Wasting no time, dropping straight through the floorboards, we found ourselves beside the open door of the room containing the box.

Inside the cellar, Simon had dragged the injured Marion to the entrance of the glass case. He cast her down among the sage while fiddling in his pockets for the key.

Unconscious but not dead, she lay across the leaves, the fingers of her right hand on top of one of the larger shards of selenite.

Simon swung the pane of glass inwards and bent to drag her inside.

Coming round, she reared up over him, the sharp shard a dagger clutched in her fist. Roaring at the top of her voice, she plunged it into his neck.

Blood gushed from the wound, spraying out over the sage and selenite, dripping down the panes of glass. But the barrier remained: we could only watch as the shard rose and fell, rose and fell.

We could hear the girl now. Sobbing, she curled herself up into a tight ball.

Simon stopped defending himself.

Marion, drenched crimson from head to foot, fell against the wall of the prison, panting hard.

"I'm not sure that was such a clever idea."

She swung round to look at Caroline. "Self defence! He went mad. You saw. It was him or me. I'd have been a ghost..." She waved her hand at her prisoner. "Like her: dead."

The girl stared first at Marion then at us. Her hands flew to her face. "I'm a gh...?"

And knowing the truth, she no longer needed us to guide her; the box could no longer hold her. She was no longer there.

Marion staggered out of the box. "It doesn't matter she's gone. I've got Simon now. He died inside and can't cross the selenite. Oh yes, I know the glass doesn't do anything, but he didn't. And it was such a nice way to contain and display a spectacle."

Caroline grinned. "I'd forget that idea if I were you. Death didn't come suddenly enough, Simon was aware of what was happening. He didn't need telling it was time to go."

"Oh, so now you're an expert on ghosts, are you?"

"I ought to be," she replied and vanished.

I gave Marion a low, sweeping, if rather mocking, bow before following Caroline.

Mission over, we returned to Hell feeling rather pleased with ourselves but the common room was empty. Josh must have sent the other two out on a mission. I hoped he would keep out of my way for a while. I wasn't sure I could trust myself, and confronting him would achieve nothing.

Caroline picked up a magazine.

I wanted a little time on my own to work out what had happened between us and whether or not it meant anything. "I'm going back to the library."

I sat at the same table as before, had the same book open and was giving it the same amount of attention.

A shadow loomed across the table. It was Caffiaes. And the daemon, who now considered me his friend, couldn't wait to tell me his news. "Guess what, Ross. They've given me one all to myself!"

"Good. That's quite a promotion, isn't it?"

"Not much, not really. I don't get to throw any ashes or brimstone over her."

If I had one, I would have felt a nervous shiver go down my spine. "You said 'her'?"

"Yeah, some silly little girl who poisoned her ma and pa. Turns out her idea of Hell is as boring as they come. No fun for me at all."

I didn't dare ask but I knew he was going to tell me.

"I've put her in a glass box, not too wide, not too tall. They're easier to store that way, you know."

CHAPTER 22

Whatever horrors Hell might hold, it was an excellent place in which to get an education. By now I was able to read and write with some fluency, which was a great deal more than anyone else in my family had ever learned to do. My father was able to add and subtract but that was all life as a blacksmith required of him. He would not have been impressed by my growing skill because he'd be too ashamed his youngest son was residing in Hell. My mother and he both took pride in their honesty and industry. I was more than a disappointment to them. When they found out I had become a highwayman, they disowned me altogether.

Shaking away my thoughts of the past, I turned the large manilla envelope Caroline had just handed to me over and over in my hands. It bore my name, and it had to be some kind of official notification: I had never heard of anyone below team leader receiving any mail. Who would send letters to a ghost?

"Well, aren't you going to open it?"

"I suppose so." I would rather she had left me to it, but her curiosity was understandable.

I slit the envelope, trying not to let her see how nervous I was. It had been a while since I had seen Josh's note accusing me of being a spy. Nothing had happened since then. But could this be connected to that? Had he taken his suspicions to whoever was above him? "It's a summons to Interview One. I'm to have an appraisal."

"An appraisal? Are you sure?" She took the paper from me and frowned. "I don't understand this. As a rule, an appraisal is just an excuse for Josh to tell you how stupid he thinks you are and how, if it were up to him, you'd be going straight through the Final Door without further delay. But this..." She sighed. "This looks much more serious. Have you done something idiotic recently and not told me about it?"

"Like what?"

"I don't know, but the only time I ever saw anything like this was when..." She bit her lip. "It was when your predecessor was taken away from us."

It is possible to shiver in Hell despite the heat. Was I to be questioned about Anya? If so, why? I knew nothing. It didn't help that most of us referred to the place I was to go as "Interrogation One" rather than by its official name.

I knew it was impossible, but the corridor seemed even longer and greyer than it ever had before. The door to Interview One was already standing open. I was expected. I had better not keep whoever was inside waiting.

I didn't recognise the man on the other side of the table. He was about fifty, tall and thin, with short grey hair and piercing pale grey eyes. He did not stand to welcome me, nor did he give me a friendly smile. And, as usual, there was no chair on my side of the table. So, I stood like a naughty schoolchild with my hands clasped behind my back.

"Now you have arrived, Mr. Ferris, let's get this over with, shall we?"

"I'm afraid I have no idea why I'm here."

"All will become clear in due course. Now, tell me. Do you know any daemons?"

"Daemons? I've seen one or two, of course, usually in the distance."

"None closer? What about the one you Hell hounds call Caffiaes?"

"Oh, yes, I do know him. I've come across him on a couple of occasions." In fact, it had been quite a lot of occasions by then. But I was not about to admit that. I experienced a flash of memory of the hotel and later game the daemon had played shifting ghosts around. If it had been worked out Caroline and I had not turned him in when we should have, we would no doubt both be finished.

But if that was the case, should there not have been two envelopes? As team leader, she would have been in hotter water than I.

"Can you be more specific? Under what circumstances have you 'come across' this particular daemon?"

"Er, well, I sometimes meet him in the course of my work." And sometimes well away from it too. We had taken to meeting in Caroline's study. There was always the risk she might find us there, but we could think of nowhere else which offered any kind of privacy. And, since we were breaking the rules as it was, we could hardly sit together in the library.

I was trembling: my borrowed body was letting me down. I wanted to run. But there was nowhere to go. Fighting to regain control, I told myself I had been in much tighter situations. And managed to lie my way out of them. I had, hadn't I?

"Tell me about your work."

What was the point? He knew what my job was as well as I did. Well, here we go...

"My role at the moment is as a Reaper, Third Class. We're sent out onto the temporal plane to find those souls which belong to Hell but haven't yet realised they're dead. Our task is to inform them the time has come for them to begin paying for their evil lives." Oh, how I loathed it. But at that moment it seemed far better than any alternative on offer. I wanted to delay having any of Caffiaes' colleagues set loose on me for as long as possible. If ever. And eternity is rather a long time.

"Mr. Ferris, are you aware of Rule Fifteen and its implications?"

"Yes, I do know about the official attitude to friendships. That rule states it's forbidden for beings from the different circles to fraternise with each other. And I'm not stupid. I don't break the rules." ...unless I think I'm going to get away with it.

Was that what this was all about? Not Caffiaes' massive transgressions but a minor matter of the odd friendly conversation?

"Look at my record. I didn't have any friends when I was alive. Why would I start now?" Strange how I never realised that fact at the time. What had seemed to me to be friendships were really only transactions. I gained something, they gained something. It was always an exchange, a bartering. Sometimes fair, sometimes not but never unconditional. I would not have risked my life nor even my comfort for any of them, let alone the eternity beyond.

And now this. Caffiaes and I had never expected to become friends. How could we? In his true form I couldn't even look at him without my eyes hurting. The heat alone would make charcoal of my bones. If I had any. For a fetch like me, being friends with a daemon in this place is like being a fly allied with a spider while both balance on the rim of a cup of boiling water. If it were noticed, we would be flicked into the liquid in the blink of an eye. I had to be careful. This was indeed an interrogation. "What you're suggesting is ridiculous! How could anyone ever be friends with a daemon?" Ooh, I shouldn't have said that. The last thing I wanted him to do was use his brain.

Caffiaes and I should have had nothing in common. Minor daemons are supposed to enjoy throwing sulphur and ashes around all day. Only he didn't. He found it boring and longed for something more stimulating. He was too clever for a denizen of the outer circle. I was too clever for a Hell hound. And we both simmered with resentment at the way we were treated.

It was a good basis for friendship, that resentment. Gave us more in common than anyone could ever know. We both had dreams and liked to talk about them. I wanted to escape, so did he.

The difference was he wanted admission to the inner circles of Hell. There he'd be able to do the torturing himself, rather than look in from the outside at other daemons enjoying themselves. All I wanted was to get the hell out of Hell. Yes, Caffiaes and I had a great deal in common. Why would we not be friends?

The man drummed his fingers on the table. "There have been comments, Mr.

Ferris. You have been seen talking with this daemon in the library and other places."

"Erm, talking yes, but I wouldn't have described it as anything remotely friendly." I leant toward my interrogator, closing the physical distance to draw him into the web of lies I was about to spin. I had to get this right. "If you must know, he's a bully. He likes to pick on those weaker than himself, the petty fiends and the Hell hounds. Of late, I've been a bit of a special project of his." Not true in the slightest but this was the point where I had to bring all my talents into play in defence of my friend and myself. I had always been an accomplished liar. It was, after all, one of the main reasons I had ended up in Hell.

"You want me to believe this daemon beats you up?"

"No, he doesn't beat me. Nothing like that. He doesn't do anything physical. How could he? I'd be incapacitated, unable to do my job, if he so much as brushed me with his smallest claw. No, I think he's practising his psychology on me, trying to upset me; destabilise my thoughts. And he's doing a pretty good job of it."

"Are you afraid of him?"

I nodded, as though the words were too difficult to say. Then I gazed at my feet as though I was embarrassed and ashamed of my weakness. Victims always are. So of course I was.

"In that case, given the choice, I suppose you would not want to see or speak to him ever again."

Oh, the fake joy in my face as I raised my head. "No, I wish I didn't have to speak with him again at all. Doing so seems to me to represent a punishment I never merited and that, as you know, is against all the rules. Besides, the mere fact of being here in Hell is punishment enough, isn't it?"

Good. I had amused him. "Don't you believe you should be in Hell? Was your being sent here nothing more than an unfortunate mistake?"

"No, I do agree the way I spent my life means I deserve to be here. Yet I was under the impression, while working as a Hell hound, I would be kept away from the Final Door and from those, like him, who dwell in the darkest depths." I had to be careful not to lay it on too thick. I wanted to save my friend from trouble and get through this without making things any worse for either of us.

"Does this daemon cause similar problems for all of your colleagues?"

"What? No, he doesn't tease anyone else from my team. He doesn't know any of them and, to be honest, I don't believe he'd find them interesting. They're a pretty dull lot." Whatever happened, I had to make certain I kept Caroline and the others out of this mess.

"Well, I have to say your story is consistent with the version we had from the daemon."

"Oh, you've already interviewed him, have you?"

"He says he doesn't like you; you're an ugly, ignorant, idiot."

"I see. Well, it's not a surprise. I don't think he likes anyone." I was no longer afraid. If this had anything to do with Caffiaes' escapades, it would be clear by now. No, this felt like speculation: curiosity even. All that remained for me to do was convince this man Caffiaes was the last being I would ever want to talk to, and the perverse logic of this place might even dictate I would see more of him.

It could be so much easier for the two of us to get on with our plans: a permanent holiday home for him, an escape for me. So long as he could control his urges and keep the number of souls he tortured within reason, we might well get away with it for close to eternity.

"I think this interview is at an end, Ross. I will admit I am somewhat impressed with this daemon. For one of so junior a rank, he has shown a high degree of initiative in selecting a Hell hound as his own personal torture victim. It will look good on his appraisal. And, while I will see he is warned off going too far, I have no intention of protecting you. However, if he carries on like this, he may well win himself a promotion. And if he does, you'd never see him again.

"Now, off you go. I have a report to write up." He bent his head to the papers now on the table in front of him and began scribbling. There was no doubt I had been dismissed.

"Thank you. I hope they do promote him."

No, I didn't. Because if they did, my best chance of getting away might disappear into the furnace with him. I would be faced with an eternity without even the slender hope of escape. And that hope was all I had.

CHAPTER 23

I had just returned from another unpleasant mission. The couple of wraiths concerned had quickly realised what I was, and clung together, begging me to leave them alone. I would have done so if I could. But, alas, I was only the messenger. Their fate was out of my hands.

Caroline met me at the common room door. "You'd better tidy yourself up, Ross. You've got visitors."

Over her shoulder I caught a glimpse of Louise and Greg. I was sure they were listening in as hard as they could, while at the same time trying their best to pretend they weren't interested in such a unique event.

"Visitors? No one ever comes to see one of us." Unless... "Oh, no! Am I in trouble again?"

She shrugged. "I've no idea, but I wouldn't keep them waiting if I were you."

Was this it? Had Josh taken his suspicions higher? "Where are they?"

"Over in Interview One."

Not my favourite room. I was getting a bad, bad feeling.

Setting off along the featureless, grey corridor that never changed, I passed the doors on either side, the ones without handles that led into the rooms without windows. As I arrived at Interview One, as usual its door swung open for me in silence. Whoever waited inside was not going to give me enough time to collect my thoughts. Ah well, there was nothing to be gained by hanging around outside.

"Oh!" Whatever I might have expected it would never have been this.

Two angels were sitting on tall stools on the far side of the wide, mahogany desk.

"Please join us, Mr. Ferris." The female angel was familiar. I had met her before. Once again, her perfect smile dazzled me. "Yes, do come in. You have nothing to fear from us."

There were a couple of unusual additions to the room's furniture. On my side of the table, where there had never been one before, was a seat. And it wasn't even an office chair; it was a well stuffed, comfy armchair upholstered in a fluffy, yellow polka dot fabric (far too colourful for Hell). Beside it stood a tiny, occasional table with matching coasters. And was that... could it possibly be a glass of cognac?

"Is that for me?"

"Indeed it is. I understand it's one of the things you have missed the most. Am I right?"

I didn't bother answering. Instead, I made myself comfortable and took a tentative sip at the liquid. Like everyone else, I always hesitated at such times until I could work out whether Hell was going to permit me to enjoy a drink or not. This was one of the good days. I closed my eyes: not only to savour the incredible flavour of the liquor but also because I feared I might only be dreaming. Either that or this was some sort of elaborate trick.

But when I opened them again nothing had changed. Except the glass had topped itself up.

"What's this all about? Have you realised you've made a mistake, discovered I shouldn't be in this place after all? Are you here to rescue me from Hell?"

"Don't be ridiculous. We don't make..." The male angel broke off mid-sentence. He shuffled his shoulders, which made his wing feathers rustle.

"Leave this to me, Fred. Mr. Ferris and I have already made each other's acquaintance."

Fred? The angel's name was Fred? Surely not. It had to be a nickname or something. But if he was Fred, what was she called? How about Doris?

"Call me Ross. If I'm not in any trouble, we ought to be civilised with each other, oughtn't we?"

"We're never anything other than civilised." She sighed. "That's the reason we've got this little, er, problem."

"Is Mr. Barnes not settling in as well as you hoped?"

They both stared at me.

Fred slapped his hand down on the table. "Who told you about that?"

"'It's a bit obvious, isn't it? Why, out of all the operatives of Hell, would you have singled me out for a chat if it wasn't for the one thing your colleague and I have in common?"

"How very astute of you to work it out, Ross. You're right, of course." She smiled at me again. If you could have bottled the intense light reflecting off her teeth, you could have sold it for moonshine... or even something stronger. "Mr. Barnes has indeed not, as you say, 'settled in'."

"He's on strike." Fred's interruption switched her smile off, which was a pity.

"Well well, imagine that. What's his grievance? I didn't think you had any money in Heaven. I know for sure we don't here. So, I don't suppose it can be over pay. Is it the eternally long hours?"

"Please don't be flippant, Mr. Ferris. This is a serious situation. We haven't had anyone go on strike in Heaven for millennia."

I was surprised he was admitting there had ever been any unrest in Paradise. Here in Hell, we tended to believe the other place was all calm harmony, soft music and delicious dinners.

She regarded me as I sipped a little more of the brandy. "We require your assistance. Mr. Barnes has been nothing but trouble since he arrived. He wants..." She took a deep breath. "He wants equality."

"What's that supposed to mean?"

"He wishes to share in some of the benefits the deserving residents of Heaven have earned by their good deeds and exemplary conduct while alive, but which, despite his presence among us, he himself does not merit."

"I see. But if he's making things so difficult for you, why don't you just boot him out again. You know by rights he belongs here. We're perfectly willing to deal with him."

"We can't do that. She made a mess of it, didn't she?" Fred jerked his head at his companion who, since she hadn't volunteered her name, I decided I would continue to think of as Doris.

"I did not. It wasn't my fault."

So, angels were not above blaming each other. How interesting! Where was the forgiving nature Heaven was always boasting about? These two were not impressing me: their behaviour was no different from any Hell hound trying to stay out of trouble by covering up an error.

"What did you do wrong?"

"Nothing. Angels can't do anything wrong." She pouted. "It was just a small oversight."

Fred spluttered. "An oversight? You forgot to tell him he was in Heaven to work and when the job was finished, he'd have to leave. And you call that a 'small oversight'?"

"I was under pressure. Mr. Shakespeare was shouting at me. He was in a hurry to start rehearsals."

"You should still have made sure he understood. Now, thanks to you, Mr. Barnes believes he is entitled to stay in Heaven forever."

Stifling a smile, I set down my glass. "I don't see the problem. All you have to do is explain it's time to go and shove him through the Gates."

"What!" I thought Doris was about to faint. She fanned herself with her hand as though the heat of Hell was getting to her. "That would be like going back on our word. No angel could ever do such a thing."

"Well now, isn't that a shame. It sounds like you're stuck with the chap. But I don't see why this would have anything to do with me. I didn't want you to take him in the first place."

"Never mind that. You can help us now, Ross. And help yourself at the same time. Your bosses are annoyed you failed to complete your mission to collect Barnes upon his death. And the matter is pending. What we're offering you is the chance to put right your omission."

Oh? Did they think I was born yesterday? (Instead of over two hundred years ago!) "I'll thank you for the brandy but this is not my problem. You should stop worrying about how you got into this fix and find a way to deal with the matter yourselves."

Doris leant towards me. "But we can't. We're too good. Angels are above lying and deception. We would never stoop to playing tricks on people. No, it requires someone like you: someone both dishonest and unreliable."

"I'm not unreliable! And, frankly, I do have some sympathy for Mr. Barnes. You took him to Paradise but you won't let him enjoy it. He can watch the fun but he's expected to work all day instead of being allowed to play like everyone else."

"What else could we do?" Now it was she who shuffled her feathers. "I told you the last time we met: Mr. Shakespeare had written a special role for Barnes in his most recent tragedy. Also, quite a lot of our residents like to watch the man perform. Besides, he does a stunning Hamlet."

Was that a hint of a blush on her alabaster cheek?

"So, you want me to do your dirty work?"

"What else is Hell for?"

I doubted my bosses saw their role in that particular light. "I think there's something you're not telling me. Why can't you isolate Barnes, pop him into a secluded bit of your Eternal Garden and just forget all about him?"

"He's stirring others up. And the unrest is spreading. Some of our residents are so nice, they think he has a point and want to support him. Now, will you help us or not?"

"What's in it for me?"

They looked at each other. As I awaited their response I took another sip of the brandy.

"You would be permitted to spend a little time in Heaven. What else could anyone in your position ask for?"

"I want more than that." Placing the glass on the side table, I folded my arms. "If I do this, I want to see and talk to Tessa Noyles."

Doris shook her head. "Out of the question, I'm afraid. She's happy and settled. She has forgotten all about you."

"I haven't forgotten her."

Fred rubbed his chin. "That's part of your punishment here in Hell. But we could sort it out for you: take away all your memories of her. It would give you just a little less to regret."

My mind flooded with images of Tessa: how she had looked on that last day, the concern in her eyes at my injuries, the sweet words we had exchanged. Who knows? I might even have married her if things had not turned out the way they had; if I hadn't died that night in the tavern and so been unable to defend her from Robertshaw.

"No, I don't want you to take those memories away. I want to hear that she no longer cares for me. And hear it from her own lips."

"You want to upset her?"

"No, I just want to talk to her."

They were not fooling me. Given my conversation with Doris when she took Barnes away, what other request could they have expected?

"Very well, though it won't do you any good. Why would she want to leave Heaven and come here? It might even make things worse for you. But we'll allow you to meet with her just the once." Fred was attempting to make it sound as if they were doing me a huge favour, when we all knew they couldn't sort Barnes out without me. He stood. "Shall we go now?"

The Pearly Gates were exactly that: two gold and pearl barriers so tall I couldn't see the tops and so wide they could have accommodated an entire army marching through them. Impressive, yes, but the immense scale made them more daunting than beautiful. To one side of them was a smaller structure. At the front of this a normal sized wooden door stood half open.

We entered a room set with low couches and small tables. A long counter ran across the middle and behind it were two more angels. One of them gave me a smile I could have basked in for a lifetime.

"Welcome to Heaven, Mr. Ferris. As you are no doubt expecting, before we proceed, I am obliged to make you aware of the terms and conditions of your visit here." A long piece of paper fluttered down from her hand, unfurling itself like a banner, but the widest one I had ever seen. "Your stay shall be limited to the equivalent of three days on the temporal plane and shall be for the express purpose of collecting one Kenneth Barnes and removing him from our environs. You are permitted to converse only with those residents and staff necessary for the execution of your duties."

I opened my mouth to protest but she hadn't finished.

"There is to be one other meeting permitted, limited to not more than one hour, and shall be with a Miss Tessa Noyles. Have you any questions?"

"Can I enjoy food and drink while I'm here?"

"Of course you can. You can do whatever you wish, though I must point out alcohol has no effect on visitors to this place. You have to be a resident." From the disapproval in her tone, you would have thought I was some sort of drunkard. She waved the paper at me. "Sign here, please."

On the table appeared a long, white plume and beside it a pot of liquid gold.

This being Heaven and she being an angel, I trusted her so I signed.

Well, so this was Heaven, was it? Not at all what I had expected. But then Doris took pains to explain to me what I was seeing: in effect the servants' view. Barnes was a long way from being the only unworthy resident of Paradise. To keep things running smoothly and to make sure the millions of good souls resident there had everything they desired, required a substantial workforce. Even so, the working conditions couldn't fail to be a thousand times more pleasant than anything Hell had to offer. I would have liked to have spent some of my allotted time looking around, finding out more, but Doris was anxious to take me to Barnes right away.

"Don't be in such a hurry. I need to observe him for a while, come up with a strategy. And it won't be possible to fool him at all if he sees you with me."

"So, what do you propose?"

"I think I'll pose as someone in the same position as him and try to win his confidence."

"Oh, but that's so sneaky."

I wanted to laugh at her horrified expression. "Madam, I understood that was why you brought me here: to be sneaky. Now shall we get on with it?"

We arrived at the theatre. It was infinitely bigger than the original on which it must have been based. It was circular and constructed of what looked like wood, but I couldn't even conceive of a tree with a trunk thick enough to have yielded such planks.

Doris left me at the main doors, but I knew she wouldn't be far away. Besides, I was sure there had to be other angels around keeping a close eye on the proceedings. It felt as if I were being accused of wanting to steal the curtains.

Inside was an uncountable number of tiers of stone seats, each with an elaborate embroidered cushion. I sat on one of them and right away the stage seemed to be much closer. It was as though I were now in the front row. I guessed the view from every angle would be the same. Only a perfect line of sight could be allowed in this place.

The stage was empty except for a solitary man sitting cross legged in the centre.

I had found Mr. Barnes. But would he want to talk to me?

It was then I discovered one of the little tricks that made Heaven function with such efficiency. I had no sooner risen to my feet with the intention of seeking a way onto the stage, than I was there standing next to Barnes.

He looked up at me. "Nothing doing, mate. I've told them I'm not acting today or any other day until they give me what I want."

I joined him on the floor, crossing my legs like a mirror image. "I don't think you should perform. I've heard about the stand you're taking and I'm with you all the way, brother."

"Got the same problem as me, have you?"

"I think a lot of people round here have. There should be equal rights for everyone. Heaven for all and not just the Heavenly!" I shook my right fist in the air.

"Think you're clever, do you?" I got the feeling he wasn't impressed with my brand new campaign slogan.

"I know I deserve better than I've been given." Well, I never said to the angels I would tell lies all the time.

"So, who are they keeping you away from?"

I blinked at him. Was it so obvious?

He heaved an overdramatic sigh and wrinkled his brow. "She is my lawful wedded wife, you know. A man should not be prevented from seeing his own wife."

"Who? Tessa?" What was the man talking about?

"I don't know any Tessa. It's Marjorie I want to see: my wife. I know she's here. I spotted her in the crowd at my first matinee performance. But those interfering angels keep denying me access to her. They say she's got everything she wants and that doesn't include me!"

"All this trouble is about your wife?"

"What else? I told them I'll be staying out on strike until I see her. I don't care if she did think I was a horrible husband. She's still my wife after all. It's my right. She never did know what was good for her. And now I want her back."

"So, you haven't been trying to pursue some sort of rebellion?"

"No. Why would I want to do that? This place is wonderful and the Bard's latest play script, The Life and Death of Elizabeth the Second, is an absolute masterpiece. But I will never be happy until I have Marjorie once again by my side."

Inwardly I cursed the angels and their deliberate misdirection. "I think the point of all this is you're not meant to be happy. In fact, you're not meant to be here at all."

He stared at me. "Where else would I be?"

"Haven't they told you about your death in the dressing room at the Adelphi Theatre and which way the scales tipped?"

"What are you burbling on about?"

"You, Mr. Barnes, were destined to go to Hell. I was supposed to collect you, but they brought you to Heaven because Mr. Shakespeare insisted on having you here. If you don't want to work for him, I suggest you leave now and come with me."

He scuttled across the floor, away from me. "Leave here?"

"You don't fit in. Stay and you will only ever see Marjorie in the distance enjoying herself. They'll never allow you to get any closer. And they won't stop trying to get rid of you. I suspect they'll find ways to make you more and more miserable every day."

"You think I'd enjoy Hell more than here?"

No, no. Emphatically no. But I wasn't going to tell him that. There was too much to lose. Besides, he might be behaving like a spoilt child, but there was something nasty in the tone of voice when he spoke about his ex-wife. I remembered, from my research prior to the aborted mission, she had been the first of several, and all his divorces had been acrimonious. There had been many accusations of cruelty, both physical and mental, with even the suggestion of murder in one case. "At least they would understand you better in Hell. And, you never know, some of your other exes might well be in residence. You say you've only seen Marjorie here, but you were married... how many times?"

"Five. Lots of affairs but I only wed five of them."

"There you are. Marjorie might be the only one here."

His brow furrowed and he stroked his chin. One more push and...

"You could always give Hell a try, see what you think. I'm sure Mr. Shakespeare would grant you leave of absence for a day or two."

"Oh? I didn't know you could travel between here and there."

"Oh yes, you can. I've only come here today myself for a quick look round, though I have to say, so far, I'm a bit disappointed. It's all rather boring so I reckon I'll be heading back in a few hours." If you want to be convincing, it always pays to add a few morsels of truth into the mix.

"Just a visit?"

"Why not? In fact, why don't we sneak out right now, making sure no one sees us, of course. Then later, if you want to, we'll sneak back in again and no one will be any the wiser." What a load of rubbish! But he was lapping it up, not even

Page 115

considering how unlikely it would be for Heaven and Hell to permit free travel between them. I suppose he must have been getting used to everyone around him always telling the truth.

I hoped I was right about the angels and they hadn't let me out of their sight. Or, more importantly, their hearing.

He rose to his feet. "I'll go with you but just for a quick look. I have to be back for rehearsals later on."

"I thought you were meant to be on strike."

"I am, but how will I get my point across if I don't keep making a nuisance of myself?"

We left the theatre by the stage door.

The street outside was empty. I so hoped the angels were not going to overdo this. The lack of passers-by would have made me suspicious but, to my relief, Barnes was unfazed.

I wasn't sure which direction to take. Where could the Pearly Gates be?

We turned a corner and there they were: magnificent and daunting. The door to the side building was open and I peered round it. There were lots of people inside: so many, I couldn't see the desk for the crowd.

No one paid the slightest attention to us as we wove our way to the opposite door, the one leading out of Heaven.

As we crossed the threshold it slammed shut behind us.

At the noise, Barnes turned to look and took a single step back the way we had come.

Fred appeared between him and the entrance. "Thank you, Mr. Ferris. You have done well. And in only a few hours too."

"It wasn't difficult."

I saw the truth dawn in Barnes' eyes. "I'm not leaving. Just having a quick look at Hell, see if any of my exes are there. Tell Will I'll be back before too long and ready to get on with the play."

"Ha!" Fred laughed. I have to admit it was a glorious sound: all bells and music, but there was an edge to it. "You have left Heaven of your own volition, Mr. Barnes. We have no further use for you. This lady here..." He pointed over my shoulder. "She will conduct you to your true home. Mr. Ferris has a reward to collect."

"A reward for betraying me? How fitting!" All of a sudden Barnes was different. He was standing straighter, his face twisted into a sneer. He wagged a long finger at me. "Ah, how ignoble art thou, Brutus. I should have known. But never fear. We will meet again, and I shall not forget thy iniquitous and cowardly treachery."

"Enough of that." Fred stepped between us. "Mr. Ferris was only doing his job. If you had only done yours, no one would be sending you anywhere. Now, get a move on. Your escort doesn't want to wait around here all day, do you, miss?"

"Oh, I don't mind one little bit. But we are expected. Do come along, Mr. Barnes. See you later, Ross." And Caroline was gone again along with her charge.

CHAPTER 24

Fred waved his hand at the small door and ushered me inside. "There is still time to reconsider. You have done Heaven a great service and there are many other things we can do by way of reward." He held out a bottle of brandy. "Have a look round, think where you wish to be: a garden, a beach, anywhere at all. You can remain there for the rest of today and all of tomorrow, help yourself to unlimited drinks and the finest food."

He clicked his fingers and we were standing in a stable yard. I was dressed in the fashion of my own time: a long, dark cloak brushed the tops of burnished leather boots. And I had a pistol strapped to each thigh.

A horse was watching me over the half door. "Midnight!" I couldn't help it. I had to walk over. My own horse, my own favourite, pushed at me with his velvet nose.

"This is all yours, Ross, for the next thirty-six hours. Ride over the moors. Go wherever you wish."

"Tell me the way to Tessa's inn."

Fred's brilliant smile faded away. He shook his head. "Believe me, my solution would suit you so much better."

I took a step away from Midnight. "We made an agreement. Unless you intend to break your word, you will take me to Tessa now."

"Very well, but you can't say I didn't warn you."

The stable faded, the pistols were gone but the clothes remained the same.

"You have one hour. When that has elapsed, you will find yourself back where you belong." He vanished.

I was standing in the garden of a small manor house. Tall flowers swayed in a gentle breeze. The humming of bees and the scent of herbs, rosemary, marjoram and mint, enveloped me. Vines heavy with bunches of ripe purple grapes spread their wide, green leaves up and across a wall constructed of cool, white marble. Beyond them a summerhouse stood to one side of an ornamental pool filled with bright scarlet water lilies nestled among huge, dark green pads. The long fin of a golden fish broke the surface; damsel flies, glowing blue and purple, flitted among rushes and a clear stream flowed away from me beneath a small, wooden bridge. Ahead lay an arbour, shaded by willow trees. The scene was all too perfect to be real. I was ungainly and out of place.

Following the paved path to the centre of it all, I came across a bench and on it sat Tessa.

So beautiful, her long, blonde tresses falling around her face; a pale green dress sprinkled with a thousand summer daisies clung to her slender figure and a fine lace shawl was draped around her shoulders. Was she reading? How very strange. When we had been together, she had known nothing of books, had never learnt her letters.

"Tessa?"

She looked up. "Hello. Who are you? Are you here to see Jerome?"

"Tessa, it's me. Ross."

"I'm sorry. Have we been introduced?" She frowned as she placed the book down onto the seat beside her. "Did we meet at a party or was it the theatre? I do apologise. As a rule, I'm good with names."

"It's all right." No, it wasn't. I ached to take her into my arms, to kiss her.

But she looked at me and talked to me as though I were a complete stranger.

"Do you live here, Tessa?"

"Yes, this is my home. Isn't it lovely? Jerome says he couldn't imagine a nicer house." There was a warmth in her voice and a slight flush to her cheeks. Whoever Jerome was, there could be little doubt he had taken my place in her heart.

But my hour was not yet over. I had to try again. "Don't you miss the sea?"

"Why would I?" Her brow wrinkled, then she laughed. "You're new here, aren't you? You've only just moved into the area. Come on. I'll take you to the shore." She rose to her feet.

I followed her along the same path which had brought me to the arbour but now the garden was gone and we were standing on pebbles. High rocks rose up on either side of us. A taste of salt carried on the breeze and I could hear the whisper of waves.

We emerged onto an endless beach of golden sand. Seashells in impossible bright colours winked up at me. A circle of small, smooth boulders held a rock pool with tiny, scuttling crabs and delicate anemones. Overhead, gulls turned silver wings to the brilliant but not too hot sun in the cloudless sky. A kittiwake called and, in the distance on the calm, deep blue, a yacht rode at anchor.

Tessa shaded her eyes but could not hide her delight. She bounced a little on her heels. "Jerome is coming. Look! There's the boat he's named after me. He'll be here soon and you can meet him."

A bright green rowing boat appeared between us and the yacht. I did not want to meet Jerome. I had no doubt Heaven was a faultless matchmaker. This man would be perfect for Tessa in every way; her ideal lover. I could never hope to compete with any of this. What had I to offer her? Nothing... except unhappy memories.

This Tessa was not mine. The angel had told the truth. I would gain nothing by remaining.

Apologising for having disturbed her and blinking back tears, I fled away through the gap in the rocks. It was no surprise to emerge in the garden.

Fred was waiting for me beyond the manor house wall, holding Midnight's bridle. "I did try to make you understand. I did say she wouldn't remember. Memories of her past make her sad, you see, and no one is permitted to be sad in Heaven."

I was sure it was something like the same speech Doris had once made me. "Does Jerome make her happy?"

"Oh yes. More than you could ever know. They're quite the couple: perfectly suited to one another. She has everything she wants. For her, this is true Heaven." He smiled and tilted his head. "You are unusual for a Hell hound, aren't you? To care so much for someone is not a virtue in that place. But it is one here. It has therefore been decided you may remain for a further day. Enjoy yourself!"

He was gone and so was the manor house. I was alone, mounted on Midnight's back. Ahead of me a lonely road crossed a bleak moor. I knew there was an inn somewhere beyond the horizon, where there would be food and drink, good company and a feather bed. Before that there would be a wild ride with the wind streaming through my hair.

But there would never again be Tessa.

CHAPTER 25

"Ross? Ross, can you hear me? Wake up!"

The couch in the corner of the common room was nowhere near as comfortable as the feather bed in which I had been lying when my eyes closed. Not wanting to miss a moment of my limited time in Heaven, I fought to stay awake as long as I could, but in the end had to give in. Yet, it had been a pleasure to feel the need to sleep. There is no slumber in Hell.

I sat up, swung my legs round and faced Caroline. It was no surprise she was not alone. Louise and Greg were observing me from the other side of the room. In their places I would have been there too: dry tinder waiting to be set alight by my words. Curiosity crackled in the air like sparks from a blacksmith's anvil.

"Come on, then. What's it like?"

"Heaven? It's..." I wanted to tell them about it. Really I did. "It's..." But the words just wouldn't come. I had arranged them, made them ready to paint a picture for my colleagues of all the things I had seen, heard and experienced: of the heath and the wild ride, of the tavern, so welcoming, of the taste of the roast beef and the mellowness of the brandy; and before that, the town with its curious mixture of buildings, the theatre, the gardens.

Everything, of course, except Tessa. I would not include her. My time with her had left me with nothing but new scars to add to the old ones. But it made no difference what I wanted to say. I couldn't utter a single word about any of it. The smallest of syllables refused to pass my lips. All I could manage to verbalise was the one phrase: "It was Heavenly!"

Caroline tapped her foot. "We know that, but what was it really like? Was it as wonderful as you hoped it would be?"

"He can't tell you. They never can." Josh had entered the room. "Somehow Heaven stops anyone who visits them from reporting back; ties their tongues, so to speak."

"Are you sure about that? I thought it was only a rumour."

"But you can see it isn't, can't you, Caroline? Besides, I happen to know it's true. That's one of the things you learn about when you're promoted to supervisor."

Not only could I have told him he was right, I could also tell him why. Heaven has its own secrets and some of what I saw there disturbed me. Tessa was happy, even beyond happy, but at what cost? Both Fred and Doris had told me the same thing. No one was allowed to be unhappy so no memories which got in the way of total joy could be retained. Fred's notion of rewarding me was to offer me a little of the same: to remove all traces of Tessa from my mind. But my memories, whether good or bad, and my experiences, even the worst of them, were all that I was: all I possessed. I would never be willing to give up a single one.

Overnight my intentions had shifted. I no longer harboured any dreams of finding a way into Paradise. Yes, I wanted to escape from Hell more than anything, but even if it were on offer, Heaven had now proved it was not an acceptable alternative destination. It might be a fine place for others, but it wouldn't be right for me.

Something else changed too. It was true I missed Tessa, but after our meeting the pain had become more a dull, rasping ache than the searing agony left by the slash of blade into flesh. I was even starting to question whether I ever had loved her as much as I'd thought. If she had fallen so completely for this man, Jerome, did she ever care for me at all? If our love had been true, surely the memory of it would have been too strong for even angels to erase. Perhaps it was as well I would never see her again.

But at least my mission to Heaven had been a success. I wondered how Barnes was settling in to his new accommodation.

"Did our friend have a smooth journey to the Final Door, Caroline?"

She frowned. "No. We never got there. One of the high ups from the training team intercepted me. It appears Mr. Barnes was not only the greatest actor of his generation but an expert on manners and etiquette across several centuries. They're going to give him a post as a supervisor. He's been engaged to lead courses on blending in. He'll be teaching us, Ross."

"Blending in? Is that what he was doing in Heaven? Oh well, no one can say there's no irony in Hell!" I was trying to be flippant but the idea of Barnes having any say in my training worried me. How much of his performance in front of the Pearly Gates had been an act and how much had he meant? Plus, I didn't need another supervisor on my back. Josh was annoying enough as it was.

And Josh had not come to the common room merely to check whether I had returned safe and sound. He was never one to waste sympathy. He came with instructions. Caroline and I were to prepare ourselves for our next mission.

Only moments later we were walking along the endless corridor into the grey, swirling mist.

We emerged into a scene of chaos. Hundreds of living people were crushed up against a long, low fence. Every one of them was angry and making a great deal of noise. Fists were being shaken, pieces of paper were scrunched into balls or ripped to shreds and trampled underfoot. We held back, waiting until the shouting was over and the crowd showed signs of calming. Then Caroline and I made our way through the fence and onto the churned up mud of a racetrack.

To our right, twelve horses snorted and tossed their heads as they formed an improvised herd. Four of them had shed their jockeys. One had reared and caught another as his legs came down. It was a miracle none of the animals or riders had suffered serious injury. But the fear was contagious, even if to the riders it could not be explained. Eleven men were doing their best to soothe eleven mounts, trying to urge them to put one hoof in front of the other. And all without success. There was no way these animals were going to proceed any further.

The twelfth rider sat stock still, his mouth gaping wide as he peered at something which all the horses, but only a tiny number of the people present, could see. Caroline and I, of course, counted among that tiny number.

Just beyond the winning post a dead man and a dead horse were celebrating their second win of the day.

"I'm sorry we have to interrupt them. Did you ever see a ghost so happy?"

Caroline was right. This was a unique sight. "We could give him a few more minutes, I guess."

But we couldn't. Josh had sent us out on short notice with strict orders to "sort things before they get out of hand". This was a serious situation. Perhaps one of the most serious so far in my long career as a Hell hound. As a rule, an active ghost is nothing more than a minor irritation, but this one was the cause of major disruption, creating havoc which could not be ignored.

Mickey Trent and his mount had both died almost six months earlier during a race at the meeting before last. It had been a big scandal at the time. The horse, injected with far too much dope, had collapsed mid stride and rolled over on top of the jockey. Most of the rider's bones had been crushed. The pain alone should have sent him the message he was never going to survive.

But here he was and here also was Summer Lightning.

Animal ghosts are rare and, I have to say, have never been anything to do with us. I had always assumed, since they don't understand the difference between good and evil, the other side took them all. Though I suppose Caffiaes and his fellow daemons might find a use for the odd mosquito and such like.

Mickey Trent wasn't the only human ghost connected with this racecourse. Gamblers are notorious in being difficult to convince when their time is up since so many are used to deceiving themselves. We knew there were two of them lurking somewhere around. We were also aware of a trainer who had shot himself, at least one other jockey and a young stable hand. Josh had given us no instructions regarding any of those, only the disruptive Mr. Trent and his stubborn horse.

By the time we arrived, our ghost was in the winners' enclosure, patting Summer Lightning and whispering something into his ear about carrots.

"Hello there."

Both rider and mount turned their heads to look at Caroline. "Hello yourself, miss. Come to congratulate us? You shouldn't be in here, you know."

"Neither should you, Mr. Trent." I took a step towards the pair.

Summer Lightning snorted at me. It was no surprise to discover his breath was as cold as an arctic blast.

"You do know you're dead, don't you?" Sometimes it's best to be direct if you're in a hurry.

The jockey's eyes narrowed. "Boss threatening to kill me now, is he? Given up on persuasion and bribery? Well, I won't throw this race. My career is more important than his profits. Tell him I don't care if his stables do go under."

"We weren't sent by your boss. You're overdue for a most important appointment." Caroline extended her hand to stroke the horse's nose but with another snort Summer Lightning jerked his head up and out of her way.

"You're right there. We're racing in an hour. Come on, boy."

He didn't even grasp the halter; just started walking away and the horse followed on behind.

Both then vanished.

CHAPTER 26

I'm sure my expression was as startled as Caroline's. "How did he do that? And where has he gone?" She turned in a slow circle, as though checking he was not hiding behind us.

He had not gone to Hell. That much was certain: we had not yet convinced him he was dead. "I don't know. I think we may be out of our depth here."

"Unless this is the extreme edge of the area he haunts."

I hadn't thought of that but it made sense. Under normal circumstances we arrive before a ghost can become established. It doesn't have time to discover there are limits on its movements.

"I suppose he'll be in the stables now, getting ready for the three thirty. We'll have to find a way to get through to him before he has the chance to cause any more chaos."

Easy for her to say, I thought, as I tramped in her wake towards the distant stable block.

A small, restless crowd stood outside. It was clear the living horses were unwilling to share the same space as Summer Lightning, and their jockeys and owners were unable to persuade them.

As we approached, I heard people muttering about the probability of having to abandon the rest of the meeting. That would not be good news for us. We had to come up with a plan without delay.

To save time, we slipped into the building through the wall hoping no one would spot us. We didn't wish to give anyone even more confirmation the place was haunted.

On seeing us, Summer Lightning snorted again and pawed the ground with his front hoof. It was as though he were drawing a line and challenging us to cross it. I had the oddest feeling our real problem was not a clueless jockey who believed he was still alive but an over-intelligent horse that had realised it was dead but had no intention of acknowledging the fact.

"Mr. Trent, you have to listen to us." Caroline took a step over the imaginary line.

Summer Lightning bared his large, yellow teeth and bit her.

She leapt back, treading on my toes and coming close to knocking me over. We might not be able to feel pain but that doesn't mean we can't be startled.

The horse was now tossing his head and whinnying. But it sounded to me a lot like laughter.

Mickey Trent joined in. "Ha! You shouldn't get so close to my horse. He's highly strung, you know."

"So I see. I understand why you don't want to leave him, but you can't stay here and neither can he."

"You want me to just give up, do you? Like I told you before, this is my race and, after I've won, it won't make a blind bit of difference what the boss thinks. The other stables will be queueing up to give me rides. Now, buzz off. I'm busy." Mickey Trent could be rather threatening when he waved his whip at someone.

Caroline took another step back. "Aren't two wins in one day enough, then?"

"Didn't you hear me? This is my race: mine and Summer Lightning's. We did Goodwood and it was more like good practice. You'll see, I won't waste my last chance."

He leapt up into the saddle and, without a backward glance, Summer Lightning strode out of the stable.

Caroline bit her lip. "He's not listening. We're just not getting through to him. Have you any ideas at all?"

I got no chance to reply as a terrible din started up outside. There was a great deal of shouting but most of it was frenzied neighing. Summer Lightning was making his way to the starting post.

We pushed through the maelstrom of churning mounts as their jockeys struggled to calm them. A couple of bewildered stewards stood together, watching what was going on but powerless to intervene.

Seconds later the loudspeakers made an announcement. Due to unforeseen circumstances the meeting was to be abandoned for the day.

"Oops, that's not good for us," Caroline whispered into my ear.

That was some understatement if ever there was one. All kinds of betting are looked upon in a favourable light where we come from. On that afternoon someone, maybe more than one person, might well have begun their personal journey towards corruption. Gambling might lead on to a bit of pickpocketing, maybe then they'd get involved in a little animal doping. Ever worsening acts would ensue. But now those people wouldn't have the opportunity to place that first foot on the slippery slope. Hell was not going to be pleased with us at all.

We went over to the now deserted rail and seconds later Summer Lightning thundered past us on his way to the winning post.

Once again rider and mount vanished soon after. Instinct and experience told me they had returned to the stables.

As I trudged towards the building, Caroline called me back.

"He's not going to stop until he's beaten."

"I know but since no horse will race him that could take quite a while."

"No living horse you mean but perhaps another dead one...?"

"Where are we going to find another ghost horse and rider?"

"I'll go back to the office and explain the problem. The way I see it, we only want to borrow a fast mount, not necessarily a jockey as well. Either you or I could ride it."

"I'm not a jockey, Caroline."

"Neither am I, but I used to ride to hunt and you, being a former highwayman, ought to be used to galloping away from pursuit."

Well yes, I had been but I wasn't sure it was the same thing. A thoroughbred racehorse would be twice as fast as anything I had ever ridden; even Midnight would have been left far behind. To be fair, though, the likes of Summer Lightning wouldn't have the stamina of even the slowest workhorse from my time. Oh, but the idea appealed. To be once more on horseback like I had been in Heaven and to ride fast, the wind whistling round me and...

No, we were working for the wrong side. Our masters were not about to let us feel that much pleasure.

"Keep an eye on Mr. Trent. I'll be back as soon as I can." She walked away from me and was gone.

About a day later I was still there, which meant her request must have been heard and considered. Hell would never let any of us stay on an assignment unless it was still being pursued.

Inside the stable block, Summer Lightning stood alone in a stall. There was no sign of Mickey Trent. He could have been anywhere within the radius of the course, wandering about, still not understanding what had happened to him. I wondered what he had done to make him one of ours.

Eventually Caroline reappeared. I have to admit I've not often seen an expression as smug as the one she was wearing. "I've been lent one of the best ever: almost never beaten. He won the Epsom Derby by several furlongs. Summer Lightning has no chance against him."

The air rippled and a glorious bay stallion with a long white blaze stood on the straw beside us. "He's called Shergar."

He was stunning and I didn't doubt he would leave Summer Lightning standing. Assuming his rider could stay in the saddle.

Caroline put out her hand to stroke the long, velvet nose and Shergar stuck out his tongue. He then gave a whinny. Once again a horse was laughing at us.

"I'm not sure he's going to let you on his back." Was I pleased at the thought? Oh, yes. I couldn't wait to take her place.

Only, I discovered it wasn't just Caroline who was to suffer the stallion's disdain.

Shergar took a long pace forward as I stepped alongside him. He turned his head and gave out another whinny. He didn't need to be able to speak. It was obvious he had no intention of being ridden by either of us.

"Most racehorses don't like amateurs on their backs." The voice came from behind me. A young man was watching us from the doorway; another of the course's ghosts. Judging by his clothes he had died some time during the nineteen fifties. "He's a bit special, isn't he? You the owners?"

"We work for them and, as luck would have it, our jockey has let us down." Caroline gave him that beaming smile of hers, the one that never fails.

But he had eyes only for the horse. "Shame. I bet he'd walk it."

"Could you ride him for us?"

"Are you joking? I'm not an experienced jockey. I only take the horses out on the gallops to get them warmed up. One day, maybe someone will take a chance on me, a maiden race perhaps with a mediocre mount."

"Why not today and this horse?" Caroline stepped forward. "You'd be doing us a favour. Shergar will be unhappy if he doesn't get a gallop."

"Shergar? Is that his name?"

The horse gave a much more enthusiastic whinny and took a pace towards the young jockey.

He reached up and the velvet nose came down to meet him.

There was such temptation in his eyes. "I've no silks."

The impossible of course happened and a full set of deep green and red silks appeared in front of us, draped over the wall of a nearby stall. Below stood a pair of riding boots, their shine like that of an ink black mirror.

Excuses forgotten, our jockey made off with them, heading for the dressing rooms.

Mickey Trent and Summer Lightning reappeared at half past two. They took no notice of us or Shergar. Trent checked his horse's harness and ran his hands down each leg in turn. It was as though we were not present. This, then, was his haunting; nothing else existed: doomed to repeat over and over the actions leading to his death. He had a black leather holdall and from it he drew a syringe.

Caroline grabbed my arm. "He's the one who did it. He doped his own mount."

"Yes, and from the way he had no problem with the injection, I'd say it's not the first he's given. No wonder he's one of ours."

Any sympathy I might have felt for Mr. Trent evaporated. His death was his own fault. Shame about the horse, though.

We heard the Tannoy calling the next race: our race.

Mickey Trent mounted and he and Summer Lightning walked past us.

The horse nipped at Caroline, even though his jockey still appeared oblivious to our presence. But there was no doubt Summer Lightning could see us. And he did not want us there. Once again, I had a sense of an intelligent, aware animal and a stupid, unseeing human.

As the previous time, the living horses were refusing to approach. A couple of the living jockeys were lashing out with their whips but most had already given up. Three were on their way back to the stables. The voice on the Tannoy was more resigned than angry as it announced another abandoned race.

Even so, our jockey was already behind the starting gate. I wasn't sure if I had imagined it, but could Summer Lightning have hesitated for a moment before taking up his position?

From somewhere a starting pistol fired and the gate rose. The two ghost horses leapt out onto the track, neck and neck. A flat race of two miles and four furlongs had begun.

For the first mile they were together, stride for stride. But it didn't last.

Shergar was soon five lengths ahead. Summer Lightning was being left behind.

Caroline cried out and maybe I did too as, for no reason I could see, Summer Lightning pulled up.

Mickey Trent flew over his mount's head and crash landed on the track. The horse rolled over him again and again, pounding the jockey's body into the earth. Had they both not been dead already, there would have been no survivor. But a ghost, whether it be human or equine, cannot die.

Summer Lightning was back on his feet. His neighs of triumph rang out so loud I was sure some of the living must have heard them. He turned, kicking the fallen, crushed body as he did so, then galloped away and was gone.

Mickey Trent remained where he had fallen.

"Good! Oh, good, good! He's ours now. Come on. Let's get him!" Caroline's nails dug into my arm. "After what he's done, it would have been so wrong for him to be happy." Her eyes sparkled. "Don't you see, Ross? There is a point to what we do, after all."

If this was what triumph looked like, it was the ugliest expression I had ever seen.

For this moment at least, all her doubts were gone. But I was being torn apart. If only I had been able to agree with her: rejoice at Mickey Trent being sent where he deserved to be. Indeed, no mission had ever had so clean an end before.

Or such a blurred one. I had seen no good in the dead man, but was an eternity of pain not excessive? And why did I have to be the executioner?

My eye was drawn to the end of the course: Shergar in lonely majesty, his jockey waving his arm in the air, flushed with elation.

Something was approaching them. I could just make out a blurred figure, no doubt one of my more fortunate opposite numbers from upstairs. I bet he enjoyed his job, never endured a single instant of regret.

Caroline had left me behind. She drifted across the mud and stood over the splayed, broken body. I saw her reach out.

Mickey Trent took her hand. On his feet. Talking. His shoulders slumping. A whimper.

Gone.

CHAPTER 27

Nadine flowed into our common room. Casting a glance at her reflection in the tall mirror by the door, she patted her hair and smiled. I wasn't surprised she was pleased with her appearance. Considering the woman had been dead for such a long time, she looked good. We all did. One of the few benefits of working for Hell is you don't show your age.

But what was she was doing away from the office she shared with her two colleagues, the bald man and the one with the earring? Maybe she was just after a bit of company.

My team were relaxing for once; a rare, almost unknown treat. Sitting in comfortable armchairs around a pair of occasional tables, we were reminiscing over our last few missions. We were not expecting anyone else and if we had, it would not have been Nadine. She was a bureaucrat, a member of the panel who had interviewed me as well as other prospective Hell hounds. Her kind did not mix with the likes of us.

Besides, Josh hadn't told us of any changes that would necessitate us working with someone from Recruitment and Records, not that we had seen much of him in recent times. He had been on rotation, attending something called the "Ongoing Permanent Conference", whatever that was. I so hoped his would be a long absence.

"Hi, Caroline."

"Hello, Nadine. Are you here for a chat or have you brought some new instructions for us?"

"Neither. I'm to go with you on your next mission. Louise is staying behind."

Louise let out a stifled cry. We all knew what "staying behind" meant.

"She's a vital member of my team. She pulls her weight."

"No one is saying she doesn't." Nadine half turned to face Louise. "It's not a punishment. You're not going to lose any of your privileges. Trust me. It's just this single time. Don't look at me like that. It's not so unusual. The team needs to take a specialist with them for this one. The mission is... delicate. We have to get it right and resolve the matter as soon as possible."

Louise gaped at her; she didn't believe a word of it. Neither did I. We were in the natural home of liars. For a moment I thought she was going to protest, not give up without a struggle, but her shoulders slumped and she bowed her head. I hoped she was not about to burst into tears. We could offer her no consolation.

Her goodbye was a faint whisper, drowned by the sound of a door closing in the distance. She was gone. We would never see her again. It made no difference how we felt: we had a new team member now. Why was I suddenly feeling so guilty that I had never made much of an effort to get to know her?

Well, there was nothing I could do about it now. And Nadine would have to do her best to settle in.

She shrugged. "Hey, come on. I didn't ask for this. It's as much a shock to me as it is to you. It's not my fault."

Caroline was on her feet. "I never said it was. We all have to do as we're told but I thought you were part of the assessment team. Why have they taken you off that duty?"

"They didn't tell me. But I suppose it's because I wasn't any good at it. Yours wasn't the only session I made a mess of."

So, Caroline also had a strange interview. I thought the slip Nadine made in mine was a practised deception. I must have been wrong, though being assigned to us did not seem an appropriate punishment. And since when had our masters ever given anyone a second chance? Even among the usual bad odours of Hell, something didn't smell right about this.

"What did Louise do wrong?"

"I haven't a clue. They didn't tell me that either and I've no idea what they're going to do with her. Perhaps she'll replace me on the interview panel."

There was no point in pushing her. She might even have been telling the truth. Louise could have been retired from the team on a whim. There did not have to be justice. This was Hell after all.

Our first mission together was a breeze. Nadine, it turned out, had lived in a much later time than mine. She had died up against a wall, shot by the French Resistance when they realised she had betrayed them. Like most of us she had bought her place in Hell with the blood of innocents while trying to profit from them. And she'd had plenty of time to repent since.

Not that repenting does you any good: it's just something you're expected to do once you're faced with the prospect of eternal damnation. No one takes any notice, whether you mean what you say or not. It's far too late. In life you are responsible for constructing your own bed; cutting down the tree with your weapons of choice, be they verbal or physical. You put it together one splinter at a time using the tears of others as the glue. The big lies are the headboard, the smaller ones an elaborate footer. When you've finished, and you are claimed by

Hell, you're not handed a feather mattress to complement all that hard work. In death, all that remains for you is to lie down and wait for a daemon to tuck you in. And they will provide their own matches.

When our second outing as a team began, I could no longer deny something was going on between Nadine and Greg. I tried to ignore it at first, but they made it difficult. They sat so close together and whispered as though they shared some secret. Occasionally their hands would touch.

I wouldn't have minded giving Nadine a bit of a squeeze myself. She was a typical French miss: heart shaped face, short-cropped hair, black as printer's ink, and dressed in the height of the fashion current in the period we were next to visit. As with everyone else, her clothes had altered to fit the mission. Hell possesses an infinite wardrobe. It's all part of the necessary deception.

Away from the Inferno on a mission, fetches are difficult to distinguish from the living. We are trained in the phrases currently in use and the manners to display in order to fit in. Ghosts, yes, there is no doubting the fact, able to pass through any solid surface, but we are in disguise. If you come across one of us in the street and are sensitive enough, the touch of a chill wind on your skin may make you shiver. But there will be nothing more.

We look much as we did in life, in my case a tall man with jet black hair, dark blue eyes, a short beard and a curling moustache. I would be considered by some a lady killer. They would never guess how accurate the title had once been.

To my surprise, the grey tunnel led us near to the place where I died but more than two hundred years later. We passed in front of the farmhouse where Robertshaw murdered my sister. I choked back a wave of anger. I would never forgive that man for the deaths of Jayne and Tessa. I hoped by now he had been tucked away on the sixth or seventh level of Hell for a long time, suffering agonies beyond enduring.

But as we arrived, smoke was rising from the chimney; the garden beside the building was full of herbs and flowers; in the yard a dozen hens pecked and scratched. A contented marmalade cat was curled up in the sunshine beside the steps. We passed a flock of creamy white sheep grazing in a field bordered by strong fences. A tall crop of waving wheat awaited harvesting. I smiled at the evidence all was well with my descendants. I was grateful this was not our destination.

No, our business here was with a car crash. Two men and a woman had robbed a bank in the nearby town. There was a perilous high-speed chase along country lanes as they fled their pursuers. Hitting a patch of rough road, the vehicle skidded across the camber, over the edge, down a steep slope and ended up in a shallow river at the bottom. Unable to stop in time, the police in the car behind had followed them down: the patrol car wrapping itself round a tree.

The robbers were not our target, having already departed. It was the two corrupt, young policemen who had intended to help themselves to some of the loot but died instead, whom we were to collect.

Caroline and I slid down the slope. This was surely a task for two, not four. I asked myself why the rest of the team had been sent. Had Josh miscalculated?

"Good afternoon, gentlemen."

The policemen turned as one to look at my team leader.

"It's all right, miss. We don't need any help. We've already radioed in our position." He was about twenty-five, a pale young man with a receding hairline. Well, he wouldn't need to worry about that any more. Given the amount of blood he had lost (the left arm of his uniform was soaked through and a steady stream of drips crimsoned the grass at his feet) I guessed the shoulder was severed through and the artery was close to having bled out. That alone would have been enough but, from the way he hunched over, I could tell there was other damage, less visible, though, now being dead, he was no longer in any pain.

Caroline waved her hand at him. "You're injured. Haven't you noticed?"

"It's nothing. I've got a few cuts and bruises, that's all."

"Oh, I think you've got more than that."

The second policeman was, if it were possible, in an even worse condition. After all I had seen while working for Hell, I was far from squeamish, but I found him difficult to look at. Most of the glass from the windscreen had been crushed into his face.

He took a step towards Caroline. "There's an ambulance on the way. We'll get checked out when it comes. For now, you can help us. Did you witness this accident? If so, what did you see?" He fished in his pocket and brought out a bloodstained notebook. "We can take a provisional statement right now if you like."

I pointed to the wreck of the other car. "Don't you think you should check for signs of life?"

"No, they had no chance, they're..." He froze, staring at me, mouth wide open. He dropped the notebook and his hands rose to a ruined face. "I'm..."

He was gone.

His companion did not appear to notice. His hold on life might be over but he was tenacious in his determination not to acknowledge the fact.

It was time for drastic action. I walked over to the patrol car. "This is a mess." I poked at the thick tree branch which had been driven through the windscreen, the one which had skewered his shoulder.

"Leave that. It's evidence."

"Evidence of what?"

He frowned as he joined me beside the wreck.

"Don't you think it would have been a miracle if you'd survived this?"

"Miracles can happen."

"Not to the unworthy."

He swallowed, walked round the vehicle, peered inside at the blood, licked his lips. I knew he was tasting the dark, salty iron still trickling from the wound where his left eye had been.

His voice was a whisper. "No one could survive this, could they?"

"Nope."

He gave a tiny nod and also vanished. The familiar tang of sulphur drifted in the air as he was claimed.

Leaving the two vehicles and the five empty carcasses, I followed Caroline.

She called out, "We've finished!"

There was no reply. The road was empty: no sign of either Greg or Nadine.

"Where could they have got to?" Caroline grasped my arm. "We have to find them. They'll be in such trouble. And so will we for not reporting them."

"Reporting what? Maybe they saw there was nothing for them to do and went for a walk."

Her fingers dug into me. "You can't be that naïve. You must have worked out what's going on."

"Tell me."

She snorted. "Do you imagine Nadine joined us by random accident? Open your eyes, Ross. I overheard her telling Greg it had all been much easier than she'd expected."

"You think she somehow influenced the interview panel to let her work with him?"

"Don't you?"

"I suppose it's possible. They were an odd trio." Had she reached the same conclusion as me? "To my mind, the only one worth persuading would be Claude."

She nodded. "Sleeping on the job? It wasn't a very convincing act, was it? And he was also on the panel when Greg was assigned to this team."

"So, he selected all of us."

"I guess so. But I don't know why he would be willing to break the rules for

Nadine. Perhaps he owed her some kind of favour, or she found a way to trick him."

Imagine that. "If she did, she's much cleverer than I took her for." I couldn't help grinning. "Playing the system and winning! We'll have to get her to give us lessons. What? Why are you looking at me like that?"

"You can't be saying you approve of what she's done."

"Why not? Come on, Caroline. Think about it. If someone you cared for was here and it was possible to manipulate events to let you be with them, wouldn't you do it?"

"And put everyone else in danger for such a selfish reason?"

Yes, I'd do just that. But Tessa wasn't here and I would not have wished her beside me in Hell. "I don't think I could resist, not if I really loved someone. Hasn't there ever been anyone you would take a risk for?"

She turned her back on me and started out for a clump of trees on the other side of the carriageway.

But before she got there, Nadine and Greg pushed their way out. They were holding hands.

"You idiots!"

Greg smiled and, letting go of Nadine's hand, slid his arm round her waist. "No, we're not. We know what we're doing." He kissed her.

For just an instant I hated them both. Memories flooded through me. I felt Tessa in my arms once again, the pressure of her lips on mine. I so craved what Greg and Nadine had.

Flapping her arms like an enraged mother hen, Caroline advanced on the couple. "Stop it. Stop it at once!"

Greg and Nadine kissed again.

"You mustn't do that. You can't."

"Why not? We've got bodies, haven't we?" Nadine laughed. "You should give it a go yourself. It's almost as pleasurable as it was when we were alive. A bit colder of course, but we don't mind that. Come on, Caro. You must remember what it's like."

Caroline flushed.

I stared at her, but it was Nadine who spoke. "You don't remember, do you? Didn't you ever have a beau? Were you never in love?"

No, she wasn't. On the occasions in the common room when Louise, Greg and I talked about our past romances (though he never mentioned Nadine) Caroline sat in silence. I thought her a product of her time, embarrassed by the subject. Now I understood this young, sheltered debutante had nothing to tell.

She tossed her head. "It doesn't matter. The only thing that matters is you are going to give them an excuse to send us all through the Final Door. I don't want to suffer because you can't keep your hands off each other."

"I'm sure they could manage to be discreet."

"Don't you start, Ross. There's no way they could be discreet enough. We are watched. Or have you forgotten that?"

"I haven't forgotten. But I still say..."

"Shut up!" She bit her lip. "The mission is over; we have to return to Hell. We won't speak any more of this. Nadine, you will go to the panel and ask for a transfer. That is the only way this can work."

"No, I won't do that. I'm staying with Greg. It's you who'll keep your mouth shut, Caroline. You don't have any choice. If you say anything, they will punish all of us. You're our leader: you let this happen. And it's not as if it's the first time for this team, is it? Think about it. They're not going to give you any more chances."

The two women were toe to toe. I was afraid one was about to strike the other.

Instead, Caroline clenched her fists. "I won't do it. I'll take my chances and tell on you. At least that way, it won't be hanging over me."

"That would be the worst mistake you could make. I had myself transferred because I found out how Anya got away. Yes, I know how she escaped. Greg and I are going to use the same route." She paused and her eyes met Caroline's. "And we could do with your help. If you were to give it, we could all go together."

"Impossible. There is no escape."

"Oh, but there is. And Anya wasn't the first either. This route's been used by a few people over the centuries. You hear things when you work in the offices. She didn't mean to, but she left several clues and not long ago I put them together. I assure you escape is not that difficult. It's not difficult at all."

"If you're telling the truth, why are you still here? You and Greg ought to be long gone."

"We would be, except the escape route doesn't start here." She was so earnest, so determined. And if it wasn't true, would she have taken such a risk for a few stolen kisses?

A strange, unfamiliar feeling was surfacing within me. I was afraid of it. "Where would be the right place to escape from, then?"

"I can't tell you that. If you knew, Greg and I would be at your mercy. So, we will hold our secret until we find ourselves in a situation where the time and place are both right. And then we will all escape together."

I couldn't help it. I wanted to believe her. The unfamiliar feeling now flooded through me, drowning my arguments.

I glanced at Caroline.

Her lips were a little apart, her eyes wide. I knew she felt it too; the most forbidden feeling in the whole of Hell; the one capable of undermining everything.

We felt hope.

CHAPTER 28

"I can't stand this any longer. I have to find out what happened to Louise." Caroline and I were alone in the common room. Even so, she was standing close beside me and hissing into my ear.

"You know what happened. And there's not a single thing we can do about it. Louise is gone. We have to accept we're never going to see her again."

She bit her lip, turned away from me then started towards the door. "Come along. We can't talk in here. Greg and Nadine could be back at any moment and..." She lowered her voice further. "You know we can't trust either of them. They're so absorbed in each other and it's more and more obvious. Every time they are sent out together, I'm afraid they'll do something really stupid, maybe even try and run away."

"Perhaps they will. If they were telling the truth about having found out how Anya escaped..."

"Don't be ridiculous. You know it's hopeless. There's no point in dwelling on dreams. There is no escape. Greg and Nadine only said what they did so we wouldn't report them." She took another restless, nervous step. "Come on, Ross." It was more a plea than an order.

Following her as she drifted along the corridor and into the library, I had an inkling about our destination. If right, I would have to act as though it was my first time inside her private study. Which it wasn't, not by a long way. I had met up there with Caffiaes only a short while before. Trying to think back, I hoped we had not left any trace of our presence.

But we had.

Caroline stopped beside the table and stared down at the small, gold coloured object on its surface. "What is that thing?" It wasn't really a question. She might have been in Hell a good while, but I knew she couldn't fail to recognise a wristwatch.

Why had I trusted Caffiaes to hide his little toy? I should have taken care of it myself. Now Caroline had seen it, she was going to want an explanation.

When he first showed it to me, I was impressed, having thought it impossible to bring anything down the tunnel. Yet Caffiaes managed the feat; he brought a treasure into the Inferno. But there was a catch: even though this watch functioned on the temporal plane, it would not work in Hell.

We tried to set it but it refused to tick. So, now we used it to signal to each other. If Caffiaes was about, he set the hands to twelve o'clock. When I found it, I would change the time then wait for him to return. It was a mystery to me how he knew, but he would always arrive soon afterwards.

Between meetings we hid it behind a set of books.

The hands stood at three o'clock, the same time it showed when I left. Yes, an oversight for sure.

She picked it up, the leather strap slipping through her long, slender fingers. "I don't understand. I never use this room. Who could have been in here and left this?"

I was struggling to come up with a convincing answer. She knew me too well to be taken in by an outright lie.

But I was saved the need to think of one because, as she leaned forward to replace the watch, her crimson nails brushed the edge of a deep scorch mark carved across the table: a souvenir of the last occasion Caffiaes had been in a bit of a strop due to his frustration with his superiors.

"A daemon has been in here. Why would…?" She broke off. Her eyes narrowed. "Oh, I see. You've been using this room, meeting with that creature we ran into at the hotel. Well, are you going to deny it?"

What would have been the point? "Come on, Caroline, you might get on with Caffiaes if you try. And some day having a daemon for an ally might turn out to be useful."

"Useful in helping pass through the Final Door, you mean. You're such an idiot, Ross." She pushed the watch away from her. "I forbid you to use this room ever again. Is that understood?"

It was, but I had no intention of obeying her. Why give up the only place where it was possible to be alone, out of sight and able to plan? I was still working on a way to escape, with Caffiaes' help, even if so far we hadn't managed a single good idea between us.

It would be best to distract her. "Didn't you bring me here to talk about Louise?"

She frowned but then nodded. "Yes, I did. And even if we're right and Claude was behind it, helping Nadine for some reason, surely he wouldn't just send Louise through the Final Door. I can't stand not knowing what happened to her." She perched on the edge of one of the seats, small, sharp teeth chewing at her lower lip.

I leaned over her. "What do you want to do about it?"

"I'm not sure but I can't get over how different this is to Anya. If Claude is doing this, how is he getting away with it? With Anya it was all so official: more than just the interview panel involved. She was given the bad news by Nadine and her colleagues during long meetings in Interview One. And she was allowed to say goodbye to the team. Whatever happened to her after that, I have no idea. But procedure was followed up to that point."

"What you're describing sounds rather gentle for Hell."

"I suppose so, but it's what happened. Also, she had her lodestone removed just before she was sent away."

Now that was interesting. The lodestones could be removed, could they? "Caroline, perhaps that's the key. Once the lodestone was gone and she was no longer a fetch but a wraith, Hell would have had no means of tracking her. Could that be what Nadine was referring to when she said the circumstances weren't yet right for an escape to be possible?"

Her eyes widened. "I suppose it could be if Anya had help getting out of Hell. Once outside, without her lodestone she would be next to impossible to locate. But, Ross, it would be such a risk. There would have to be so many others involved. You're talking about a conspiracy. I don't see how that would be possible without leaving any trace."

"I think Anya did leave a trace and that's what Nadine discovered. She had access to Records. Perhaps if we look, that's where we will find it too."

"And we might also find out what happened to Louise." She got to her feet. "The records are kept in a storeroom behind Interview One."

I had seen the door: another nondescript, plain piece of grey wood with no window and no handle and assumed it led into another corridor.

"I got a glimpse inside once. It's a huge room full of files."

I didn't ask what else she had expected to see in a records office in this place. I knew on the temporal plane things had moved on since my time. I had read about computers, even seen them in action on a couple of missions, but Hell continued to use nothing but paper. Perhaps those in charge liked the way it burned. This was after all the home of fire and ashes.

"Come on, then. What are we waiting for?" She walked over to the door.

I followed her, past the shelves groaning with too many books, and out of the library into the grey corridor.

I had always waited for someone in Interview One to let me inside. You don't drift into an appraisal uninvited. But this time, in the full knowledge we were crossing another line and perhaps the final one, we strode through the door.

The room was empty: no one behind the mahogany table; no papers littered its surface.

"They mustn't be interviewing today." Caroline was already standing, poised in front of the records office door.

For an instant I hesitated. This had to be the ultimate stupidity: risking the Final Door just to satisfy our curiosity.

Caroline put her head against the wood. "I can't hear anything."

"They might be very quiet workers."

"Only one way to find out." She vanished inside.

Seconds later she was back. "It's all right. There's nothing but a load of metal boxes: no sign of any people at all."

Well, this was it. We would be in just as much trouble if we stayed where we were. If caught, one further transgression would make little difference.

I stepped through the door.

The room stretched away from us. We couldn't see an end to it. Not unusual for Hell. It was crammed floor-to-ceiling with filing cabinets. Most were double width and the same grey as the walls. But there were the occasional single width crimson ones. The greys were labelled "Personnel": the reds had no labels at all.

A string of large numbers was embossed on every drawer. I was a little shocked. Had there been so many Hell hounds? Or was this Hell's entire workforce? I hoped it was the latter. I supposed, given eternity, you might run through a pretty large number of staff. Even if none of them did expire.

Caroline slid open the top drawer of the nearest grey cabinet. Inside were at least a hundred individual files. As far as I could tell, they were in perfect alphabetical order. I didn't recognise any of the names. Neither did she.

I wasn't certain we were going about this the right way: trying random drawers in the hope of spotting some reference to either Anya or Louise. But what else could we do? It would have helped if we had a clearer idea of what to look for.

Even though it was deserted, the room was lit by a constant, soft glow from the ceiling. Hell has no need to be concerned with shortages of energy. I wondered if heat and light was syphoned off from beyond the Final Door. One thing we could not complain about was being cold!

My mind drifted and it was difficult to concentrate. I could not summon up the slightest desire to root through the papers inside the metal cases. What was the point? For all we knew, the records we wanted might have been packed up to accompany our colleagues on their journeys through the Final Door.

Caroline was by one of the red cabinets. I didn't want her to open it, though I could not have said why. She placed her hand on the metal surface.

A blast of air whipped around me, rattling the cabinets and carrying upon it a sound like a thousand voices whispering in the far distance.

Her arm fell to her side. She turned to look at me. "Oh hello, Ross. Are we on a mission?"

Before I could reply, she crumpled like a marionette whose strings have been cut. Her limbs sprawled out across the grey stone floor.

A flash of lightning from somewhere ahead became a ray of bright light illuminating a pathway towards us. Caroline's head and shoulders were bathed in a golden glow which encroached upon my toes.

I could not move.

Someone or something was approaching us: a massive shadow cast ahead of a moving body. I did not want to look. It would not be Caffiaes. And I had no other friends in this place. Except for the woman lying at my feet.

What idiots we had been. We should have realised Hell would protect its secrets. Even those of little importance or none at all.

"Ross? Is that you?" The light faded and the shadow resolved into a woman.

Able to move again, I bent to grasp Caroline by the shoulders. "Louise? Help me, she's hurt!"

"What are you doing here?" She peered at Caroline. "I suppose this was her idea. What did she imagine she was playing at?"

"We came to find out what had happened to you. We thought..."

"Oh, what fools you are. Right, we'd better get her up and out of here. You're so lucky it was me on duty." She made to grasp Caroline's feet. "Come on."

I waved her away and gathered Caroline into my arms, letting her head rest on my shoulder. I followed Louise through the maze of cabinets. They towered above me in unbroken rows like the crenelations of some massive, steel castle. After a short while I was lost. The way in had vanished behind me.

We arrived at another identical door, another identical common room. I laid Caroline on a chaise longue exactly like one of ours and knelt beside her.

Louise took a seat at the table. "This is such a mess. She could be out for a long time. She'll have overloaded her lodestone. I do hope she hasn't done too much damage to herself. If she has, I'll have to report what has happened. And that won't end well."

"End well for whom? If Caroline needs help, we have to find it. And this is your fault. We only came here to find out what had happened to you." I stared at her, sitting, watching me. I detected no concern for Caroline, only for herself. "You owe us an explanation. You had us..." I struggled not to shout at her. "...mourning you. We thought they'd sent you beyond the Final Door. Caroline wouldn't have got hurt like this if you had only trusted us."

"How could we trust you? The more people who knew, the greater the danger.

You know that."

We? Of course: Nadine and Greg. "And you did all this just so those two could be together?"

"No, it isn't like that. We had to change places." She rubbed her cheek. "It's a secret."

"Well, it doesn't matter now." I took hold of Caroline's pale, cold hand. Still she did not move, did not react.

Louise was continuing as though there was no urgency, as though her tale was more important than what was happening to Caroline. "Nadine and Greg, they've found a way out: an escape route. But they have to be together to make it work." She gave a deep sigh. "I couldn't take being a Hell hound any longer. I would have given up soon enough." She waved her hand towards the door which led into the Records room. "Every one of the hundreds of files in the red cabinets represents the end of a Hell hound. No one dies, but everyone makes a mistake or resigns in the end. What is the point?"

She was waiting for an answer. If she was trying to absolve herself, I was not going to make it any easier for her.

"Most Hell hounds take to the corridor and make for the Final Door all on their own. No one has to force them." She tried to smile. "You never knew a ghost could commit suicide, did you, Ross?"

Caroline continued to lie silent and still. Her skin was pale. Would she ever come round? With no pulse or breathing to check, I had no idea as to her condition.

Louise heaved a deep sigh. "I think it would be best if you left. Take her with you and lay her out in your own common room. You could tell anyone who asked you found her like this. Or maybe you carried her from the library after she fell from one of the ladders."

What nonsense. "You mean tell them anything I like but keep you out of it?"

"I didn't ask you to come here. The higher ups take so little interest, I could hide in Records for a very long time... unless something happens to make them suspicious."

"We came because Caroline cared about you."

"Well, she shouldn't have. We can't afford friendships in this place. You know that."

There was no point in arguing. Louise wanted rid of us. She was not about to take any risks and had no intention of helping us.

I lifted Caroline into my arms again. It was a long trek across the Records room. I counted myself lucky she had all the weight of a wraith, which I guessed was about equal to an angel's feather.

Louise refused to set foot outside the office. She would not even enter Interview One. Indeed, as I melted through into the corridor, she was already running between the cabinets. Away from me.

The passage was empty. I decided against going into the common room. I did not want to have to explain. Better to take her to her study. No one except Caffiaes would be likely to walk in on us there. But I had forgotten the library might be in use.

Three members of another team were grouped round a table close to the door. They had an array of books and several large maps spread out in front of them: all raised their heads to stare.

"Training exercise: what to do if a colleague passes out. New idea by that Barnes chap." It was idiotic. My words would not have borne the slightest scrutiny. But often, the most outrageous lie works best.

I received two nods and a sympathetic smile in response.

I pressed on through the towering stacks of encyclopaedias and atlases. Once inside the study, I settled Caroline on the sofa, took her ice-cold hands in mine and tried rubbing them.

She didn't react. Worse, I realised she was beginning to fade away, becoming translucent.

I was losing her.

A gentle shake and her body fell forwards. I ran my fingers over her head. They were drawn to the lump.

Except now there was no lump. Through the silken strands of her hair, I could feel burning points of extreme heat. Had the lodestone fragmented?

As I cried out her name, tears ran down my cheeks. I knew she was beyond my help. "Caroline, I have to leave you but don't worry: I'll be back soon. I'm going to find Caffiaes. He will know what to do. Please! I can't lose you." Wanting to gather her in my arms but realising it would be a waste of precious time, I kissed her on the brow. The cushions on which she lay were already visible through her body.

I set the watch hands to twelve o'clock. I didn't know why but it felt right. Then through the door, fleeing past the hounds: only two of them now.

The corridor stretched away into the distance. I passed the common room, Interview One and half a dozen other doors. Never before had I taken a path so deep into Hell. But where else would Caffiaes be found?

It was getting hotter. The air around me tasted more and more of sulphur. My feet drifted above the floor. The flags were scorched. Here and there thin rivulets of molten metal flowed in the cracks. But worst of all was the sound: a continuous, long, low howl reverberating from the walls.

Ahead was a barrier: blood red, floor to ceiling. The Final Door blocked my path. Just as last time, the surface was alive: contorted bodies, writhing shapes, heads with screaming mouths, fists and fingers; men, women, children.

I was shaking. Terror took hold of me. My lodestone reacted with increased heat in response to the rising temperature in front of me.

The door's surface was a myriad of disembodied hands; impossible, snake-like arms; fingers stretching towards me; clutching tentacles with claws reaching out to grasp and imprison me. To drag me inside.

I could stand no more.

"Forgive me, Caroline!" I cried out. Forsaking the woman I cared about, abandoning all hope, even for myself, I fled: a deer before hounds poised to tear it apart.

At my back the howls became a continuous scream of rage.

I tore on, certain any second I would feel those ropes of flesh grasp my ankles and wrists.

The first of the doors was still ahead. I swear I could feel the heart I did not possess thudding, as though it were the instrument of an insane drummer.

I could not bring myself to try again. My eyes were blinded by tears for Caroline, now lost forever; for myself and for the future I knew awaited me; for all those who dwell in the shadow of those doors.

The library was silent except for the rustle of papers from a new group at another table.

If she was still in the study, my intention was to wait beside her, though not accompany her to her end: I was too much of a coward.

Passing through the door...

"Leave her alone!" I screamed. How could her eternal torment have begun so soon? And how could Caffiaes, whom I considered my friend, be the instrument of her agony?

Standing over her and... and... his fingers, the impossible, long fingers of his right hand, were inside her head.

"Be quiet, Ross. Let me concentrate."

So, of course, I threw myself at him.

He swatted me away; a mere touch, no force behind it, sent me spinning across the room and back through the door.

I picked myself up and re-entered the study. "No! You will not do this to Caroline."

Caffiaes had finished his probing. He held his hands up, clear of her, high in the air in mock surrender. On the table lay a pile of tiny, sparkling fragments: pieces of lodestone.

"You were taking it out?"

"Actually, I was replacing it. Without a lodestone she wouldn't be a hound any longer."

Unable to take any more I collapsed onto a chair. "You had your fingers..."

He shrugged. "How else did you imagine the stones get inside? Not that they are stones as such." He held his right hand in front of my face. The nail from the middle one of his seven fingers was missing.

"The lodestones are made from daemons' fingernails?"

"One for each of you, not that I have ever done it before. I'm not of a high enough rank. In fact, I have to warn you that what I've just done might not work and, even if it does, it could fail at any time. If it is successful, it will prove I'm a far more powerful daemon than any of the others give me credit for. Well, aren't you going to thank me?"

"Thank you very much, Caffiaes."

"You're welcome. But don't forget: this is another favour you owe me."

"Caroline and I both."

He frowned. "No, I wouldn't have done it for her. She doesn't like me. And it's best you don't tell her about this: she strikes me as the squeamish type."

"How did you know we needed you?"

Caffiaes flicked his hand towards the watch. For an instant it changed and I was looking at another long, pointed fingernail.

"You should know nothing physical can be brought into Hell. Everything here is either made of clay or it's an illusion. Nothing but clay ever endures. It's the heat, you know." He approached the door. "See you later, Ross, and, like I said, it's better for everyone if this stays another of our little secrets. I think you should look after her now."

I stared past him at Caroline. Her eyelids were starting to flicker.

When I looked back Caffiaes was gone.

"Ooh, my head! What happened to me?" She massaged the lump at the back of her skull.

"You had an accident." Not only was I going to keep Caffiaes out of it, I was going to tread with caution until I'd found out what she remembered.

"Louise: we were looking for her records, weren't we?"

"Yes, we broke in, and you started searching through a filing cabinet, but there was some kind of booby trap. You fell over clutching your head. I think it was a reaction from your lodestone."

Once again, she rubbed the lump. "It must have been. It still hurts. I didn't think anything could hurt us any more."

She stood up. "What did we find out? Was her record there?"

CHAPTER 29

The old manor house was on fire. Bright tongues of crimson flame shot up into the dark sky. I'm not all that keen on hot places so I didn't want to be there. None of us did.

Caroline, her face lit up by the fierce glow, paced away from the rest of us and approached the side of the building. "This reminds me of home."

"You mean Hell?"

"No, Ross, I mean my home, the place where I died. It was a house similar to this and it happened on a clear night just like tonight."

"I'm sorry. It's not easy dealing with sad memories."

"I don't have sad memories, not of this anyway. I'd do it all again." She shrugged. "Don't look so shocked. I was barely nineteen, a sheltered young girl never even permitted a beau. Then suddenly I'm being fitted for a wedding dress and expected to marry my distant cousin, whom I last met at the christening of his baby daughter."

"That's awful, Caro. What happened to his wife?"

"Died after breaking her back in a hunting accident." She gave Nadine a weak smile. "I was told she didn't suffer. After all, she expired in the arms of her loving husband. The same man who asked for my hand less than three months later."

"And your parents were in favour of this?"

"I told you, Ross. I've no regrets. My parents always viewed me as more of an investment than a daughter. I was to marry well, and this was the best they could do."

"Even so, burning down the house was a bit drastic, wasn't it?"

She gazed up at the windows, lit from inside by the encroaching conflagration. "My room was up on the second floor. I thought I would have time to get out, but the fire travelled too fast. When Josh came for me, I was on the landing. He took me from the midst of flames only to lead me to more of them."

"It was Josh who collected you?"

"Yes, why wouldn't it be? I came for you at the Farrier's. It's not unusual to join the same team as the hound who brought you in."

"I suppose not."

She sighed. "Josh told me the fire killed five of the servants, two dogs, one cat, six rats, twelve mice and an awful lot of assorted cockroaches and other insects, besides my parents. I was sorry about the cat."

She drifted across the grass toward the house.

I couldn't help wondering what she had left out of her account; no innocent, shy debutante would be as skilled at deception as Caroline. The girl she described would never have had the ability to lead a team like ours.

So far, this mission was not going well. We were the third team to have been sent to this spot at this point in time. The first two groups had reappeared in Hell empty handed and, what was even more mysterious, with no memory of what had gone wrong. Now it was our turn. The task was on the face of it a simple one: to collect a dead man from inside this building.

After Caroline had finished leading us in a close circle round the house, we stepped into a wide porch. The air was hot and dry and the bodies we had been clothed in were sweating hard. But that was nothing new for us.

We pressed on, through into the great hall. Ahead of us the wide, Gothic staircase was a seething mass of leaping flames. Charred spars of timber tumbled down around us. One of them passed straight through Nadine. She gave a sharp yelp: a natural reaction but we all knew nothing physical could harm us. We would not burn. Not in this conflagration.

Still there was no sign of our target.

"Up or down, Caro?" Greg placed a foot on the bottom stair.

"Down always feels more natural, don't you think?" She turned away and headed along a corridor leading deeper into the ruins of the house.

"I think we ought to split up." For once Nadine had made a sensible suggestion.

"I agree. I'll go with Ross and take a look at the kitchen. You and Greg go up the staircase but if you do locate the client, don't try to tackle him on your own."

Greg gave her a nod and grabbed Nadine's hand. "Come on, honey. Let's see what the bedrooms are like."

Did he have to remind us of their forbidden affair? Besides, for once I would have preferred to be the one to work with Nadine. I was waiting for an opportunity to tell her I knew what she had done to Louise; not that there was any way she could put things right.

Caroline was pretending she had not heard what Greg had said.

I followed her to the back of the house. The kitchen was a complete ruin: there was not much left of it. Judging from the extent of the damage, it had to have been the place where the fire started. Even so, there was no sign of anyone, living or dead.

We dropped down into the cellars, taking the easiest path, straight through the flagged floor. Right away I experienced an odd sensation. It was as though my flesh were shaking, trembling, even though I could see no reason to be afraid.

Caroline held up her hand. "What's that sound?"

I listened. There was a faint noise, a kind of buzzing. No, it was voices, an indistinct sort of chanting. The words might not be clear but there was something threatening about them.

"It's coming from over there, further along that corridor. There must be another cellar down here."

She was about to rush ahead. I didn't know why but I had to stop her.

My hand closed around her wrist. The unexpected shock of flesh on flesh made me forget for a second why I had grabbed her. We both watched as my fingers slipped over the back of her hand, my thumb sliding on top of hers. Oh, the soft, tickling sensation as she returned the touch. I shivered a deep, deep shiver: a fragile shiver.

She closed her eyes as I stroked her cheek with the back of my hand. I watched her swallow. It was hypnotic. I couldn't help myself. I just had to kiss her. Oh, the softness of her lips, of her body…

"Told you it felt good, didn't we?"

I let go of Caroline and whirled round.

Greg, with Nadine at his side, was standing behind us. "There's nothing upstairs, not a single thing. The floors have gone and most of it's open to the sky. Not that you care, eh?" He sniggered.

"Shall we go away for a while and look outside? Let you two…"

A blushing Caroline pulled further away from me in response to Nadine's words. "No, we have a job to do. Let's get on with it, shall we?"

Oh, such an ache inside, a yearning, as Caroline glided to the doorway. I had to get a grip on myself. Since the incident in the Records office, when she was so nearly lost to me, I had come to realise my feelings for my team leader were more than simple friendship. But how did she feel about me? Recently she had kept her distance and avoided being alone with me, even to the extent of spending time in her study if the other two were not around: an action which was as inconvenient as it was pointed.

I shook myself to clear my head. It must have done something because a few of the words of the chant reached my ears. One was "daemon", others "be gone".

"Stop, everyone! Don't go any closer. I've a pretty good idea what's happening now. I think there's an exorcism in progress."

"What? You can't be serious. They wouldn't have sent us if that were the case." Caroline, her dark brown eyes wide, swung round to stare at me.

"I'm certain I recognise some of the words. I witnessed one once. It was in a church. I was hiding from the sheriff's men after a rather messy robbery had gone wrong. The priest was attempting to drive out an evil spirit."

"You mean someone like us?" Greg pulled a face.

"That's right. Just like us."

Caroline backed away from the door. "Perhaps, as we're already working for Hell, we're immune and it can't harm us."

"No, I think it can. Or at least it might drive us back to Hell. I'm pretty sure that's what must have happened to the other two teams."

Another word rang out and this time we all heard it. "Spirit!"

We fled through the ruined building. Outside, we regrouped on the lawn in the ornamental garden, next to a fountain which was still playing.

Nadine perched on the edge of the basin and trailed her fingers in the water. "What do we do now? We can't just give up."

"I don't know." It was so difficult to concentrate. I could still feel the exquisite pressure of Caroline's lips on mine. And she had not resisted...

"Ross, are you still with us?" Greg's grating voice possessed the harshest of tones. I had never liked listening to it.

"Yes, I hear you."

"How do we shut this exorcist up? We can't persuade him to come with us if we can't get near him."

Caroline was standing on the other side of the fountain. I observed her through a fine spray. I wondered how those cool droplets of water would feel against my overheated skin.

"So, do you agree, Ross?"

With what? Oh, he must just have said something to me. I had to pull out of this distraction or I would be no use to the team. No use to Caroline either.

We had to solve our various problems one at a time. And our first task was to stop the man in the cellar from chanting. Then we had to complete the mission. Yes, the mission. And when we had completed it, what then? Only another mission... and another... and another.

I so hoped Nadine had been telling the truth for once when she said she and Greg had found a permanent way to escape.

I looked across at Caroline again. Was she arguing with Nadine? I couldn't make out any of the words for the falling water, but I could see she was shaking her head. I hoped she was not regretting even the slight intimacy we had shared. If only I knew what she was saying, could hear the words, hear...

"Ah!" The solution to our other problem hit me like a tidal wave. "Listen. We have to stuff our ears so we can't hear him."

The other three got my meaning at once. "Yes, of course. If we can't hear a command, we can't obey it." Greg scratched the side of his head. "But what can we use for earplugs?"

A soft, green moss was growing around the base of the fountain. I pointed to it. "That ought to do the trick."

We had a quick discussion about how many of us this job would take. I wanted to go in alone, but Caroline wouldn't hear of it and, in the end, she was our leader. Her argument was I might not be able to overpower the man on my own if he was good in a fight. We must be certain of victory.

First stop his mouth to prevent him chanting, next talk to him and somehow persuade him he was dead. I was to go with Greg. She and Nadine would give us ten minutes before following. It was imperative one of us should succeed.

The moss was uncomfortable. Slimy mud clung to my skin and I had to pack the lichen in tight enough so as not to hear anything at all, not even the falling water. I wondered if I looked as strange as Greg, with green fur descending from his ears and dark splashes of wet soil on his shoulders.

He pushed me ahead of him. The women, to my surprise, blew us kisses. Perhaps we had indeed just crossed a threshold without realising it. Now it looked as if all four of us were willing to break the rules.

I entered the hall first. The flames had started to die down but it was still far too hot. There was no point in wasting time. With Greg a second behind me, I slid through the floor into the first cellar. The only sound was a strange whooshing, as though the sea were in my head.

We passed into a corridor and through to the cellar from which the chanting had come, perhaps still came, though I did not think so, since a tight-lipped man was sitting on a low stool in the centre of a chalk circle. I couldn't see anyone else. He had drawn what he must have believed were magic symbols around the edge.

He attempted to shoo us away. If he thought he had created a safe space, he was wrong. The circle lacked candles and the symbols he had drawn were like the scribbles of a child. Wherever he had copied them from, it would have been too much of a compliment to describe them as merely inaccurate. I walked into the circle. He windmilled his arms at me. I could see he was shouting something but I couldn't hear: the moss was doing what it was meant to do.

We reached out to him and dragged him from the stool. I held his mouth closed with my hand.

Greg pulled the moss from his right ear... and vanished.

There was only one possible explanation: the chant must still be continuing. Someone else had to be down there.

But there was no sign of anyone. Nothing. The only objects out of place in the room were a shiny silver box next to a black satchel on an old, rickety table opposite the door.

The man was slippery. I began dragging him out of the circle, but he writhed like a sack of snakes and I made little progress. It wouldn't do me much good in the end anyway. If he didn't leave this place of his own free will, he would only vanish from my arms as we passed through the door and reappear in the ruins of his now half rubbed out circle.

I was at an impasse. I believed the chant was continuing so I didn't dare remove the moss from my ears, yet I couldn't persuade the man to come with us without being able to hear him and speak to him. I would have to wait for Caroline and Nadine, though I couldn't think what use they would be either.

Several minutes passed. The man kept struggling. Neither of us had the advantage. I did wonder why his companion, who must still be somewhere in the cellars keeping up the chant, did not come to his aid.

Caroline entered first. She crossed the boundary of the circle and sank down beside me.

Nadine hesitated. She mouthed some words. I guessed she must have been asking what had happened to Greg. I couldn't explain because she had moss in her ears.

She wandered round the outside of the circle, peering into the dark corners of the cellar as though she hoped to find him there.

On reaching the table, she leant over the silver box, picked it up and smashed it to the floor. Caroline shrugged at me as Nadine then proceeded to drag a thin, brown ribbon out of the wreckage. Once it was nothing more than a tangled mess around her feet, she gave us a little curtsey and dug the moss out of her ears. I waited for her to vanish.

But she remained where she was.

I nodded to Caroline, and we both followed Nadine's example.

The chanting had stopped. The only sounds in the room now came from our prisoner, who knew more oaths than even I did.

He took some time to calm down, all the while insisting we had ruined his séance. No, he did not know there had been a terrible fire in which he had died of suffocation when the cellar filled with smoke.

At last, we persuaded him to come with us to take a look and, as is usual, once he had at last volunteered to leave the room, reality hit him: his empty corpse crumpled to the ground and he disappeared off to Hell.

Page 154

I turned to Nadine. "How did you stop the chanting?"

"Oh, that was easy. He was using a cassette recorder."

"A what?" Sometimes I regretted the gaps in my knowledge. All the information we could ever need for the era in which we operated was there in the library. We were supposed to familiarise ourselves with anything we might meet. But technology did not interest me. And, from what I could tell, it all changed too fast to keep up with anyway. How could I be expected to know everything?

"Oh, Ross, I'd forgotten you come from more primitive times. It's a twentieth century contraption which copies sounds. Our friend had recorded the words of an exorcism onto a cassette tape, but I destroyed his machine." Nadine looked around her. "We have to get back now. I must find Greg, check he's...."

"Don't worry. He won't be in any danger. You'll see. He'll be waiting for us in the common room." Caroline gave her far too bright a smile. "They're bound to want to keep the team together; we're more successful than most, you know." I hoped she was convincing Nadine more than she was me.

If we were to have lost Greg, we might also have lost any reason for Nadine to share her secret with us. And a way out of Hell was the only thing I wanted: the only thing I was determined to find.

CHAPTER 30

"I've got to go; it's not a choice, you know."

"Yes, but Caroline, does it have to be Barnes? He's such a pompous ass. You'll be bored to tears."

"I really don't know why you dislike him so much. Besides, I've never been to a masterclass on impersonation before."

"Well, I hope you enjoy it. I'm sure you'll find him scintillating company!"

She wagged a finger. "Don't be like that, Ross. I need you to leave my office right now and keep an eye on those two for me."

I knew what she meant. Nadine and Greg were becoming ever more blatant in their behaviour: whispering with their heads close together and even kissing in the library.

"I don't know what you expect me to do. If I've seen them, tucked away behind the Eastern Europe section, so have members of other teams. You should order them to stay in the common room."

"Oh, there's no talking to you!" She flounced out into the library.

Greg and Nadine were taking a very real risk. And not just them; since Caroline had not reported the illicit affair, she too was in danger. And so was I. Once the unauthorised job swap between Nadine and Louise came to light, I had little doubt the entire team would be taking a stroll together. It was a precarious position to be in.

I returned to the common room to find Greg out on a solo mission, which meant I could at last corner Nadine. "We have to talk."

She shrugged. "Why so serious, Ross? You think we should put on a surprise party for our glorious team leader or something? It would be a lovely idea if only we could eat and drink. And I'm not sure where you would get hold of a cake or any balloons."

"This isn't funny. I know what happened to Louise."

"Then you know she wanted to leave the team. All I did was give her a hand."

"You conned her into believing your story about there being a way out."

"No, it wasn't a con. There really is a way out. But even if there weren't, Louise is better off where she is." Nadine pursed her lips. "How did you get into Records and not hurt yourself? That place is full of tricks and traps. The worst of them are those red filing cabinets, the ones that contain the most confidential records. They make them like that to attract and then disable anyone who shouldn't be there. And it works every time. We're so starved of colour down here."

I had no intention of telling her the trap had been sprung by Caroline. "I'm asking the questions."

"True, but that doesn't mean I have to answer them." She perched on the arm of the nearest chair. "But maybe I just might."

"Go on, then. Explain."

"Why not? You were going to be told soon enough anyway. We'll need at least six of us working together if the plan is to succeed. You and Caroline will complete the group."

"Six? I thought Anya was supposed to have escaped alone."

"She did, but this is a different route and it needs more people. Six is the minimum required."

"So, that's the four of us, Louise and..." If the answer was in Records... "Your bald friend from the interview?"

"What? Paul? No!" She sighed. "And not Louise either, I'm afraid, though she hasn't worked it out yet and I hope she never will. The other two are members of another team. Don't worry. It will all be sorted out in good time."

"How and by whom? I don't like entering into things with my eyes closed."

"Who does? The idea came from Claude. And I don't see why it won't work."

"Claude? Ah, so he's dreaming of getting out of here while he's snoring his way through interviews, is he?"

Nadine leant further into me. "You had a good, long sleep yourself last night, did you? And Caroline always gets her full eight hours too, doesn't she?"

Oh! How could I have not seen that one coming? "We don't sleep, do we?"

"Daemons don't either but Claude loves pretending."

"Claude is a daemon?" Go on, Ross, state the obvious. It might give you time to think.

"Did you really believe Hell would leave the decision over who gets to be a hound to a panel of amateurs with no idea of what they were looking for? Paul and I were only window dressing. And as for Claude, he's not the only daemon involved. There are three of them who take it in turns. We're lucky two are willing to help in the escape attempt, which leaves only one to avoid. And he's easy to spot: no sense of humour, that one. You can tell he didn't choose the name they all share when they're interviewing."

"Their name?"

"Oh, come on, Ross. Claude… Clawed!" She scratched the air with her fingers. "All daemons are, aren't they?" She giggled. I didn't.

"So, what is the plan?"

"I'd rather Greg explained, and it might as well be to both you and Caroline at the same time, don't you agree?"

"Fine but do make it sooner rather than later, won't you?"

"Yes, the moment all four of us are together again." Nadine ran the back of her hand over her mouth. "I'm sorry about Louise. She doesn't know it but it's her who set this whole thing in motion. I found her in the corridor one day, trembling from head to foot. She had wanted to give it all up, finish with being a Hell hound, and had already made an attempt to reach the Final Door but couldn't go through with it. I can't imagine what she saw that scared her so much; not that I'd want to.

"Claude suggested the place swap. He said, since he had planted lodestones from his own fingers in both Louise and me, it was difficult to detect any difference between us: we give out near identical signals." She smiled at me. "Every member of the team is the same. Claude selected us all personally and had a hand in our implantations."

I tried to resist the urge to shudder. And I knew I had to be careful. No one must guess that a claw other than Claude's was inside Caroline's head.

Greg never had the opportunity to explain anything. He and Caroline were no sooner back than we were all sent out again together.

This time we were on a motorway. Banks of fog swirled around the crowded lanes of multiple crashed vehicles. Horns sounded out a mournful dirge for the unfortunate dead. Many aimless souls wandered to and fro between the wreckage. And six of us hounds stood beside the crash barrier, staring at each other.

Greg clasped hands with Nadine. "Here we go. This is it. Remember, not the first or the second. We must send a few others down before we can select our little gift for Claude."

I was aware of their words but was too preoccupied trying to remember where I had seen one of the final members of the group before. Then it came to me: his name was Michael and I had done my basic training with him. It all seemed such a long time ago.

He gave me a nod but there was no time to exchange greetings since my lodestone was already drawing me towards a blue van and its three occupants. It was so strong a pull, I found it near impossible to resist.

Caroline drifted alongside me. She touched me on the shoulder. "Why are we going over there, Ross?" What a strange question.

I stopped a few feet from our target and turned to look at her. "We're going to collect the driver of that van and his friends."

"Why are we doing that when they're not ours?" She spun round on the spot, her arms extended. "None of them are. I can't feel a thing: no heat at all. They must all belong to the other side. There must have been a mistake. We shouldn't be here."

She started walking back towards the crash barrier, passing straight through two cars, one of which was on fire and also blazing with heat as far as my own lodestone was concerned.

There could only be one explanation for what was happening to her. This was our third mission since her original lodestone had been destroyed. Caffiaes had been right to worry about his repair only being temporary. The new one he had fashioned for Caroline must already be malfunctioning: perhaps it had been overwhelmed by the multiple signals coming from all around us. Why couldn't it have lasted a little while longer, given us time to carry through our escape? Whatever the situation, I could not have felt more out of my depth. With Caroline in her present condition and the attempt already in progress, could things get any worse?

"Stay there. I'll be back in a moment."

She nodded, took a few steps up to the twisted metal barrier and seated herself on top of it. "Don't be long, Ross. I..." She bit her lip; she didn't need to tell me she was scared.

Nadine was the closest so I made my way over to her. She was engaged with the soul of a man who had already shed his body, crushed by the steering column of a four by four. He leaned in through a window now made up of cracked and splintered glass, trailed a hand over his corpse and vanished.

"Well, that's the first one down," said Nadine as I reached her.

"We've got a problem."

She frowned. "You're not feeling squeamish, are you, Ross?"

"Not at all, and I must know what's going on right now. Caroline's lodestone has stopped working. We have to get on with Claude's plan without delay. We can't take the risk of being drawn back to the common room."

She shook her head. "If we'd had time to explain, you would know returning there is an integral part of the plan. Claude is only going to show us the route out of Hell once we're back and we've done a little job for him. But you're right in a way. We have to do what's needed before the Pearly poodles get here."

A shout from behind me. "This one is perfect!"

I swung round.

Michael and his colleague were driving the wraith of a young woman in our direction. But something was wrong. My lodestone was not reacting to her at all. Had it also started to malfunction?

Nadine nodded. "Yes, she's just right. Now, Ross and I will go and arrange some camouflage."

"What do you mean, 'camouflage'?"

She leant into me. "We're taking this one back with us. She's the price of our escape: an innocent soul for Claude and his little gang to play with. They're after something different, you see. They're bored with torturing souls who deserve their torment."

"Are you mad? You can't do that. Her soul belongs to the other side."

"Claude told us, all we have to do is place her in the middle of a bunch of ours and she won't be noticed. Come on. Weren't you a smuggler yourself once?"

"No, I was a highwayman. And, believe it or not, there was a little bit of honour in what I did, at least compared with this." In life I had tried to steal only what my victims could afford to lose: and nothing that came close to equalling their eternal salvation. It also struck me, besides being cruel and immoral, this was also the most stupid and obviously flawed plan ever conceived. Had the details been revealed in advance, I would never have agreed to be a part of it.

I glanced across at Caroline and froze. She was no longer on her own. Josh had a hand on her arm and a hound I recognised as another supervisor stood on the other side of her, while behind her floated three hazy beings: the poodles were arriving.

There were only seconds in which to react. Grabbing hold of Nadine with my right hand, I dragged her toward Josh, while at the same time waving my left in Michael's direction. I didn't want to do it, but there was no choice. It was Michael and his friend or all of us. "Those two have made a big mistake. They're trying to harvest an innocent soul."

The other supervisor began to glide toward the two hounds and their captive.

On seeing him, Michael and his colleague released her. Then, instead of waiting, they ran away.

Josh pointed at Caroline. "Stay here, Ross. Take care of her. I need to deal with this." He was gone, racing off to join in the pursuit.

I took his place beside Caroline.

Nadine lowered her eyes. "You won't tell them I was involved, will you?"

"No, I don't suppose we will. There's going to be enough trouble as it is without us turning on each other."

Greg arrived seconds later. "They've got Sam Phillips, but Michael Brent headed off across the fields. I don't know why he's bothering. They'll only use his lodestone to rope him back in."

He was right. Michael stood no chance. And the pursuit did not last long.

There was still work to do and when Josh returned alone, he insisted we finish it. The other supervisor had already taken his two prisoners and returned with them to Hell.

We were now a depleted team. Unable to tell the difference between the good and the bad souls, Caroline could do nothing except watch. Greg, Nadine and I left her at the barrier while we got on with helping the poodles sort the wheat from the chaff.

There was not as much fallout as I had been expecting from the "escape attempt". Indeed, it was not even described as such. Before anyone else had a chance to speak, Michael confessed he and his colleague, Sam, had gone rogue. They'd had the crazy idea of hurting an innocent for a bit of fun. He claimed it had been his idea and his alone; no one else had been involved. He made no mention of anyone from my team and made no reference to the daemons. It was difficult to acknowledge it, but in the end I would have to admit admiring him. I could never have been as brave when faced with the Final Door.

After this fiasco I would have been inclined to believe there really was no escape route, had it not been for Angel Doris' words when she took Barnes out of my hands at the Adelphi theatre. She said I was to "follow the crowd". I still had no idea what she meant by it, but I was certain angels could not lie.

Meanwhile, Caroline was treated as an invalid. Later I learned this was not the first instance of an unexplained, non-functioning lodestone. She was taken aside and a replacement inserted. I was still the only one who knew of Caffiaes' involvement.

Caffiaes himself went into a long sulk, having been given proof he was not up to the task of being a senior daemon: no point in my friend applying for promotion just yet.

CHAPTER 31

"We have to rescue my nail!" Caffiaes had never sought me out in the common room before. He and I had both avoided involving the rest of the team in our various conversations. And I had never seen him like this: gone was his usual blustering arrogance and in its place was a nervous fidgeting. He frowned at us. "Well, do you hear me?"

Caroline unfolded herself from the chaise longue. "Yes, we hear you but you're talking in riddles."

Not to me he wasn't. But, then again, I had not told anyone what had happened to Caroline after we had broken into Records.

Nadine however gave a little gasp, and I realised she must have worked it out. "Ah, so you didn't get out of there totally unscathed. My guess is Caro must have touched one of the red cabinets." She raised her eyebrows. "That is what happened, isn't it?"

I nodded. But before I could respond and try to explain the situation to Caroline, Caffiaes cut across me.

"They've got hold of my nail. And they know it's been used as a lodestone. But I'm sure they won't have examined it yet. We must rescue it before they can."

"Are you certain they'll be able to tell it's yours and not the original?"

The face he pulled left me in no doubt I had asked a stupid question. "They'll soon work out it's different and then they'll open an official investigation to find out where it came from. Unauthorised tampering with a lodestone never looks good on a daemon's CV and to get caught replacing one..." He shook his head. "I don't know what they would do to me. One thing I do know is that this is all your fault."

He was right. Or at least if not mine, it was Caroline's. She had chosen to open the cabinet, though that made no difference to this situation. Caffiaes would not be the only one to get into trouble if we were found out.

"How will they match it to you? How long will it be before you grow another one?"

Caffiaes took two strides. He stood right in front of me. "I already have grown another." He was so close; too close. His hand raised, transformed into a seven fingered claw. "Look!"

A razor-sharp talon raked across my face.

I was in agony. Gripped by a burning, searing pain. I screamed. A red-hot blade scoured through skin and cartilage. It carved its way right inside me. My flesh stretched for an instant. Then it tore.

I fell to my knees. Reaching up, my fingers found the open wound which was once my nose.

As one, the others gasped as I regained my feet.

Straight away the pain began to ebb, but it had been so severe I would never be able to forget it. Ever. I just had to see the damage.

Oh but I regretted the impulse. My body may only be borrowed but I had become accustomed to it. Somehow it was now my own but reflected in the ornate mirror by the door was a complete ruin of a face. Unable to turn away, I gazed in horror upon the long, deep, dry scar across my lips and the yawning chasm between them and my eyes.

"Why, Caffiaes? Why would you do this to me?"

He shrugged. "It's only temporary."

"But you've hurt me."

"That is what daemons do, you know: hurt people. And if you don't get my nail back for me, I can promise a much worse fate will be waiting for you on the other side of the Final Door."

My face began to itch: it was as if a thousand minuscule ants had crawled into the pit which had been my nose and were milling around in there.

"Mind you don't touch it or it'll scar."

I turned back to the mirror and stared, fascinated by the process, as my skin began to knit and meld itself together. I clenched my fists, fighting to resist the urge to disobey Caffiaes and scratch. If anything, this feeling of discomfort was worse than the original pain.

But after only a few minutes it was over. No sign of the damage was left at all: not even the tiniest of scratches. It was as though I had imagined the whole incident.

"You ought to know, Ross, damage caused by daemons always heals rapidly. If it didn't, a soul's eternal torment wouldn't go on for very long, would it?"

"I suppose not. I hope you don't expect me to thank you for giving me a personal demonstration."

"No, you can have that one for free. Maybe it'll act as a reminder of what's at stake here."

He was right about that. It also made me question my willingness to have any trust in this daemon. Was it wise to consider myself a friend of a being as capricious and as dangerous as Caffiaes?

"Why can't you rescue your own nail? You must know your way round Records a lot better than we do."

"I can't go anywhere near that place until this is over. It's my nail, you see. Mine. If I get close to it, everyone will know."

"How could that be?" Nadine folded her arms. "After all, it's only a fingernail. They're all the same, aren't they? Apart from the shade of polish, you wouldn't be able to tell one of Caro's from one of mine."

"Yours may all be the same but ours are very different from one another's. You're not a daemon so I don't expect you to understand. We're made from the clay of Hell itself. We are finite. We never change. My nail may have been separated from me for now, but if it gets the chance, it will do its utmost to reunite with the rest of me."

That sounded hopeful. "Once it does, won't the problem resolve itself?"

"Not if someone sees it happen. And, compared to you, we daemons are a much more observant lot." Though the rest of his face did not change, wide, grey eyes with glowing golden pupils raked over me. He was becoming impatient.

Nadine sighed. "If we were to go and look for it, where would we start? It won't be just left lying around on top of a cabinet or something, will it?"

"No, it'll be on the conference table in the Joint Meeting Room."

"You're kidding. Why would it be in there?"

"Lodestone accuracy affects both sides. They will want to be sure it was a one off and not a fault that might be repeated."

I had a funny feeling I already knew the answer but hoped I was wrong. "Joint Meeting Room? Does that mean Heaven is involved as well?"

"That's what I said." Caffiaes shuffled his feet. "You should be able to sneak in there when it's empty, grab my nail and be back here before anyone realises it's missing."

"How will we know when the room is empty? I doubt whether anyone's going to give us access to a schedule of negotiations. If we were unlucky, we could walk in on some high level discussions."

"Huh, they don't discuss: they squabble. And none of the important daemons or angels ever get involved. It's just a talking shop for supervisors."

"Does Josh attend?" Caroline's question startled me. I wondered if she realised the lodestone involved had been hers. If so, she was taking it rather well.

Caffiaes shrugged. "It's possible but I don't think he will help us, do you?"

"No, but if he attends these meetings and he's here, not there, then it might be safe to assume there's no one else there either."

She had a point. But, since none of us could walk into the supervisors' rooms to check, I didn't see how we were any further forward. Until...

"I'll go and find out. He'll either be in the supervisors' common room or his own study. I know where that is."

"What excuse can you give for needing to talk to him?"

She shrugged. "I don't need an excuse, Ross. He'll be more than happy to see me. I just hope I'll be able to get away from him afterwards."

"Perhaps it's not such a good idea after all. Tell me where the rooms are and I'll go myself."

A long finger curled over my shoulder. Caffiaes gave me a tug towards him. "You are going to rescue my nail. She can go and check. This Josh likes her."

I had rather worked that out for myself. I also knew she did not like him in the slightest. But Caffiaes was not giving me a choice, so I decided to give him one. "If we know there's no one in the conference room, there's nothing to stop you coming with me."

I thought he was going to refuse but instead he nodded. "So long as nobody is going to see me. And I do so miss my nail."

"You shouldn't have put it inside my head then, should you?" Caroline, always so clever, was already on her way out of the door. "If I'm not back soon, you'll know the coast is clear, and if I'm not back by the time you are, you'll know you have another rescue attempt to make." She was gone.

We waited. Caffiaes cracked his knuckles. The sound reverberated round the walls.

He did it again. "I think we've waited long enough."

I hoped he was right.

Nadine was on her feet. "Come on, then. Let's get it over with."

"No, I don't think we need you. Caffiaes knows the way and I'm going with him. Two should be enough to handle whatever we might encounter." I wasn't being heroic. I just didn't trust her. As for Greg, he hadn't said a word since the moment Caffiaes had entered the room. He simply sat with his arms folded, observing us all.

I followed the daemon along the corridor to the door of Interview One. The room was empty. We were over the first hurdle. I did not want to run into Claude.

The Records office was also deserted. As we passed through, I was careful to keep my hands by my sides, not wanting to risk an accidental brush against any of the red cabinets.

Caffiaes reached the far end. As well as the door into Louise's common room there was another in the opposite corner. It appeared to be a small, narrow, rather unimportant entrance but as we passed through it, I gasped. We were in a huge space; more on the scale of a concert hall or arena than anything which could be referred to as a mere meeting room. And taking up the centre was a table: the longest I had ever seen. It would have seated more than a hundred if there had been any chairs present. Wide enough to lie across, it had a raised gold line along the centre. On our side, the room was the usual, uninterrupted grey, but over the line was a rainbow of shifting blues and greens; a forest under a cloudless sky: a glimpse of Heaven. It was distracting, and it took me a moment to realise we were not alone.

"Hello, Ross. I knew Caffiaes would have to bring someone with him but I didn't expect it to be you." Doris the angel emerged from the trees and shimmered her way to the far edge of the table.

Caffiaes leant towards her. "He was handy and..." There was a moment's hesitation. "I trust him."

It was then I discovered the smile on the face of an angel can take your breath away, even if you are a fetch. "Then I will trust him too."

"Trust me with what?"

Caffiaes shrugged. "The truth, I suppose."

This situation was becoming far too weird for me.

I looked at Doris. "Are you going to help us recover his missing nail?"

She pouted. "Oh, do I really have to give it back?"

Stunned, I stared as she drew a heavy, golden chain from out of the neck of her dress. Suspended from it was what appeared to be a large diamond in the shape of a long, tapering claw.

Caffiaes let out a soft, rumbling purr. "Oh, you've made it so pretty!"

"What else could I do? It's a part of you, after all."

Another purr from beside me. "I've missed you so much."

Doris placed her hand beside the golden line dividing the two sides of the table. "We don't have much time."

"We never do." Caffiaes turned his head and glanced at me. "Do you understand now?"

"Think so. Your story about the nail giving you away was just that: a story."

"I had to have some sort of excuse. And so did *******."

If that was her real name, I would have to stick with referring to her as Doris. I would never be able to pronounce all those musical notes: like an exquisite arpeggio played on a silver harp.

They both leant toward the line. I wasn't sure what would happen when they kissed each other. And I had no doubt they were indeed going to kiss. Would there be some sort of explosion perhaps, like matter and antimatter colliding?

Doris put up her hand. "What shall we do with Ross? I don't want an audience."

"I'll turn my back."

"Not good enough. You might peek."

"No, I wouldn't. I give you my word as a gentleman."

Doris pouted again. "A gentleman? In Hell?" She reached out and my arm was caught in a vice. "This way, Mr. Ferris."

I was suspended above the table, then branches scratched at me as we passed through the trees.

"There. You can enjoy a little time here while ######## and I have a little privacy." So that was Caffiaes' real name. I could never have pronounced that either. It had a lot in common with a loud fanfare from a hundred brass instruments, all playing out of tune.

Doris frowned. She wagged a finger at me. "One thing: don't you go disturbing anyone, especially that girl you liked. What was her name?"

"Tessa."

"Hmm, her. Why don't you find yourself a tavern? And do keep out of trouble!"

She was gone and I was once again a day visitor in Heaven.

Now, where would I find a tavern? Only... I didn't want a drink. I wanted to find Tessa. Since when could a Hell hound be relied upon to do as he was told?

CHAPTER 32

I had no idea where to start looking, and no way of knowing how much time I had. All I could do was start walking.

An instant later I found myself in the arbour. Without turning to look, I knew the pool with the water lilies and the summerhouse were behind me. My feet were once again on the paved path and there, on the bench just ahead, sat Tessa.

This was so similar to my last visit. I was sure the pale green dress with its sprinkling of daisies was the same one she had worn on that occasion; the lace shawl over her shoulders and the book in her hands: nothing had changed.

I should have turned and fled but...

"Hello, Tessa."

"Hello. Who are you? Are you here to see Jerome?"

I shivered. "My name is Ross. Don't you remember anything at all, Tessa?"

She smiled, but her blue eyes were vacant, and I could have recited her next words along with her. "I'm sorry. Have we been introduced?" She placed the book down on the seat beside her. "Did we meet at a party or was it the theatre? I do apologise. As a rule, I'm good with names."

"It doesn't matter. And I mustn't take up your time. Jerome will be here soon, won't he? Once he's rowed from his yacht, the one he's anchored in the bay."

For a second a frown hovered between her brows. Then she laughed. "Yes. Yes, I expect he does have a yacht. And he will have called it after me."

"Indeed he has."

I was confusing her. It wasn't fair on either of us. Nothing I said was going to make her remember. "Goodbye, Miss Noyles."

"Goodbye. Please do call again. I know Jerome will want to meet you."

I turned my back on her, hearing the faint rustle of paper as I did so.

The paved path led to a tavern: not the same one as last time. This was a low, thatched building with ivy covered walls. It stood to one side of a perfect village green where a game of cricket was in progress. The landlord was plump and friendly. Without needing to be asked, he pushed a double brandy across the bar.

I took it outside and, of course, a table awaited me beneath the spreading branches of an oak tree. I was the only patron not smiling, not talking, not enjoying the eternal company of friends I believed I had known forever.

I must have drunk a whole bottle by the time I saw Doris approaching, not that I ever had to refill the glass: the liquid retained its level. Whatever it was, it had none of the effects of real brandy. I might have been gulping down brackish water from a horse trough for all the pleasure it was giving me.

"Finally tired of Caffiaes' company, madam?"

"Hush. Don't say that here." She sank onto the stool which had just appeared opposite me and peered across the table. "Oh, I can tell by your face what you've gone and done. I told you to keep away from her."

I took a long, slow mouthful of the brandy. "You can tell me all you like, but I'm not yours to command, am I?"

"We angels don't command. There's no need. Everyone is happy here."

"Are they? Well, I'm not."

"Why would you be? You don't belong. And you're not staying."

"I don't like what you've done to Tessa."

"I didn't do anything. And all that has happened is for her own good. She has no regrets, Ross. Not one."

"Tessa has nothing at all. Not a single thought in her head."

"She has her Jerome, and that's what's making you angry, isn't it? You're jealous!"

The taste of the so called brandy was cloying, far too sweet. I pushed the glass away. "If the powers that be found out about you and Caffiaes, you'd both be in deep trouble, wouldn't you?"

She flushed. "Is there a point to this conversation? Because you have to go. Your kennel mates will be out sniffing around for you."

"That's not nice language for an angel. Are you getting a tad worried?" I leaned across the table, closing the distance between us and lowered my voice. "You will find a way to restore Tessa's memories and in return I will forget about your little liaison."

"Are you trying to blackmail me?"

"Yes, I believe I am."

"Then you are a fool." She rolled her shoulders. There was the familiar blur of white behind them. Was she trying to intimidate me? The very fact she was reacting gave away how nervous I was making her.

"I can't do what you ask. And, in any case, it wouldn't have the result you're expecting. Tessa had so many regrets. Her contrition for her sins was a large factor in tipping the scales in her favour."

"I don't want excuses."

"I'm not giving you any." She tapped the table. "All right. There is only one way to show you how wrong you are. Come along with me."

I took her hand. Warmth flowed through me. It was as though she were a flesh and blood woman. But the illusion did not last.

Her wings opened, enveloping me. We were above the tavern. But no one below was staring up. I wondered if they could even see us. Or was it that an angel flying was an everyday sight, something not worthy of comment.

"Don't let go, Ross. I don't want to lose you on the way."

"Where are we going?"

"It's not a where: it's a when."

This was not like the corridor; this was a spinning kaleidoscope of stars in a black sky; a whisper of seasons; a descent through centuries.

We were standing on a beach.

"Do you recognise this place?"

"Yes." As she furled her feathers, I took a step away. "Just over that headland is the Farrier's Arms." I pointed.

"And between these rocks?"

"A cave, madam." More than that: it was the cave where I often used to meet with Tessa. A smile came to my lips as I remembered the floor of silver sand and the ledge where we would spread a blanket, come together and for a short while forget the world.

Doris drifted her hand toward the entrance. "Shall we?"

Shall we what? I might be with a creature more beautiful than any mortal woman could ever be, but I didn't... well, "fancy" her. Caffiaes was welcome to this vision of perfection. I preferred...

A laugh from inside the cave.

"Tessa?"

Doris raised an eyebrow. "Who else did you expect? Today is the twelfth of July seventeen ninety-six. It is one p.m. as the locals reckon their calendars."

"I died just a few days later."

"So you did."

My mind was racing. Was this the last time I had lain with Tessa? And why was Doris showing it to me?

We were inside the cave now.

"Don't worry, Ross. We can see but can't be seen."

I wasn't certain I wanted to see, though I was curious about being a voyeur on my own tryst. Except…

I was so close to them: Tessa locked in the arms… of Luke.

I fell to my knees. This could not be real. He was caressing her. They were both naked. My eyes closed, then flew open again. His hand on her breast...

I wanted to be sick. I wanted to fly at him. I wanted to kill him; her; both of them.

My fingers balled into fists. I staggered forwards.

Doris was a restraining hand on my wrist. "Just listen."

Luke, raising himself on one elbow, gazed into Tessa's eyes. "I know it's not nice, love, but it'll soon be over. He'll be dead and gone. And think what we can do with all that money."

"But they'll hang him."

"You don't have to watch. We can be miles away by then."

"Yes. Yes, we can. Oh darling, we can be together forever."

He rolled her over onto her back.

I could take no more. Doris let me flee.

Outside, I doubled over, retching. Waves of anger raged through me as I yelled their names at the uncaring sea.

"Do you understand now?"

I fought for control. There was nothing I could do. The scene behind me had played out so long ago. Everyone involved was dead: Tessa in Heaven… And Luke?

"What happened to Luke? Is he in your happy place too?"

"What good will it do you to know?" She shook her head. "I shouldn't tell you any more. We've broken enough rules between us as it is. But you still won't let it rest, will you?"

"No."

"You shot him. Remember? Your bullet sent him straight through the Final Door. So, I suppose in a way you had your revenge."

It didn't feel like revenge. "I loved Tessa so much."

"Did you? Did you really?" Doris pursed her lips. "Should I show you some more, take you to a few other places? You have such a bad memory, Ross. Even that last summer you weren't faithful to her, were you? How many ladies did you take to your own bed? A man who truly loves does not look for pleasure elsewhere, does he?"

"That was different." No, it wasn't. Tessa had never been the only one.

Questions crowded in on me. Why did it have to be Luke? Why did she have to betray me with him? Had he been in love with her? Which of them had come up with the plan to collect the reward on my head?

"We have to go back now. ######## is taking a risk by waiting for you in the conference room for so long."

"One last question. Did she love him?"

"No more than you loved her. She wouldn't have married either of you. She wanted what you could never have provided: security, a family and a few pretty baubles, a lace scarf or two…"

"Take me home, lady. I've seen enough."

Doris spread her wings. We were again claimed by the spinning kaleidoscope.

Returning to the conference room, once again a daemon and an angel embraced.

But this time it was different for me: I understood. I would never have risked anything for Tessa yet these two were prepared to jeopardise their very existence for a handful of stolen moments with each other.

Beauty and its opposite could not have been less relevant. I would never betray either of them. It was my privilege to be in the presence of true love. The problems of Romeo and Juliet had been mere molehills when compared with the mountains which faced this couple. Who would ever want to deal with the disapproval of both Heaven and Hell?

I would have given anything, everything for a love as deep as theirs.

CHAPTER 33

Josh and Caroline were at the far side of the common room, snarling at each other. I couldn't understand it. If they wanted privacy, they had a choice of her study or his, so why have the row in this room where three pairs of ears were bound to be wagging? Nadine was no more reading an article in Cosmopolitan than Greg was studying Country Life or I was playing patience.

The argument ended abruptly and Caroline advanced on me. "Come on, Ross. We have to go." She turned back to Josh. "I mean it. I want my objections recording and I'll be making them official."

He shrugged.

I left the cards where they were. As I reached the door, I glanced behind me. Josh had the oddest expression, one I could only have described as a delighted sneer.

"Where are we going?"

She didn't break stride. "You'll see. And he's out of his mind sending us on this one."

The grey corridor seemed longer and less straight than usual. It ended in a car park. But not any car park. I shuddered as I stared around me. I had hoped I was done with this place forever.

The Farrier's Arms was trying to pretend it was still the eighteenth century. The walls had been distressed and the mullion windows had more bullseye glass than could ever have been afforded when the tavern was constructed. The heavy, black door was of wood from a tree not even planted until around a hundred years later than the carving suggested; while around the building were expensive, modern cars and the occasional, slightly older model. Tessa's former home had become a "destination pub", with signs proclaiming "gastronomic delights" and, for this weekend only, a "Folk Festival with Real Ale". I wondered if Pete Noyles would have recognised the beverage as such.

"I can't go in there. I've too many memories."

Caroline did not reply.

"I really can't. You should have brought Greg or Nadine."

"Don't you think that's what I told him?"

"Josh chose me specially for this?"

"Chose us both."

As we arrived at the door, it was thrown open and a gaggle of young people pushed past us. The blast of heat from inside would have been worthy of the place we had come from.

The bar was crowded: too many people in too small a space; no room to move except right at the back, where there was a small, raised dais. A trio of women in what I supposed were meant to be eighteenth century village outfits, complete with straw hats, were singing some strange sea shanty while waving large pieces of fishing net at the audience. I didn't recognise the song.

My lodestone was giving off a gentle heat. There was someone here waiting for us to collect them. But where were they? Not in the bar for sure. Perhaps upstairs: the very place I did not want to go.

Caroline was fidgeting. I knew she was as unhappy as I was. Best not to think too much: just get on with the job. The sooner we found the target, the sooner we would be out of there.

Another performer stepped onto the dais, seated himself on a stool and hefted a guitar onto his lap. "Evening folks. In honour of The Farrier's and our famous ghosts, let's have the one you all know: The Lay of the Highwayman and the Publican's Daughter."

"What?" I staggered back against Caroline.

"Oh no!"

The singer's voice swirled around me. Unable to move, I found myself standing in the exact same spot and hearing the exact same words as the night Caroline had collected me from the inn: the exact same night Tessa had also been murdered.

I was shaking. And I could feel Caroline trembling against me. "Future echo," she whispered. Except this time it wasn't. This was happening. It was real and it was now. "We have to get out of here. Never mind the mission."

"I can't move."

The song went on and on. I looked round, looked for Tessa. But Tessa couldn't be in the Farrier's; she was in Heaven: I had seen her there. And yet...Was that her, the girl half in shadow behind the singer, the one in the long, blue dress?

"Ross, please. Don't you see it's a trap?"

"A trap...?" No, the girl was not Tessa.

Caroline grabbed my arm.

I wanted her to let go. I could stay here. The singer had said there were ghosts. Why could I not be one of those haunting this inn? Haunting it with Tessa? Yes, why not? I didn't like Hell. I'd rather be...

Before launching into another chorus, the singer turned his gaze towards me.

His voice was so melodic for… for someone with eyes that colour… For a…

"Ross! Come on!" She tugged at me.

I couldn't stop staring at the singer. The door… We fell through the door; a tangle of limbs on the stone path.

Caroline was sobbing. "We've failed. We can't do this. It's so wrong. Josh has no right. But they won't listen. We're finished."

The cold night air drifted through us. For an instant we were wraiths with no bodies and no purpose. But now, away from the singer, the spell had been broken.

I clasped Caroline to me, kissed her tears, held her. "Josh hasn't won yet. There must be something we can do, some way to get past his friend in there."

She shook her head.

It would be so easy to despair. But I knew the tavern, not this playground they had made of it. No, I knew the real Farrier's. And under the façade, the ancient structure was still intact. Over Caroline's shoulder I studied the walls.

"This way." Holding her hand, I led her to the foot of the stairs which had been there in my time, now filled in with builders' rubble and stuccoed over. Only the faint tracing of a shadow on the wall told the tale of a bygone way to the upper storey. On more than one occasion a highwayman had climbed those steps to a warm room and a warmer woman. Tessa would leave the door unlocked and drape a shawl over her casement to signal the coast was clear.

If anyone had seen Caroline and me, they would have screamed: half in and half out of the wall as we ascended a stair only I could perceive.

We entered the building to find the inner landing occupied: a young man was sprawled out across the passage. He was not dead, at least not yet.

But in the room where I had myself died, there was someone else. Her ghost blinked at us as we entered. "I don't think Robbie's very well."

"No, he's taken an overdose. What about you?" Caroline, suddenly all business, walked across to her and smiled.

"I'm OK. I think." The ghost frowned. "I'm… Oh!" She was gone.

With our task completed, we should have been gone too, but the walls of the room which had held my deathbed still surrounded us. And from beneath the flowery wallpaper, a plain, whitewashed surface peeped through. The past was bleeding into the present. And the speed of the transformation was increasing.

"What's happening?" I could hear the panic in my own voice.

Caroline rocked back and forth. Her eyes were wide and she was so pale. "We've been caught. We can't leave here now. It's ensnared us, making us part of it."

I grasped her by the shoulders. "Tell me. What are we up against? Is this the same as Caffiaes' hotel? But with Claude in charge?"

"If only it were that simple." She perched on the end of the bed. "There are places haunted by spirits so ancient, malevolent and evil even the daemons avoid them if they can. The Farrier's is one of those. It's the reason I was sent to collect you with such haste; the reason the other side will have come for your friend, Tessa, before she was even cold. These spirits collect others, take them over, possess them and so become ever stronger. They can reach into other time periods and join them together. Sometimes they create echoes like the one we experienced."

"If that's the case, I'm surprised Claude was risking himself down in the bar."

"The bar was crowded: enough living souls in there to hold even the strongest manifestation at bay."

"Then we have to get back to the bar, join the crowd and enjoy the singing. And we must go now."

Around me the picture was becoming confused. What remained of the wallpaper was stained and tattered. The bed head bore a carving of entwined letters. Somehow I knew they were far older than the current building. Strangest of all, the floor was now solid rock. And damp, as though it were in a cave: a long, cold, grey cave, curling back into a mountain which had never stood within a thousand miles of the Farrier's. I could hear water flowing close by. The door was still there, though it too had changed. It was now inside a narrow, pointed arch.

I struggled towards the exit. But it was so very far away. And Caroline made no move to follow.

Reaching out, I grasped her arm. "Come on! We're not finished yet. We can do this if we work together."

My feet were touching stone. I looked down. My boots were gone and the trouser bottoms were dirty rags. Without warning I was wading through water, icy and full of clinging, dark green weeds. I didn't understand. There had never been a river where the Farrier's stood.

"It's the sea." Caroline was now helping instead of dragging me back. Perhaps the shock of the cold water had cut through her fear.

I don't know how we reached the door. We entered the passageway. Strains of a raucous song drifted from the stair well.

The voice was no longer that of Claude and the song was "John Barleycorn", not some sad tale with too many connections to me.

I joined in. It felt like the right thing to do.

But Caroline's nails dug into me. "Stop it. Those words don't belong in this time. You're helping it keep us here."

I set foot on the top step. The stairs twisted beneath me. A spider's web of thick, sticky strands bound itself around me.

We were not going to make it.

But a young man was in front of us. Dressed all in black, silent, sneaking around, trying not to be seen by the people below. I recognised his intentions. We had found ourselves a burglar.

At the sight of us he froze. Before we could move, he lost his footing, tumbled over and over, screaming all the way down the steep staircase. His head struck the wooden spindles, then the stone wall.

My lodestone sent a shock of intense heat through me.

The scream had been heard. The singing ceased. From the crowded bar, people ran to the foot of the stairs. The first to reach him tried to move him. I could have told her it was a waste of time. My lodestone had now settled to a steady heat: another soul to collect.

But a flowing, shifting darkness was writhing through the crowd, swirling around and between the living: an indistinct shape reminding me of the grasping hands of the Final Door. A blur of what might once have been figures swallowed up the thief's body.

"Ross! Move!"

We fled, now insubstantial, chilling blasts of pale smoke.

Through the door. Into the car park.

Arms tight round each other, clinging together under the stars, we waited for our fear to ebb.

Nothing followed us.

I don't know how long we stood there.

The silence was broken by the arrival of the police. I wondered what the officers would make of the confused story they would soon be hearing; how there had been two people on the stairs with the victim: a man and a woman who had mysteriously vanished. No doubt someone would suggest the young man had been pushed.

Meanwhile, my lodestone had gone cold: there was nothing here for us; no soul remained to be collected. It had already been possessed and absorbed.

For once we were grateful when the grey corridor surrounded us.

CHAPTER 34

It started after they'd all returned from attending one of Mr. Barnes' "masterclasses", from which I had, as usual, been excluded. Whenever I walked into the common room, conversation would cease or the subject would change. But for accomplished deceivers, my team were doing a pretty lousy job. I could tell they were trying to pretend everything was normal, but they were not convincing me. Something odd was going on.

Although still polite enough, they were also distant, as if sharing some secret between them. Even Caroline was keeping it from me.

When I asked her what it was about, she laughed. "Oh, Ross, you've got such an overactive imagination. I do hope you're not developing a persecution complex."

"Maybe I am, but I haven't imagined I've been left off the training rota, have I?"

"No, that's true. Whatever it was you did to upset Mr. Barnes, you're going to have to sort it out. He's still refusing to allow you to attend his lectures."

"And he gets to choose who he teaches, does he?"

She shrugged. "Seems like it. But if you disagree, you'll have to take it up with Josh. Because it's nothing to do with me."

Now there was an unhelpful suggestion if ever I heard one! I wasn't Josh's favourite soul either. No doubt he supported Barnes' refusal.

Even though I was beginning to get annoyed, I decided to leave them to their whispering. I went to seek out Caffiaes; he would be much better company, and he might have some idea what was going on.

Caroline's office was empty. But it was clear someone had been in there since my last visit. Six chairs were arranged round the desk, whereas before there had only been the one. The surface of the table was littered with papers, which was strange because Caroline never wrote anything down.

I picked up the top one:

"Union Of Reapers: Official List of Demands.

A nice garden with pretty flowers and a little stream, for use in off duty hours.

An improved decoration scheme. We are all sick of grey.

The ability to enjoy food and drink on every assignment.

A private study room for each team member.

The ability to sleep when we want to.

Negotiations to commence immediately on the possibility of the removal of lodestones and their replacement with hand held devices."

This had to be the worst joke there had ever been in the history of Hell.

As I was reading the list for the third time, Caroline arrived. "I had a feeling I would find you in here. Even though I ordered you to keep out, I knew you wouldn't. You're still using my room to meet with that daemon friend of yours, aren't you?"

"Caffiaes is often better company than anyone else around here, especially at the moment." I waved the document at her. "What is this? A collective suicide note?"

"Not at all. Mr. Barnes says it's a more than reasonable list of requests. There's nothing on there that could cause any possible offence."

"It uses the word 'demands'. I'd say that one word was more than enough to cause offence."

"Mr. Barnes told us you wouldn't understand. He thinks you're too corporate: not to mention too scared of our masters to be able to see what a strong negotiating position we're in."

"He's dreaming. Our masters won't bother to sit round a table with Barnes or anyone else. They'll just open the Final Door and shove you all through it."

"Oh no. You see, Ross, that's where you're wrong. Mr. Barnes has explained everything. It takes a long time to complete the training of a Hell hound, and if all of us stand together, they couldn't get rid of that many of us without leaving an enormous gap in their operations. Think about it. Until they could replace us, all the souls we would have brought here would be left to languish on the temporal plane. That would lead to a massive increase in hauntings up there. And if the strike went on long enough, it might well create a backlog they would never be able to clear."

Strike? "This is insanity. Hounds can't go on strike."

"Why not?"

Because Hell wouldn't stand for it, that was why not. There had to be a fundamental flaw in her reasoning: or rather Barnes'. But I just couldn't quite put my finger on it.

She snatched the paper from my hand. "Why don't you join us, Ross? Prove to Mr. Barnes he's wrong about you. You're a stunning speaker. He might even be able to use you on the negotiating team."

"No, thanks. I've no faith in your Mr. Barnes. He'll end up leading you all into the fiery furnace. Unlike some, I'm not a sheep and I'm not looking for a shepherd to march me to the slaughter."

"Suit yourself. But if that's the way you feel, I'll thank you to keep out of my room in future. These papers are private: they're exclusively for members of the union."

Turning my back on her, I drifted into the library. I thought I might be able to work out which particular trade union leader Barnes was pretending to be. The man had no personality of his own, so it followed this was just one more of his many roles. But after a short while I realised it was a waste of time. He could be modelling himself on the Pied Piper for all I knew. And what difference would identifying the original make anyway? The man had already done too much damage.

Nothing happened for a few days, but even so, the atmosphere was tense. Since I knew Caroline's office might be in use for meetings (and I didn't want to bump into Barnes), I was obliged to spend a lot more time in the common room. I waited with increasing dread for the storm to break. I was sure the longer this went on, the worse the outcome would be.

Caroline flounced in. "It's happened. Hell's representatives have agreed to come to the table. They're creating a debating chamber next to Interview One. We're on our way!"

"Yes, but where are you on your way to?"

She glared at me. "You're still not going to join us?"

"No. I told you: this is beyond stupid."

"You won't work against us though, will you? I mean, if it does come to a strike, you won't try to break it: you won't become a scab?"

"There isn't going to be any strike, Caroline. It won't get that far." The fact was I really didn't know how to answer her. Would I be the only hound in Hell to go on working or, when it came down to it, would I discover a sense of solidarity with my comrades? I wasn't sure.

After several hours, Caroline went to take a look at the new room. "It's huge," she reported back to the team. "And there are lots of seats. It looks as if they're going to allow observers. Oh, I can't wait. Isn't Mr. Barnes so incredibly amazing? With him leading us, I just know we can't lose."

I got to my feet. "Don't go, Caroline. Please stay here. Stay with us."

"But I want to go. Mr. Barnes…"

Her words burbled over my head, as meaningless as the speeches of her precious hero. Mr. Barnes this, Mr. Barnes that… She reminded me of a young schoolgirl in the throes of her first serious crush; following him around like a puppy; his name forever on her lips. But at that moment I realised, though she might have been in Hell for hundreds of years, beneath the surface she was still that same sheltered nineteen-year-old debutante. She had not lived long enough and had never had the opportunity to fall in love. While the unworthy object of her affection was an over-charismatic lounge lizard without a personality of his own, one who could make an angel blush when she talked of him playing Hamlet.

I had to at least make one more attempt to save her neck. "Please listen to me. Our masters never negotiate. They're not some overblown temporal corporation. They're not reliant on their staff's co-operation because they can't afford to lose too many skilled workers at a time. Why can't you understand? Open your eyes, Caroline. Barnes has got it all wrong. You've often said it yourself: time runs differently in this place. They have the whole of eternity available to them in which to find our replacements."

She wasn't listening. I was losing her. Perhaps I already had.

But then I got some help from an unexpected quarter.

Greg was standing between Caroline and the door. "It's a waste of time going to the debate: you're not on the negotiating team. They won't even let you in. You'd just be left outside in the corridor. Besides, something as complex as this is sure to take all day. Why not stay here. We can plan how we're going to celebrate our victory when the negotiations are done."

"Oh! Oh yes, that's a great idea. We could put together a proposal for a thank you party for Mr. Barnes." She drifted over to the table in the corner.

Greg was about to follow her when I touched him on the shoulder.

"Thanks for that. I was beginning to think everyone but me had fallen under Barnes' spell."

He shrugged my hand off him. "No, not everyone. I don't fall for charisma. Not any more. I felt its pull once a long time ago; was swept away by it all, just as badly as she is now. Perhaps worse. The cost then was millions of innocent lives. At least on this plane we all deserve what's coming to us."

We did not have to wait long. Josh swanned into the room and crooked his finger at Caroline.

"All team leaders and supervisors are to report to the negotiating chamber."

"What's happened?"

He shrugged. "I haven't a clue, Ross. All I do know is a petty fiend was in an awful hurry to give me the message. Come on, Caro. We'd better go."

She leapt to her feet. "Mr. Barnes must have got what we wanted. The authorities must have folded. I told you the requests were reasonable." But I knew she didn't believe her words any more than I did.

I paced across the room: door to wall, wall to door. I didn't keep count of how many times. And I didn't feel any better for it anyway.

She was back. "The negotiations didn't go as planned." I had never imagined even a ghost could look so pale. She was trembling.

I pulled out a chair from beside the table and steered her into it. "Tell me the worst."

She closed her eyes. Ran fingers through her hair. "There was no discussion. Nothing. Only an ultimatum."

Just what I had expected. But I felt no desire to tell her so.

"Barnes wasn't even there. He must have betrayed us. They said he had been a great help to them." She was sobbing now.

I knelt in front of her. Greg and Nadine stood on either side of me.

Caroline jerked her head back. "I'm here to say goodbye."

She grasped my wrist. "They gave us a choice, you see. All the hounds are to be lined up and then…" Again, her eyes closed. "Decimation: one in ten will be sent straight through the Final Door or…" Her back straightened. "The supervisors and team leaders could volunteer to take full responsibility for their people. In that case, it'll be one in five of us, chosen by ballot. We had a vote on whether it was everyone or just us. So here I am: to say my farewells."

"When is it going to happen?"

"They first have to process the negotiating team, and there are a few others: the ones who helped… him… draw up the demands. A few hours, I guess. Not long." She gave a loud, choking sob and fell forwards into my arms, her head resting on my shoulder. "Oh, Ross, I'm so frightened." The words were no more than a whisper.

I rocked her gently. Nothing I could say would ease her fears. Nadine stroked her back, crooning as though Caroline were a terrified child.

Greg stepped away. I could see his face: less sympathy, more relief. He had escaped a fate he knew he did not deserve. I wondered if he and I were the only Hell hounds who had not been even a little tempted to sign Barnes' list of demands.

I was not achieving anything by staying. I could try to comfort Caroline as she cried but how was that helping? What good was it going to do?

Easing her back into the chair and disentangling my arms, I rose to my feet. "Take care of her, Nadine." I raced out of the common room.

Caffiaes was already waiting for me in the office.

I didn't give him chance to speak. "You have to fix the ballot: save Caroline."

He wrinkled his nose. "Yes, I know. I can't risk her going beyond the Final Door any more than you can."

Surprised by the reply, I perched on the end of the table. "You want to help?"

"No, not in the slightest. But let me explain something. You've never been where she's going. Do you know what the first thing every soul does when it's being tortured?"

"Screams, I should imagine."

"Well yes, I agree that does come first, but very soon the begging starts."

"So?"

"Next comes the confessing. They can't help themselves: every wrong they've ever done; everything they've always wanted to keep hidden; all their secrets rise up out of them like bubbles in a boiling pot of blood."

"Oh, I see: secrets such as helping a daemon escape his punishment for having played little games with stolen souls."

"Maybe."

"No, not maybe. Well, I'll raise the stakes a little higher. I told Caroline all about you and Doris." I hadn't. But it was too good a lever not to use.

He jerked back as though I had stung him. "Why did you do that? It's a secret. You know it has to remain that way."

I shrugged.

He hissed, "All right. But explain to me how I fix a ballot I'm not even involved with."

"I don't know. And we don't have much time left to work it out."

For several minutes we tossed ideas into the air. But there was nothing we could think of that would disrupt, delay or deny the eventual result.

"How will they do it? Will it be pieces of paper?"

"No, we have special stones for events like this. There'll be a big clay pot and inside it a stone for each of them: one in five will be red, the rest white." He broke off and a slow grin spread over his ugly countenance. "That's it! That's how we do it. You are so lucky she once had a part of me inside her head; it will have left traces. It shouldn't be too difficult to find an excuse to handle the pot and then I can slip..." He raised his hand and bit off a fragment from the long nail on his middle finger. He rolled it in his palm. "I'll stick this deep into a stone. She will just have to pick the right one, which will be easy as it will be drawn to her hand."

"It's as simple as that?"

"It ought to be. I'd better get going if I'm to get a shot at the pot. They'll want this sorted out quickly, so they won't be hanging around. You'd better get back to your precious Caroline and explain to her how this is going to work. Chop chop."

He was gone. I rushed out behind him. He was not the only one in a hurry.

But the common room was empty. The summons had been received. I cursed the timing. But if I had got to her, would she have been prepared to cheat?

The grey corridor was crowded. Small knots of four or five souls clung together. Muted sobbing and soothing whispers hung in overheated air. Caroline was not the only popular team leader.

I forced my way through the throng, ignoring curses of disrupted grief.

I was too late. I had failed. Through the open door of Interview One, I watched Caroline take her place in the line of the condemned. Watched as she extended her hand. But the door closed just as she selected her stone.

Back in the common room, a weeping Nadine, held up by a thunder-faced Greg, ignored me. They did not want to know why I had deserted Caroline when she needed the support of us all.

We sat there, in a silence punctuated only by sporadic bouts of sobbing from Nadine. I wasn't certain how genuine her tears were: she and Caroline had not been close. Perhaps, like Greg, what she really felt was relief, in her case also tinged with guilt. She had been enthusiastic about the union's demands, and she was lucky to be spared. One in five from another group of people is always so much easier to deal with than one in ten from a cohort which includes you.

I held my head in my hands and stared through my fingers at the wooden table. But saw nothing.

CHAPTER 35

I felt a soft touch on my shoulder. "I'm all right, Ross, and so is Josh."

"Caroline!" I couldn't help myself. I shot to my feet and enveloped her in my arms. "You picked the right stone after all."

She pulled away and stared at me. "How did you know they were going to use stones?"

"Er, I guessed."

"Are you sure that's all you did?"

"How do you mean?"

She bit her lip. "One of the stones was hot to my touch. It almost burned my fingers."

"So, you pulled that one out of the pot."

"No, I didn't. I think you and your daemon friend tried to fix things and if you did, it was a really unfair thing to do. I was a major part of all of this, and it was only right I took my chances. There were others waiting to pick a stone who were far less guilty than I was." Having already forgotten her fear, she flounced off across the room.

Sometimes whatever you do, it always seems you are in the wrong. But I couldn't help noticing the discoloured patch on the pocket of her gown as she turned away. It looked as if the fabric had undergone a little bit of singeing.

I had little chance to thank Caffiaes because for a while the missions came in thick and fast. It was as though Josh was trying to overload both Caroline and me. When at last I did catch a break, I hurried to the office.

The daemon was waiting for me. And he did not look happy. "Have you annoyed your supervisor in some way?"

"You mean Josh? You could say I have, though it's not my fault. Why do you ask?"

"He's put your team forward for..."

Caroline swept into the office. "Aha! I thought I'd find you here. There's no time for chit chat now. We have to go. There's some trouble for us to sort out at a country estate."

Caffiaes wrinkled his nose as if a bad smell had come into the room with her. "You don't mean Fordyce House, by any chance?"

"Yes, that's the place. How did you know?"

"Never mind. Just be careful, that's all. I can't stop you having to go." He sighed. "And I don't see how I can help you this time. So, watch your step."

Caroline wasn't really listening to him. She pulled at my arm. "Come on. The others are waiting."

As we entered the corridor, she glanced back. "Does he always fuss like that? What could there be that's different about this assignment? He must know nothing on the temporal plane can harm us. If it could, they wouldn't send us, would they?"

I had no answer to give her. It wouldn't help to tell her I had never known Caffiaes to worry on my behalf before.

The dead woman stood in the centre of the kitchen. Blue sparks flew from the tips of her fingers and the waving ends of her long, dark hair.

The four of us crowded in the doorway, watching as she pointed at objects: a chair; a cushion; a folded towel, which first charred then burst into flames. We had no idea what to do about this wraith.

She turned to face us before dropping her arms. The hair draped itself over slender shoulders. The sparks subsided.

"I've given you long enough. I'm tired of waiting. Must I burn the entire building down before you see you have no choice. Either help me or go away."

We couldn't help her. We had no plan for a situation like this. She was not destined for us and we had not expected to find her there. I wondered if she was the danger Caffiaes had been trying to warn us about.

My lodestone had an odd reaction to her. Instead of giving off a gentle heat when the soul is meant for us (or nothing at all if it is meant for the poodles), I was experiencing a most unpleasant sensation: it was as though the lodestone had been dipped in ice.

She shook her head. "No, I didn't think so. No one who comes here ever wants anything to do with me."

"So, who are you?" I asked the obvious question while seeking a different answer altogether. Her name was irrelevant. It was not who she was but what she was that mattered. But to question her in such a way felt impolite. There was no point in annoying this spectre, and there would be other opportunities to find out. I had the feeling this assignment would require longer than our usual stay. So far, nothing about this place had been usual.

"Which side sent you this time?"

Even stranger. She was aware of what we were. For a fleeting moment I even wondered if this were another of Caffiaes' or Claude's games, but somehow I knew it wasn't.

"We're the side you don't want to get involved with." Caroline pushed past me. "You have realised you're dead, haven't you?"

"What else would I be? I've been in this house so many years I've lost count, and I can't be bothered keeping a tally of how many like you I've met."

This was also news. Josh had not informed Caroline that other teams of hounds had been sent to this place before us. He had lied to us again, albeit by omission, though, in fairness, Caroline would not have thought to ask.

I squared up to the ghost. "My name is Ross."

She shrugged. A few stray sparks rose from her hair. "Don't expect me to trouble to remember it."

"I might remember yours if you were to tell it me."

"Lily. I was called Lily. I came here as a bride but I didn't last long after that."

She drifted toward us, and we moved aside, four ghosts giving way to a solitary one. I wondered if the others were as nervous of her as I was.

"I don't care for this room. I prefer my cellar, the one my body was buried in, even though my remains are no longer anything but bare bones." She sank through the kitchen floor.

We made no move to follow.

"What was that?" With her toe, Nadine prodded the spot through which Lily had just descended.

Caroline set off along the corridor leading away from the kitchen. "Nothing for us to deal with. Let's just get on with our work: find the ones we have been sent here to collect. Leave Lily for the other side to sort out."

"She didn't feel like one of theirs."

I had to agree with Nadine. The few Heaven bound ghosts I had run across had been a lot different from Lily: more polite, not as mocking and, most of all, they had not tried to set anything on fire.

Greg held back a moment before commenting in that irritating, clipped voice of his, "When I was part of another team, someone once said they had met a ghost who neither side could claim."

"Impossible!" Nadine beat me to the reply.

"No, hear me out. This one was a man. He had lived a life in perfect balance: his good deeds were of equal value to the things he'd done wrong. Too good for us and too bad for the poodles. Stuck in the middle, if you like."

I didn't like. "They would either have given him the benefit of the doubt or let him choose. Whichever way, he'd have ended up in Heaven." Even as I said the words, I was thinking of Kenneth Barnes, also not good enough for Heaven. They had let him in… until they realised their mistake and had to get me to help them throw him out again. But, on the other hand, he had been special. His extraordinary talents had made his case, along with Mr. William Shakespeare. Lily, I guessed, had no such advocate or exceptional qualities.

Greg shook his head. "No, this guy couldn't go there. He wasn't quite good enough and he was unwilling to repent the sins he'd committed. He thought they had been justified."

"Unwilling to repent? He would be ours for sure."

"I told you. He was too good for us."

"Stop wasting time, everyone. None of this matters. Come on. I think our targets are up here." Caroline was standing on the third step of an elaborate staircase.

We hurried to catch up with her. Leaving the kitchen, I glanced behind me and wasn't too surprised to notice all the damage Lily had done had vanished. Like all ghosts, she was trapped, surrounded by a bubble of her own time. She could have no permanent effect on what was for her the future.

Upstairs in the present, the furniture was old and broken; a faded, threadbare carpet covered the dusty, wooden floor. Every door was open except the last on the left. We could hear voices coming from behind that one. At the back of my head the tiny spot of heat flared into life. One or more of the ghosts on this landing were indeed our legitimate prey. Perhaps I had been wrong: the ghost down in the cellar was irrelevant and this task wouldn't take so long after all.

We split up. Too many of us arriving at once can be disconcerting for a spirit. Better results are obtained when everyone stays calm. Greg and Nadine went off to check the rest of the building. They assured Caroline they would, for now, avoid the cellars and Lily.

My team leader and I slid through the oak door into what turned out to be an overdecorated bedroom. I caught a glimpse of clashing colours: purple and green with splashes of red, though the red had not been intentional.

Two men were fighting on the carpet in front of the fire. One was strangling the other, but his victim had managed to insert a long, thin blade, a stiletto, between his assailant's ribs. They were both far beyond medical aid.

The first thing we had to do was break up the tableau which had frozen at the moment of their deaths.

I coughed. "Excuse me, gentlemen."

They broke apart. Even so, something was wrong. Instead of staring at each other, at us or at the blood, they laughed. One shouted a string of words and both vanished, but not in the direction Caroline and I had intended: neither was now being greeted in Hell. They were somewhere else in the house.

"Did you hear what he said?"

I nodded. "Yes, I did. He called out to Lily."

Following Caroline, I drifted out onto the landing.

She hesitated. "We'd better find Greg and Nadine. I don't like this at all. Just like Lily, I think those two men knew what we are."

I couldn't argue. For once it would be best if we stayed together. This was not like any other mission we had ever been on.

Caroline called out to them but there was no reply. Fordyce House was a large building: four storeys plus five separate cellars, one of which was home to Lily, whom we were wary of disturbing. Our colleagues could be in any of the rooms or perhaps out in the garden with its greenhouses, orangery and summerhouse. Where were we to begin the search?

"We should be systematic, start at the top." At least she was not suggesting we split up. This place was making me more nervous than I had been since the last time the sheriff's men were on my trail. And that had not ended well.

The attics were empty except for a couple of rats and a large clan of mice. There were cobwebs in every corner and scraps of material in the crevices. No ghosts, not even one.

A room on the floor below turned out to be a nursery. Several abandoned dolls on a high shelf gazed out, glassy eyed, over their domain. A broken cot and an old rocking chair had been piled up against one wall. No ghosts.

We returned to the room where the men had been fighting and checked each nook and cranny without success. I was becoming concerned.

Caroline by contrast had decided Greg and Nadine were hiding from us on purpose and were deliberately ignoring her calls. She believed they were holed up in a bedroom, entwined in each other's arms, continuing their illicit affair, the one I was now so jealous of. I would have taken Caroline in my arms in an instant if I thought there was any chance of her responding. I had tried to kiss her a few times recently, but on each occasion she broke away from me. "Are you mad? Do you want them to send us both through the Final Door? Oh, Ross, you must know we can't do this, however much we might want to. It's not allowed. And it's not worth the risk."

It was amazing how her fear had turned her into someone who would obey rules the living Caroline would have broken without a second thought. I was certain she wanted me as much as I wanted her, but the desire for me was not enough to give her the courage to take a chance. She would not risk losing everything. But that didn't stop me hoping one day...

We drifted into the first room on the ground floor, a sitting room with the late afternoon sunshine slanting in through French windows, which gave onto an expanse of overgrown lawn. It was an elegant room, with flowers in tall vases; and a young woman arranging them. I detected no heat from the lodestone. She was dead but not destined for Hell.

Turning to face us, her arms full of roses, peonies and one long-stemmed, perfect lily, she laid down the rest of the flowers but held the lily out to Caroline. "You have to leave. We don't want you here. Lily says you have to go."

Caroline ignored the flower. "We can't leave. We have a job to do. But you can go, Heaven is waiting for you. I promise you have nothing to fear; it will be so much more pleasant than hanging around in this place year after year."

The woman swept the bloom through the air, leaving a faint trail of golden-red pollen in its wake. When it settled, she was gone, sliding through the floor, I had no doubt on her way to report to Lily.

In her absence, the room darkened; tatters of velvet curtains clung to the cracked and crazed panes of the French windows: the sideboard, the vases and all the flowers existed only in the past.

Caroline led the way into the next empty room.

We had arrived back in the kitchen, where we had first encountered Lily. There was no sign of her nor anyone else.

"Let's get to the cellars. It's the only way to find out what's going on."

I agreed. We were gaining nothing by continuing our search for Greg and Nadine. By now, if they didn't want us to find them, they could have changed location: perhaps gone up to the attics or somewhere else we had already covered. Something was strange though. I had a feeling, a strong impression our companions were no longer in the house.

On reaching Lily's cellar, we found we were expected. She was sitting, clothed in a floor length, silver dress covered in heavy embroidery, in the centre of a long settee. To her right was the woman from the sitting room. Now pink peonies were twined in her blonde hair, while Lily held the flower which bore her name as though it were a sceptre and she were holding court. The two men who had been fighting now sat in armchairs either side of the settee. Perhaps even here they had to be kept apart. Also, a girl of around twelve or thirteen sat at Lily's feet. They had such similar features, I was sure they had to be mother and daughter.

As I looked at each one of the company in turn, I collected a response from the lodestone. The two men were ours for sure. The young woman and the girl were not. As to Lily, she again sent a cold shiver through me, as though the lodestone were indeed a splinter of ice.

"Where are our companions?" Caroline never did waste time on small talk.

Lily laughed and swung the flower in a lazy arc. "How should I know? Perhaps they gave up and went back to where you came from. You all do in the end."

"They can't have returned to Hell with our mission not yet completed and without Ross and me."

"Can't they? Oh well, in that case they must have gone somewhere else."

Somewhere else? If the heart in the body I was wearing had been functioning, I'm sure it would have missed a beat. Was it possible they had at last found their escape route? I knew Nadine was still in contact with Claude even after the fiasco on the motorway. Had he now decided to help them? Or was this some other trick of Lily's?

"Do you know where they are?"

She smiled in response to my direct question but did not bother to answer.

The girl got to her feet. "I'm bored. Can I go now?"

Her mother's hand shot out to grab her. "No, I told you. These creatures are here to harm us. They want to take you away from me. Stay still until they have gone, Rose."

Rose? What else would a Lily call her daughter?

Caroline extended her hand to the girl. "Your mother has it wrong. We are not here to harm you. We're not interested in you. All we want is to find our companions."

"Liar!" The man on the left, who bore a long, red stain on his jerkin, snarled at us. "You've come to take me and Harry away. Lily's told us all about you and we believe her."

"Fine. Yes, we would like you to come with us, but we have no hold on Rose or this maid. They belong in another place."

"No one is leaving." Lily raised the flower to her face. "We like it here. You're going to be just as unsuccessful as the team from Heaven who were here only a short while ago. We don't need or want your intervention."

It wasn't the right thing to do but I was curious. I had only ever met a couple of members of the opposition, and I was sure the likes of Fred and Doris were not sent to deal with routine tasks, as this one was supposed to be. I couldn't believe ordinary ghosts, however well behaved they had been, would be awarded an escort of angels. Close to, I was sure the blurred, indistinct shapes would hide members of teams like us. "What were they like?"

"Who?"

"The team from Heaven. Were they beautiful? Did they... Did they have wings?"

Lily began to laugh and the others joined her.

I deserved to feel foolish. And I did.

"No, they don't have wings. They look just like you. Just as ugly."

"Oh, Mama. Ross isn't ugly." Rose blushed.

I wasn't sure how to reply. So I didn't.

Caroline grasped my arm. "We're going upstairs but we won't be far away if any of you change your minds." She half dragged me up into the sitting room.

"Why have we left them?"

"Not here. Outside. Let's go to the summerhouse where we can't be overheard."

I followed her. We drifted across the damp grass of a late summer evening and into a rickety structure which had once been a graceful building with a thatched roof. She sat down on an old bench, which would have collapsed if she had any weight to her.

"Ross, you have to get to Rose. She's the key to this whole thing."

"What? She's only a baby."

"No, Rose is a young girl with a crush. As soon as she laid eyes on you, she fell for your not inconsiderable charms. The girl will talk to you."

"If she leaves her mother's side, maybe, but I don't like this idea."

"I didn't think you would." She put her hands together as though about to pray. "Sometimes I can't help but wonder how you ended up in Hell. I bet the scales can't have been far from level." She leant toward me. "If you don't like my idea, have you got a better one to offer?"

"No, but she's too young for what you propose."

"What do you think I'm proposing? I'm not suggesting you seduce her. Just be nice to the girl: gain her trust. We can use that to threaten Lily. You can tell her you'll leave her daughter alone if she stops protecting those two idiots who belong to us."

I sat beside her. She shuffled along the bench, keeping her distance.

"Caro, if I do persuade Lily to help, it won't be for any other reason than to find out where Greg and Nadine have gone. If they have found a way to escape, we should join them." I looked into her eyes. "I won't leave without you. We belong together."

She bit her lip and, without looking at me, placed her hand on top of mine. "There is no escape. We belong to Hell. They won't let us go. Stop dreaming, Ross. Don't you see it causes nothing but pain?"

"Perhaps the pain is worth it. Don't you remember how wonderful it felt to hold each other that day in the burning building."

She closed her eyes. A single tear fell onto her cheek.

I kissed it away. And, for a moment, just one single moment, Hell did not exist.

Then she was on her feet. "We can't do this. I can't do this. I'm sorry but I'm not like you. I'm not brave enough. I'm too scared."

"You're wrong, Caro. We can do this. We must do this. And we will find a way. I promise you we will."

But she wasn't listening. She floated away from me across the damp grass.

Sitting back, I considered her words. There must be a way to cut through her fear. I was now certain the others had discovered the escape route. And if they could find it, so could we. For now, though, there was still the mission. It could not be abandoned. Hell must not be given any excuse to make things worse for Caro and me.

My eye was caught by an old, wooden chest in the corner. For some reason it called to me. I opened it up. Inside were papers wrapped in an oilskin.

I unrolled one onto the dusty floor of the summerhouse. It was a large drawing of the surrounding area. There was no sense of scale and the whole thing was childlike in execution. The out of proportion house was on the outskirts of a small town at one edge of the map. Beyond was open land with forests and small streams. In one of them were what I assumed were meant to be either ducks or swans with short necks. In the woods were deer and rabbits with impossible, long ears. Three areas were named in small, precise capital letters. One was the site of a battle. The second was a churchyard far too extensive for the size of the town. The note beside it read, "Victims of plague". The third said, "Possible Roman camp": the work of a very young amateur historian, no doubt.

Folding the map up again, I replaced it in the box. There was nothing to help me there. With no other choice remaining, I would have to try to talk to Rose.

When I looked up, it was as though acknowledging what had to be done had made it happen. Rose was drifting across the lawn towards me.

"Hello, Ross."

"Hello, Rose. Do you come here often?" I had meant it as a joke, but she stared hard at me.

"How did you know?"

"Know what?"

She entered the summerhouse and hovered with her feet a hair's breadth above one of the dusty flags. "This is where I am."

It was her grave. The edge of the box was encroaching on her grave.

She watched me move it. "That was mine too. I drew all the maps and the animals myself."

"I only looked at one of the maps. I thought it was an excellent piece of work."

"No, you didn't. I was never any good at drawing but I enjoyed doing it." Her face darkened. This place was making her sad. "I wanted to be like my Uncle Paul. He was an archaeologist who worked in Egypt. He came to visit us. But my father made him go away. He looked a lot like Mama." Her fingers trailed over the lid of the box. "I had just finished the map when he murdered me."

"Your uncle murdered you?"

"No, silly. It was my father. He said I reminded him too much of Mama and he wanted to put us both behind him so he could be happy here with Laura." She shrugged. "Two summers later he killed Laura too."

"Is Laura the lady with the flowers?"

"She was our maid before he married her." Ah, so all three of the female ghosts in this house had been murdered by the same man. He was not here, which was a shame. I had the feeling Lily and the other two could have made for him a worse Hell within this house than the one I hailed from.

Rose sat on the bench and swung her legs in the air, as any living child might have done. "Laura is keeping Mama busy so I could come and talk to you. She said I should ask you about Heaven."

"I don't know much about it. In life I was not a good man." I was not going to tell her about my visits. Nor why, if the chance had been offered to remain there, I would have opted to return to Hell.

She made a humming sound and tilted her head to one side. "Did you kill your daughter too?"

"No." How could she think such a thing? "I would never have killed a child. And I never had a daughter." At least if I did, I didn't know about it.

"The pretty lady who came with the two men said Heaven was a better place than anyone could imagine. She said I would be happy all the time and wouldn't miss Mama."

"I don't know about that. If you love your mother, why would you ever forget her? But I'm sure you would be happy. There would be lots of other little girls to play with." Mentally I crossed my fingers. I hated lying to her. And it was all lies, because she would be just like Tessa: remembering nothing that could get in the way of all that joy.

"Play? I don't play. I'm too grown up."

"I'm sorry. What I meant was: there will be other young ladies you can spend time with."

"Do you think I would be able to draw in Heaven?"

"Of course. You'll be able to draw, paint, run, whatever you like. Can you ride?"

"No."

"I expect they would teach you and give you a pony too if you liked. I think in Heaven you can have anything you want."

"Except Mama. And she would be so lonely if we all left."

"You can't stay with her forever. Perhaps now is the right time to move on."

Our eyes met. This young girl was wise beyond her tender years. She was perfect and fit for Paradise. And whatever the cost, I was not going to help Caro with her scheme.

"You should go there right away."

"I don't know how."

"Your mother has some way of holding you all here beside her, but that force won't extend far beyond the house. You should start walking. Go that way." I pointed to the small, green gate separating the end of the garden from the fields beyond. "Go now."

She hesitated but only for a second, touched my hand, a butterfly on a leaf, then began walking. On reaching the gate, she looked back for a fleeting second and gave me a bright smile. Passing through it, she vanished, leaving a scent of spring flowers in her wake.

From behind me came a hideous, agonised howl. Lily already knew what I had done. There was no chance of any co-operation now. Caro would be furious, and I would have to face her. With no point in delaying any longer, I left the summerhouse to its secrets.

Caro met me at the door. Her face was flushed. She jabbed her finger into my chest. "You idiot! What were you thinking? Are you trying to buy your way into Heaven? Let me tell you it can't be done. People much brighter and nicer than you have already tried and failed."

"I know it can't be done and it never crossed my mind. That child deserved better than spending eternity as a prisoner of this house. Her mother must have known keeping Rose here was causing nothing but harm."

"It's none of our business. We have our work to do, nothing else, and you have made it impossible. Do you think Lily will tell us anything after what you've done? Do you think those two men will come with us now?"

"I don't think it'll make any difference to them. They're aware of what we represent. They've found a way to avoid Hell and, to be frank, I don't blame them for wanting to stay out of it."

For a fleeting second, I wondered if this was indeed the escape route; if clinging to Lily's skirts could keep the forces of darkness from reclaiming me. But I dismissed the fantasy. There was a fragment of Hell inside my head. My masters could pull me back any time they wished. Besides, I had to be the last person Lily would ever protect.

Caro hadn't finished. She hissed into my face, "All you do is dream. You don't get it, do you? We don't deserve to be happy. All we can do is survive, do what we're told and try not to fail. You can forget everything else."

She turned her back on me and took herself into the house. Having nothing else to do, I reluctantly followed.

CHAPTER 36

The cellar was cold and empty. Lily was avoiding us, which was not difficult. She knew the house well enough to be able to keep a couple of steps ahead.

Caro wasn't speaking to me except in short, clipped bursts. She said I had to either think of some way to make peace with Lily, which, considering what I had done, was about as likely as my growing a pair of wings, or find some way to get our targets out from under her protection.

I sat on the staircase to review my options, which didn't take long as I didn't have any.

"Is it true Rose has gone to Heaven?" Laura was in front of me. I hadn't seen her arrive.

I attempted a smile. "Yes. She'll be there by now, safe from her mother's interference. You can join her if you want. I can assure you without a shadow of a doubt it's the place you're destined for."

"I'll be going soon enough. Lily has withdrawn her protection. She's angry with me because I distracted her so Rose could talk with you." Laura glanced over her shoulder, as though checking we were not being overheard, then back to me. "Lily isn't evil, you know. She was murdered when Rose was only a baby. She believed it was her job to watch over her daughter. That's why she stayed."

"Then why hasn't she followed Rose? Ah, but you know the truth, don't you? Lily has to stay here. There's no other place for her to go. But you, Laura? She's holding onto you so as not to have to spend eternity alone. You should take your chances and leave now while you can."

"But what about Lily? How can I desert her?"

"She's not your responsibility. Leave her to us. We will seek a solution for her; perhaps somehow, we can find another companion: someone who, like her, has been excluded from both Heaven and Hell." How we would go about that, I had no idea, but I knew it was what Laura needed to hear.

And it worked. She closed her eyes and began to smile. "I can see Rose. She's beckoning to me. She's..."

For a moment Laura remained at the foot of the stairs, a slender young woman with flowers in her hair, but a moment later there was only an empty space in front of me. And a whisper in the air: "Please take care of Lily."

I leaned back against a wall. What was this strange sensation I was experiencing? My work never made me happy. How could it? And I should be petrified of the reception when we returned to Hell. Up to now I had achieved nothing as far as this mission was concerned. The other side were not going to reward me for trespassing on their territory, while my own might well punish me for not finding Greg and Nadine. Not to mention failing to gather in the two men who still clung to Lily tighter than burrs on the fur of a cat.

I found Caro in the room where the two men had been fighting.

"This is where they died, isn't it, Ross?"

"Yes. We saw them. What of it?"

"They will have to come back here at the same time today. They have no choice: they have to haunt."

I couldn't disagree. It was the rule. I had seen it often enough.

Caro draped herself over one of the chairs. "Right. We're going to stay here and see what happens." This wasn't asking: this was telling; she had remembered she was supposed to be the one in charge. Besides, she had no intention of allowing me to get close to her.

I perched on the end of the bed.

Hours passed. Outside the window, night came to an end with a soft, pale dawn. I tried to remember the time of day when we had seen the two men kill each other. It wasn't morning. I was sure of that, but it could have been late afternoon or perhaps early evening. We had a long wait ahead: a long, silent wait.

At last something was happening. A flicker of light... and the fire burst into life. The dusty, broken-down furniture was renewed and took on the sheen of polish. The fabrics regained their colours.

"Yes!" Caro hissed as she sprang to her feet.

Lily arrived first, standing by the window, her dress swirling around as though caught in a gale, her hair a wild, dark halo of tangled tresses. She ignored us.

We didn't waste words on her either. She had come to keep an eye on the two men, to protect them from us. They were the last ones left, and she did not want to spend eternity alone.

Seconds later the tableau in front of the fire resumed. The fight was at an earlier stage than when we had first arrived. The two men were unaware of us, going through the same moves as they did every time they met like this.

Caro circled them. I wasn't sure what she intended to do. But I was certain any interference from me would not be welcome.

Neither was using a weapon yet, though I knew Harry had a stiletto concealed somewhere on his person.

"I'll kill you, George. You won't leave this room alive."

The other man grunted as they barrelled into each other, hands everywhere, chopping and punching. "You won't live to see her again."

Ah, so the battle had been over a woman. By the time this was finished, she would have two suitors fewer. Perhaps she had been fortunate. Men destined for Hell don't often make good husbands.

Back on their feet, in the right position. And there it was: the long, slender knife. George, his hands tightening around...

And somehow Caro was between them.

The knife sliced through the flimsy wraith she became as it touched her.

They all froze, three of them tight together, three shadows in the firelight with Caro in the centre.

"Come with me. You don't want to go on doing this, night after night, for all of eternity only for her amusement." She extended her arm, a finger pointing at Lily.

The other woman was floating now, sparks flying from her hair. "Don't listen to her. Stay with me. With me!"

It was too late. The two men were gone and Caro with them.

I was alone with Lily.

She gave a cry more sorrowful than the owner of a living heart could ever have voiced. She dropped to her knees and bowed her head, the long hair a curtain covering her face. "Please bring them back!"

I knelt in front of her. "I only wish we could, Lily. I do understand but they did have to leave. Rose had to leave too."

"What am I going to do now?"

"I don't know. I..." There it was: the familiar sensation of being dragged back. I had no choice. The mission was over: the souls had been gathered in and Caro had already returned. Hell was now recalling me, and it was a summons I was powerless to resist.

"Farewell, Lily."

She did not reply.

For once I was alone in the common room. Following the disappearance of Greg and Nadine, Caro had been "invited" to a lengthy meeting with Josh and a few other supervisors. I was afraid for her; what would I do if she were sent beyond the Final Door? She had become so very important to me.

Looking around the room, I sighed at my drab surroundings. Could there be a more depressing colour than unbroken shades of grey?

We had been an odd group to be working together; none of us the worst of the worst. There was a surfeit of souls available who would have relished this job: sadists who would gather in the unwilling with a zeal we could never share, taking pleasure in their pain. But we had been the ones selected. Perhaps hating the task was the point: being punished by being made to punish others.

But could there be another reason? Caro once said she thought I must have been a borderline case. I thought the same of her. Though she had been responsible for the deaths of her family, she had not been driven by malice but by helplessness and fear.

As for me, I took to the highway because my brother alone would inherit the forge. My choices were to work for him, find employment with some other master or die on the battlefield. Theft appeared to be a more profitable and exciting life than that of a labourer. I had the misfortune of being luckier than I deserved: sliding deeper into corruption with each new "friendship", too many opportunities at my fingertips and basking in the admiration of too many ladies. My faults were nothing more than a handful of petty weaknesses. I never sought to cause pain, never took a life unless my own was threatened and never stole from the destitute. I would freely admit to being a bad man. But not to being an èvil one.

As for Greg and Nadine, were they any different? They spoke of nothing but escape. Perhaps they had indeed already escaped. So, it was reasonable to conclude, despite knowing so little about either of them, that they were also similar, if not the same as Caro and me.

And we had all been chosen by Claude: he was the key. Were we suffering in Hell only so he could watch? Were we the nearest thing he could find to innocents? And, when he had tried to destroy Caro and me at the Farrier's, had that been because he was now bored with us?

Well, whatever the truth, it would have to wait. Caro was back and I had to find out what had happened to her.

CHAPTER 37

The block of flats was haunted. That was a given. Hell would not have sent us there if it had not been. They don't make that kind of mistake.

I arrived to find Caro having a chat with a young lass who had been murdered in the cellar around ten years earlier. The rest of the house was out of bounds as far as the girl was concerned. Not only was her killer still haunting the penthouse, but there were two recent arrivals she claimed were making her life Hell (which showed how little she understood of the nature of eternal torment). It was fortunate for her it was unlikely she would discover how much of an understatement she had made, as I detected no heat from my lodestone as I entered the cellar. The two newbies were the ones we had been sent to collect: drug dealers who also dabbled in other, less savoury fields.

I had been told someone else would be along to deal with the occupant of the penthouse but, even though I was supposed to be in charge, as "acting team leader", I had not been told which colleague to expect.

In charge? Huh! I shook my head at the very thought of it. After my previous, disastrous mission, when Nadine and Greg had vanished, promotion to Reaper, Second Class had been the last outcome I would have expected. Hell had placed all the blame on Caro and she had been demoted to Reaper, Third Class. I had a suspicion putting me in charge on this assignment had been intended to embarrass her. If so, it hadn't worked. I still respected her; she was more than my equal. Besides, it was time I admitted it to myself: I might be falling in love with her.

The air vibrated, thickened and Josh Holdacre stepped into the room. Why was he here? As a rule, a supervisor's own missions were the most complicated ones, the most difficult to resolve, not a simple recovery of a one-time murderer. Josh could only have been sent to keep an eye on us. I was sure he would delight in reporting back if we failed. He had still not forgiven her for ending their relationship. And, believing I had replaced him in Caro's affections, he hated me even more.

His arrival changed this assignment from a simple mission into a trial.

"Why are you two just standing around? Think you're on a little junket, do you?"

"No, Caroline and I have been gathering intelligence. We wanted to work out the best strategy."

"You're wasting time, you mean. Just get on with it. The sooner everything is dealt with, the sooner we can get back."

Get back? Was that what he wanted? I glanced at him leaning against a wall, which he would slip through if he wasn't careful, and I wondered what his reward would be if he did trip us up. There was no higher rank for a Hell hound than supervisor.

"Is the weather too cold for you up here?"

He scowled. "Get a move on! We'll meet up here when we've all finished."

Caro rolled her eyes at me, then rose up and through the ceiling.

There being nothing more I could say to Josh without making things worse, I followed.

The third floor was noisy with echoes of long past troubles. The sound of laughter floated through the closed door of one of the flats.

Gliding inside, I found myself in a large, open-plan room. Despite the apparent good humour of the occupants, anger bounced off the walls in tidal waves: a tsunami threatening to swamp anyone sensitive enough to pick it up. The carpet had once possessed a complicated floral design. Now it had a dark stain in the centre that reeked of spilled blood. No amount of cleaning can ever remove all the traces of murder.

There had been five corpses in this room. All met with violent deaths. I pitied whoever had been given the unpleasant task of clearing away the carcases. Three souls left at the time of the incident. I sensed they had been willing to go. I didn't know their destination, if they were "good" or not, though I suspected the latter. Either way they were not my problem.

The two wraiths left behind were chatting as though everything was normal; as though one of them had not been ripped apart by a long knife and the other riddled with four, no, five bullets, three of which were fatal. They still had no idea they were dead!

Their conversation ceased as we entered, and they both looked at Caro then at me.

"Who are you?" The one with the knife wounds advanced a step towards me. His expression suggested he was expecting me to give ground.

"It doesn't matter what my name is. I'm here to help you."

"Help us? What sort of help would that be?"

The other man crossed the room and approached the door. "You're the ones who need help." He didn't notice but it opened a fraction before his fingers would have touched it. He leaned out into the corridor. "They're on their own, these two."

Knife-wound chuckled. His hand slipped into his pocket and emerged again holding a small revolver. He brandished it at me. "You with the cops?"

"No."

"Bit stupid then, aren't you? What do you want? We're not gonna share any of our gear with you." He pointed the muzzle of the gun at the table. At one time there had been packages strewn across its surface. He could still see them. He must have died before they had been removed. I didn't know the full story of the events surrounding this man and his death or if the drugs (I assumed they were drugs) had been removed by the police or a rival gang. It wasn't important. I could see them in the same way I saw the stains on the carpet. They belonged in the lifetime of these two ghosts but were no longer there.

"I'm not interested in your gear. I just want you to come with me."

"With us." Caro smiled and waved her hand at the open door. "What's the point in hanging around here?"

Knife-wound advanced on her. Had she been alive, I might have been afraid for her. As it was, I could only admire the way she lured him in. Another step. Not far now. When he left the room, the site of his demise, he was sure to realise he was dead. They almost all do.

He did not reach the corridor though: only stood in the doorway for a long moment before returning to his friend. "What are we gonna do with them?"

If he meant us, which I knew he did, there wouldn't be much he could do.

Caro tried another tack. "You're hurt. Look at yourself."

Knife-wound stared down at the stains on his clothes. I hoped he might be adding it all up. Only a fatal injury could have caused so much blood to be shed. "I'm fine. I'll see a quack when we've done with you."

"You mean a doctor? What doctor? You can't just walk into a hospital and expect to be treated without them asking questions."

"Not your problem, missy." He waved the gun at her. "You ought to be worried about your own skin."

"I was only going to say I do know a doctor who would treat you, no questions asked."

She did and so did I. There is no shortage of medical men down below: Dr. Shipman, Dr. Crippen, Dr. Buck Ruxton even Dr. Mengele... You can take your pick, but I wouldn't recommend any of them to treat a broken leg, much less bullet wounds or a multiple stabbing.

Gunshot had gone quiet. Catching sight of his reflection in a mirror on the opposite wall, he made a sound somewhere between a gasp and a scream. His hand trailed towards the hole in his side. He gazed open mouthed at his image as he spread his fingers a fraction of an inch above the wound, unable to touch the ragged tears. In his face I saw understanding dawn. "I'm…"

"Yes, you're both dead. That's why we're here. We're your escorts."

Gunshot faded. He was gone. One problem solved.

The other man, eyes wide, stared at the space his friend had just vacated. He froze for a second before running.

I let him go. If exiting the room didn't sort him out, we could always pick him up later. In any case, he wouldn't be able to leave the building and would have to return to the room as his time for haunting approached.

Caro stretched herself out on a long settee. "I suppose you wish we could stay here forever and become part of the resident community."

"No, I want better than this for you and me; at the very least, to be free from the grasp of Hell. And I know it's what you want too. Don't try to deny it."

"I don't, but I'm a realist. There is no escape."

"Then tell me, Caro, where do you think Greg and Nadine went?"

"I don't know. Perhaps Hell did reclaim them after all, and we haven't been told yet."

"You don't believe that any more than I do. If Hell had got them back, why keep it a secret? Besides, Caffiaes would know, and he'd have told me."

"You place too much trust in that creature. One of these days he'll turn you in; just for the fun of it. He's not your friend, you know. He's evil."

I sat beside her. "We're not good people ourselves, Caro. That's how we got into this mess."

Her shoulders slumped. She hid her face in her hands. "Oh, Ross, I've had enough. I don't care any more. I've been thinking of resigning for such a long time."

"You can't be serious. Think what they'd do to you, where you'd be sent."

She did not reply. Instead, tears fell through her fingers.

I couldn't bear it. I enfolded her in my arms.

She nestled into me.

We kissed.

I could taste the salt of her tears. "Caro, you have to trust me. I will find a way out for us. Believe me: I will."

She shook her head. "Let me go, Ross. I don't want you to destroy yourself. You're good at this… work. You find ways to help where you can. But all I ever hear are the screams of the ones we gather in."

I pulled away from her, sat back and tried to find the right words. "I hear the screams too. They're one of the reasons I will never stop trying to escape. But you... You are the real reason. If you do walk through the Final Door, you will not be alone. I promise I will be beside you." Until that moment I had not fully understood. But now I was facing my true feelings for her.

And I had spoken them out loud.

The rules of Hell no longer had any hold on us. By falling in love with each other we had placed ourselves beyond them. Whatever happened from now on, we would have shared this moment, this truth, this knowledge. Even if they purged it from our memories, they could never take it away. It would still have happened.

Caro was in my arms again. Although her skin was cold, she felt alive. She held onto me as though she would never let me go. She...

"What do you think you two are doing?"

We broke apart.

Josh filled the doorway. How long had he been there, watching us? How much had he heard?

He crossed the room in two strides and grasped Caro by the arm. "Ferris more to your taste, is he, lady? Is he really worth the risk you wouldn't take with me? What has he got to offer you that I haven't?"

"Leave us alone." She shook free of him. "Do what you want. Because the answer is he's nothing like you. And, yes, he really is worth the risk." Her voice had changed. There was steel in it now. She was no longer afraid. "Do your worst. I'm sick of shadows, sick of hiding; sick of it all!"

Josh raised his hand. Was he about to strike her? I was ready for a fight, would have welcomed it. Adrenalin coursed through me. Fists clenched, I prepared myself to defend the woman I loved; even if it were to be the last thing I ever did.

The Final Door beckoned.

But Josh turned on his heel. "This is over. I'll deal with you both when we get back." He strode out of the room.

Caro grasped my wrist. "Come on. There's no more time. We have to find that escape route. Now!"

Fleeing through the wall onto a narrow staircase, we had never descended quicker. Determined not to lose each other, hand in hand racing across the landings heading for the space between stairs and exit. But would we be able to cross the threshold or would Josh be there, arms outstretched, waiting to drag us away?

The risk he might be was too great. So, through the outside wall, swooping down into the wide-open street.

Feet now pounding the pavement. Too scared to look back.

"Fordyce House. Lily is the only chance we've got."

Caro's reply was lost in the rushing wind as we were carried headlong by the strength of our desire for freedom.

We had only one advantage: Josh was unlikely to realise where we were heading. Why should the thought of Lily, whom he had never met, cross his mind? He would first have to return to Hell for reinforcements and to ask the daemon whose lodestones were in our heads to locate us.

None of this would take him long, but if we were lucky, there might just be enough time to persuade Lily to help us.

CHAPTER 38

Arms folded, brows furrowed, Lily glared at us. "Why have you come back? You know you're not welcome here."

"Help us, Lily. We're fleeing Hell. We're trying to follow Greg and Nadine. You helped them. Please help us!"

She laughed. A familiar rain of blue sparks fell around her. "You're mistaken. I help no one. You stole my daughter and my friends. You left me to spend eternity alone."

"Then don't be alone. Come with us." Caro held out her hand. "If you know the way, tell us. We will take you with us. You need never be alone again."

The sparks faded. Lily became silent.

I wondered how long we had left. Josh would have reported back by now. Minutes we could not spare ticked away.

"This is your chance too." Caro reached out to Lily. She trailed her fingers along the line of the other woman's arm. "No one else will ever come here. There's nothing for them any more. Neither side will ever try again."

Lily frowned. "I don't know where your friends went. I can't help you. All I do know is they said they were going to a battlefield."

"Which one?"

"That was all they said: they would be safe on a battlefield."

In the end was the answer so obvious? A battlefield: a place where thousands of souls are clustered together. Who would notice a few extra ghosts among such a tangled host? Yes, it had to be the answer. But how would we find our way to one? Nadine and Greg had both died in the Second World War. They would have known where to go. But there had been no such conflict in my lifetime. Or Caro's for that matter. How could we locate somewhere we had never been?

"Not any good to you, then?" Lily interrupted my whirling thoughts. "I suppose you'll just have to stay here and wait for them to come and get you." She leaned towards me. "It's no more than you deserve for stealing my Rose from me."

Yes, of course! Rose. "The summerhouse. Come on, Caro. Rose had a map. On it was a battlefield. She'd drawn the soldiers."

Three ghosts fled together through the sitting room and kitchen of Fordyce House, then over the damp grass to where the old chest stood beside Rose's grave.

Grabbing the map, I unfurled it on the rickety table and there, among the long-eared rabbits and short-necked swans, stick men fought with swords, and the word "Naseby" was spelled out in childish capital letters.

We stared down at the image. I so hoped Rose's drawing had been accurate enough.

A sound made me look up. Shadows were crossing the ground between us and the house. Indistinct forms appeared, resolving. But into what? Had Josh and the other hounds found us? Or had Hell set deadlier seekers on our trail?

We had run out of time.

I stood between the two women. Grasped Caro's hand with my right and gestured to Lily with my left.

We sped out of the summerhouse.

But the shadows were between us and the walls we must pass through. Changing, swirling colours erupted from the nearer of them; a glimpse of a huge, towering form.

And a second one.

Fire and brimstone erupted over our heads.

But not to destroy us. Amazed, we stared as one of the daemons threw itself at the other. A crash louder than thunder and they were locked together: entwined infernos shooting out flames, consuming everything around them.

"Run, Ross. Run. Get Away!" Caffiaes, a boulder holding fast in a torrent, kept our path clear, blocking the other's pursuit.

The red-streaked sky filled with flashes of lightning and wild cries as the two daemons clashed. Blood of liquid fire mingled as claws ripped through scales. Flapping wings, now tattered banners, blocked out the sun: a friend fighting to save us, a foe to destroy us.

And while the forces of Hell were distracted, we three fled. We would not have long. This fight would soon be over. Behind us, Josh and a cluster of hounds could only look on as we flew through a realm of darkness.

But something was terribly wrong. A despairing cry, for a moment louder even than the daemons. And three became two.

Lily had reached the limit of her haunt. Fordyce House had reclaimed her, dragging her from the sky and any dreams of escape: she would remain a prisoner within its silent walls, tied to the bones buried beneath the cellar stones. We could do nothing. I so hoped loneliness would be the worst fate she had to endure.

Forced to abandon her, Caro and I, fingers entwined, continued our flight. Holding tightly onto each other and the thought, our only hope: our vision of the battlefield.

Faraway echoes carried a howl of desperate agony. My loyal friend, Caffiaes, had surely met his end.

Short of a miracle, our freedom, so hard won, was about to be wrenched from us. And Naseby was still a horizon away.

CHAPTER 39

I don't know what I expected to find, but safety never looked like this. Caro and I spiralled down into the centre of chaos.

Before us, no child's drawing of regiments of men with pikes and swords marching in serried rows, nor cavalrymen charging over pristine grassland, pennants flying over their heads. Nothing could have prepared us for these battlefield ghosts, each one caught at the moment of his death: overlapping bubbles of time creating a singular spectacle of horror: a tapestry of pain and fear.

Around us, an ear-splitting cacophony of silence: open mouths, open throats, open wounds: a hundred individual repeated deaths as the unending cycle of hauntings went on. Had we left one Hell behind us only to find another?

Was this it? Did the hiding place for unwilling souls consist of a charnel house of churned mud, ancient bone and the dust of once crimson blood?

Caro faltered, grasped my wrist. "If we stay, we'll just be two more lost wraiths. This is not the solution. It can't be."

I stared through the shifting curtains of conflict, to discover Josh and so many others gazing around them, like us, losing focus in the face of so many ungathered souls: a pack of hounds overawed by the scale of the hunt.

We might indeed become lost here, unable to find even ourselves.

In my head, the lodestone burned as hot as any furnace beyond the Final Door: the thought of surrender becoming a shadow between me and the unbearable heat.

I might have given in, but before I could stumble any further, a gust of wind rose up, stirring what remained of the grass: a coolness on overheated skin, like a downdraught from the wings of a friendly daemon.

Around us, a fraction of the tableau faded and a path appeared, leading towards a ruined building: a destination of sorts, though it held no promise of shelter, no permanent respite.

During the battle its walls had been reduced to broken, trampled, bullet-riddled, blood-spattered piles of tottering stone. But it was no time-locked visitation; what remained was real, existing in both past and present.

We drew closer. The door hung by its hinges, a gaping invitation to a final place we might find rest before Hell arrived to reclaim us.

"Stay there! Don't move. You're my prisoners." We were not alone in finding this place. Josh Holdacre, the antithesis of an angel, glided towards us through the debris of the ongoing battle. The fires to which Caro and I would soon be condemned burned in his eyes.

He led and all the others followed. Despite the confusion, the pack was closing in on its prey.

Fleeing beneath a window still possessing a few fragments of stained glass, I realised the building was a church. How ironic it would be if the forces of Hell snatched us from a place which had once granted fugitives the protection of Heaven.

But that was long ago. There would be no help for us from these cold stones. This was no escape. They were upon us. Still, though all hope was gone, my fear propelled me onwards, dragging Caro across the threshold even as she cried out over her shoulder, "Leave us! Why won't you let us go?"

Beyond the door, something was happening. Our pursuers hesitated, gazing open mouthed, while we turned to find ourselves stepping into an unexpected memory of candlelight, of incense and of peace. And before us stood a wraith: the spirit of a priest, his voice filling the building with melody, a chant sung in a rich baritone. His back was to us as he genuflected before a silver crucifix. In his time, the altar was draped in snow-white cloth, the walls rose around us and were not yet half destroyed; though the battle raged, it had not yet found his church.

Through gaps in the walls in our time, Josh shook his fist. "Come out of there."

I could not have obeyed even if I wanted to. The music cast a spell over me, offering a moment's solace.

A dark presence filled the open doorway as Josh yelled, "Come out, I say!"

The priest finished his chant.

There was no sense in it, but I had to try. "Father, we claim sanctuary."

Had he heard me?

He bowed to the altar.

Josh laughed in triumph, raising his foot to cross the threshold.

The priest turned, vestments swirling. "Sanctuary?"

"Ignore them, Father. Hand them over. They belong to Hell."

Pale blue eyes scrutinised us. "Sanctuary?"

"Don't listen to them. I say they belong to Hell. Send them out here to me."

"Sanctuary!" The priest gave a curt nod. "Claimed and granted."

Josh stumbled, as though some invisible obstacle stood in his way, his foot unable to touch the step. He hovered there, mouth twisting in his long, ashen face. A wraith had denied him access! "Don't you understand? These are no petty criminals hiding from the law. I am charged with returning them to the Inferno.

Step aside! Do not place yourself in defiance of everything you stand for."

Beside me, Caro trembled.

The weight of fear crushing down on me, my own eyes filled with tears. What comfort could I offer her when I had none for myself?

And why would this priest aid us? Josh was right: our very presence within the church was a desecration. But must it end like this? Aching at the prospect, I could already taste the sulphur.

"Good Father, I beg you. Do not let him take us. We will do anything not to have to go back."

The priest frowned at me, his eyes as cold as the silver chalice on his altar.

I shrank under his gaze. My fingers laced with Caro's as she rested her head on my shoulder.

"We go together," she whispered.

"Together," I replied.

CHAPTER 40

Turning to face Josh, the priest intoned, "These young people have claimed and been granted sanctuary. You shall not have them nor, creature of evil, shall you enter this consecrated place."

"But Father..."

"I have made many mistakes but never have I failed in my ministry. It is my solemn duty to give shelter to those beset by wanton authority. It is for neither you nor I, but for your superiors and mine, to decide the fate of these two fugitives. Though it seems to me that if a person is fleeing from Hell, they must have come some way towards a desire for the salvation of their immortal souls."

Josh shook his head. "They don't deserve salvation. And there can never be any for them. They have already been judged in the celestial court. I say again you are wrong to let them stay. Hand them over. Now!"

"Don't waste your words. There is nothing for you here. While they remain within these walls, a greater power protects them. They are beyond your reach."

Relief flooded through me; our priest stood like a shield beset by nothing more than blunted toy arrows.

Drained and exhausted, I sank down onto the flags beside Caro. She rocked slowly to and fro, eyes closed tight, fingers locked around her head.

It was a struggle to hear the words she whispered. "Josh won't go; he won't accept he has lost."

And the Hell hound did remain, standing on the scrubby grass, watching us through the broken door. It was impossible to ignore him, though I was determined to try.

Caro jumped to her feet. "Why won't you leave us alone? We're not harming you. Can't you just go away?"

He sneered at her. "I'm not going anywhere until you come with me. There's a space waiting beyond the Final Door, and the longer you defy Hell, the worse it will be when I finally deliver you up."

"Why are you doing this?" She held out her hands towards him. "You could join us. But you wouldn't do that, would you? No, you're not like us. I know how much pleasure you take in the work. And this..." Her voice, angry and accusing, rose to screaming pitch. "This is not about punishing two escaped Hell hounds, is it? You could have chased Anya or gone in search of Greg and Nadine. Instead, here you are." It was as though she had forgotten her fear or, for a moment at least, been able to throw it aside.

I tried to grab hold of her, but she evaded me and paced along the narrow aisle towards the door.

"This is about me, isn't it? About you believing I chose Ross over you." Another step and she would be past the priest; two more and she would be outside the church.

Josh raised his own arms, ready to catch her, to clutch her to him.

"Caro, come back!"

She ignored me. "So, that's it? You want me. And if I do come with you, will that be the end of it? Will you leave Ross alone?"

"No! No!" My despair echoed from the walls.

"I will."

"Do you give me your word?"

Josh cast her the smile of a traitor, the promise of a liar. "You know I do. Come with me, Caroline."

Her feet now on the threshold, his fingers about to mesh with hers...

A flash of silver. And the crucifix slashed the air between their two outstretched hands. Our priest, the setting sun through the remains of stained glass casting a halo around him, roared out, "Be gone! I will not give them up."

Caro shook her head as though to clear it, while Josh fell onto the ground, scuttling backwards, as though the cross were a brand about to burn into him. Regaining his feet, he raced away across the battlefield.

The priest pulled his vestments tighter around him. "I'm glad he's gone. He was preventing me from getting on with my work. The day is far advanced, and I have done so little. I am falling behind."

He stepped through the arch and regarded us over his shoulder. "As for you, whatever you are, there is safety here. This church was never deconsecrated, so within this building lies the sanctuary you crave. But bear in mind, beyond its walls there is no such help, nor is there anything more I can do; I cannot give you absolution."

CHAPTER 41

With the priest no longer inside, the church became an echoing, empty shell. The sun now too low, all colour faded from the stained glass, the walls grey, holding only memories of ancient pictures.

"Where do you suppose he's gone?" Caro drifted around the space where once there were pews, alone with me, where once a congregation worshipped.

"I don't know. I can't imagine what work he finds to do. But he will come back. He has to come back." Even to me, my voice sounded uncertain.

To the right of the door was a heap of curved stone. It had been carved with angels and waving lines: the font. Beside it, the flagstones were not quite even; there was a slight mound of earth: a grave. "I think they buried him here."

"Then he's tethered. He will be forced to return at his hour of haunting, if not before." She sighed. "This is not what we imagined at all, is it?"

"No, but it has to be better than giving in and letting Josh take us."

"Are you sure? An eternity inside these walls, with nothing to do and only each other for company?"

"There's always the priest. Maybe he could instruct us in holy orders!"

At least she laughed. But afterwards, we sat in silence as shadows stole across the floor.

"We will give up in the end, you know."

"What?" I stared at her. "Why would we do that?"

"Because there is nothing for us here. At least as hounds, we had purpose. And other people to talk to."

"Am I not enough for you?"

She turned her face away. And I had my answer. No, I was not enough, would never be enough for her.

I forced myself to respond. "It's too soon, Caroline. We have to wait a little. Something may turn up."

"I don't think it will."

I could not bear to go where this conversation was leading. So, leaving her, I drifted to the doorway and peered out into the dusk.

My timing was perfect; the priest was arriving.

But something was wrong. His shoulders were slumped and he was muttering as he clutched the crucifix, "Not my fault. If only I could..." He stopped and peered at me, as though seeing me for the first time. "Ah yes, here I am, giving aid to the wrong side, as usual." He was not speaking to me.

I was intruding on his private thoughts. I would have given him space, but before I could move, the dark presence returned to the steps.

Caroline and I backed away towards the altar.

The priest placed himself between us and the Hell hound. "Why are you here again? How many times must I deny you access?"

Josh made no attempt to cross the threshold. Instead, he produced a long scroll, then cleared his throat. "Father Ignatius, I bring you greetings from both Heaven and Hell. You are, it appears, in good standing with both. Your work is considered useful."

Closing the document, he wrinkled his nose. "There's no need to read any more. It's nothing important: just boring details. Why not bask in the approval of your superiors, rescind your order of sanctuary and send those two out now?"

I looked at Caroline. Was she thinking the same as me? "Oh, don't be in such a hurry. We'd like to hear the rest, wouldn't we, Father?"

The priest glanced at us, then back to the doorway. "Why not? Please go on, my son."

Josh shrugged. "If I must." He made great play of unfurling the scroll. "Sanctuary is approved."

I couldn't help it. I threw my arms around Caroline, sweeping her off her feet and whirling her round in a massive hug.

"If I were you, I wouldn't be so quick with my celebrations." He sniggered. "There's quite a bit more."

I couldn't take it: hearing that note of triumph in his voice, seeing the look of delight in his eyes. This was going exactly as he intended. His trap was sprung. He had given us everything and now couldn't wait to snatch it away again.

"Get it over with, Josh. Tell us."

He gave me a mocking bow. "Your sanctuary will last only as long as this place endures. And I wish you joy of it. What is there here? Nothing but the constant screaming of dying men and the knowledge that, when it is over, so much worse is to follow. There is no escape. You cannot go beyond the boundaries of what was once the Naseby battlefield. You'll soon wish you'd stayed in Hell."

What did he just say? Had I heard him right? The whole battlefield, and not just the confines of the church?

"That will be fine by us."

He leant towards me, eyes narrowing, voice falling to a menacing whisper. "This church will not stand forever. And believe me, when it does fall into dust, I will be waiting for you, Ross Ferris."

Father Ignatius tutted. "Have you nothing better to do than stand there threatening us? Get you gone. And if there are more words, tell your masters to send them with a different messenger."

Josh laughed. He threw the scroll onto the step. "I'll be back for them before too long. Just you wait and see." Whistling, he strode off into the darkness.

CHAPTER 42

Outside the church, the tableau was a little confusing. In the present time, a few nocturnal animals went about their business: a fox slunk past the door; an owl seeking prey swept low on moon-touched wings: an appearance more ghostly even than the battlefield's wraiths. In time past, those many wraiths sat around their campfires, or lay on hard ground nursing never-healing wounds.

Inside, the priest's voice filled the space as he sang a melodious mass for all the souls lost on Naseby field.

Caroline drew close to him as he finished. "Why are you still here on the temporal plane?"

"This is my church. Where else would I be?"

"You do appreciate you're..."

"Dead? Yes, of course I do. I died a long time ago. It's difficult to be sure how many years have passed. But you'd know all about that, being dead yourselves."

"That doesn't explain why you're still here. All you'd have to do is ask and they would come for you."

My mouth fell open. What did she think she was doing? Why remind him that he could leave? Didn't it occur to her what might happen to us if he did?

He reached out and pointed towards the door. "I have so much to do. Look out there. The field is full of helpless men. A few came to battle seeking honour or political ends, but most because they had no choice; forced to take up arms and with no understanding of what they were being dragged into. Too many fell foul of those who ruled their lives. How can I desert them when they need my help?"

"But didn't Heaven send anyone? You heard Josh. You're in good standing: there's nothing to fear from leaving this plane."

He had the strangest of smiles, gentle yet with steel in those pale eyes. "I told them and I still say now: I am not ready. When my work is done, when everyone out there has been helped, I will let them take me. But not before.

"The first time they came, I told the angels sanctuary applies to me as much as to any other soul. There is no requirement to own a beating heart. After the third attempt, we reached an understanding: I do their work for them... or I try to." He frowned, the lines on his face as deep as the sea. "I make mistakes. I can tell them they're dead, even convince them, but how do I know if I'm helping them or not?"

"What do you mean? How can you not be helping them?"

"It's simple, Caroline. He can't tell the difference between those destined for Heaven and those who, despite everything, would be better off staying here as wraiths."

"That is true. To my great sorrow, I have sent too many onward and heard their screams as they become aware of their ultimate destination. I suffer for every mistake I make."

The nave seemed to fill with a bright light as the answer came to me. His words cut through my doubts, and I knew we had reached the right place. This church was perfect for us. Where else but here would the Hell hound training we had received find a more fitting purpose?

"You must let us help, Father! We can tell. Souls who have been to one place or the other can always sense those of their own kind." No need for further explanation; if the lodestones Hell had planted in our heads could be adapted and used for good, why shouldn't they be?

"Oh yes. Yes!" Beside me, Caroline clapped her hands together and her smile was like a shaft of sun bursting through rain.

Father Ignatius put out his hand to us. "Are you sure? It will be hard work."

Maybe, but it would be no harder, and so much more rewarding, than the work we had been doing in the service of Hell.

"Why don't you let us try?"

As he led the way out of the church, I stood beside Caroline and we looked about us. This field of slaughter could never be described as any kind of Heaven, but it was the closest two damned souls could hope for.

It would do for us. Perhaps more than we deserved.

Or maybe, given enough time, we might even prove ourselves worthy.

Also by Denarii Peters

Will You Walk Into My Parlour: and other stories

Coming Soon:

Ross Ferris Book 2: House of Wraiths
Ross Ferris Book 3: Mansion of the Dead

BV - #0149 - 230625 - C0 - 229/152/12 - PB - 9781739427290 - Gloss Lamination